BECOMING
WHITE SMOKE
A TALE OF COURAGE AND YEARNING

A. B. KREGLOW

DEDICATION

For Mary Murray Shelton,
whose loving hand is always there
when I reach out.

ACKNOWLEDGMENTS

One can never do a large project like this without the kindness and support of friends. Thank you, Karyl Huntley, Lee Lewis, Kjestine Bijour, Leni Chapman Preston, Julie Haber, Jane Williams and Andrea Menard for that friendship.

I am also grateful for the wisdom and guiding hands of those who helped me bring more accuracy and authenticity to the telling of this story: Grace Dillon, Professor, Indigenous Nations Studies, Affiliated Faculty, English, Portland State University, and Elissa Washuta, MFA Faculty Mentor at Institute of American Indian Arts (IAIA), Academic Counselor, University of Washington.

Finally, there are some other people that I also want to identify as benefactors. Their generosity helped to make the guidance, resource material, editing and formatting possible: Spencer B. Gay, Kay Henderson and Tricia Johnson. Your support means the world to me.

When you rise in the morning,
give thanks for the light, for your life, for your strength.
Give thanks for your food and for the joy of living.
If you see no reason to give thanks, the fault lies in yourself.
-Tecumseh 1768-1813

1
ROCKY MOUNTAINS
IN WHAT WOULD BECOME
CENTRAL COLORADO TERRITORY

Summer, 1852

The trapper's lodge was pitch black and smelled of old whiskey and vomit. The three men were sleeping off the liquor that had inflamed their desire. Even the dogs did not stir. Her body ravaged and her clothing nearly torn off, the woman was badly injured from the men's assaults and from what had happened to her before they bought her. What remained of the embers in the stove, and the small piece of blanket they had given her, had not kept off the chill of the night. Exhausted and cold, she had not slept; but with the long night almost over she was ready to make her move.

Ever so carefully, the woman reached out for the knot in the rope that stood between her and freedom. With effort, she was able to loosen the binding enough to release the end attached to the bedpost. Her hands still tied, she eased herself off the bunk, slipping past the sleeping dogs and out the cabin door. She crept through the gate and down the pathway to the main trail, then as fast as she could, she ran. Afraid she would be followed, she turned off the trail, and with low-lying tree limbs beating at her legs, she tore through the woods. She ran through a stream where at its edge jagged stones ripped her feet, but she felt nothing. Racing up the hill onto the other side then down along the ridge, she ran staggering, out of breath till she tripped, falling down the embankment, rolling over rocks and grass and fallen tree branches, wrenching her shoulder, impaling her hip on a shaft of wood, and hitting her head on a rock.

A butterfly, orange, black and red, floated above the purple lupine blanketing the field. She lay in the dirt unable to move or call out. Blood ran into her eyes, and more came up into her throat. Her wrists ached at the knot, and now her hands were numb.

I will die here, she thought, and she began to shiver uncontrollably.

Corn Snake, who had been following the tracks of a buck for most of the morning, stood on a precipice high above the ravine scanning the forest below for the flick of a tail or the brush of antlers within the verdant trees. But just as he caught sight of what he expected to be his dinner, a woman burst into the clearing and fell, making his prey ran off.

Raiding party, he thought.

Carefully, he aimed his arrow waiting for someone else to come into view. No one came. He yanked his horse to the side, following the path down the hill to where the woman lay.

White woman, he sneered. *Let her die.*

He could not, would not, help any whites, because festering in his heart was the memory of how a young boy was once used in a most intimate fashion to please a white woman. By the age of ten, his hatred for all whites was secured. And even now the thought of it brought sourness to his mouth.

The old Yampatika Ute shaman, Quill, and a group of women walked the path back to their homes. Friends since birth, they were sharing stories about their families. Most days, Quill was able to enjoy hearing about them, free from the pain of the loss of her own two grown sons, but today was not one of those days, and her heart ached with sadness. Though she and her husband had tried to have more children when the boys were young, they had lost two at birth, and never produced any more. But she never let on how difficult it was to listen to the stories of her friends' children and grandchildren's latest achievements.

Corn Snake started to mount his horse, but when he heard the voice of Quill, he cut the rope at the woman's wrists. A throbbing pain coursed through her hands as blood filled her deadened fingers. She fought him, arms flailing, head shaking back and forth. He threw a blanket around her, and lifted her into his arms.

Let that half-white look after this one, he laughed to himself.

Corn Snake approached the women with the bundle in his arms.

"Even the grass does not want to hide that serpent," one of the ladies quietly remarked.

"The Red Wing," Corn Snake shrugged.

The Comanche raider, The Red Wing, was a ruthless and brutal bandit known for pillaging local mountain villages for prisoners, taking horses and leaving family villages in ruin, often burning them to the ground. Corn Snake deposited the moaning woman at the shaman's feet, and he retreated back up the hill.

Quill loosened the gray army blanket around her shoulders, which she wore over a striped muslin dress and leaned down to look. She tenderly opened the package and gasped. To Quill, the body was like a newborn child left at her feet.

"White woman?" one of her friends said looking over her shoulder. "Leave that white woman."

"An avalanche of trouble," another agreed.

"Is there anyone else?" Quill asked looking into the woods. She searched the path and all through the trees for any signs of more white settlers. There were none.

"One crow brings another. Yes, it will. Yes, it will," trilled a third. "Leave her. Leave her be."

So fragile and broken, Quill thought. *They are right, of course, we should leave her for her own to care for her, but there is no one near, and she may die before someone finds her.* "We will have to hurry if we are to be of any use to this one," she said aloud. She bent down to cradle the injured woman's head then barked. "Gather branches."

Barely alive, the woman scarcely felt the kind hands of the old one, but upon hearing Quill speak the Indian language, terror struck her deeply. She struggled to stand, but could only cry out helplessly, pain searing every sinew of her body.

"Shiushiushiush," Quill whispered tenderly, her face crinkling as she spoke. Then the woman lost consciousness.

"Thank you kind Senawahv, Creator of All, for putting your child into a cloud of forgetfulness," the old woman said aloud. The other ladies agreed.

Corn Snake watched from above, taking one mouthful of pemmican then another, staring in silence while the old women struggled to lift the injured white woman and drag her to their village on the travois, the sled they had fashioned out of fallen branches.

"Husband! Where are you?" Quill called out. "Old Man!"

Father Man, the tall, gentle healer from this mountain village, came from behind their tipi. He wore a black, wide-brimmed hat with an eagle feather caught in its band, and a dark wool vest over his deerskin shirt and leggings, intricately beaded with glass beads and porcupine quills. On his little finger he wore a silver ring holding a large gold-flecked turquoise. This couple was known throughout the mountains to be fine healers.

"Quickly. Lightly on that hip, and careful of her shoulder."

"White woman," he snorted. "I will carry her back to where you found her. Let her kind take care of her."

"There is no one else. Take her inside," Quill told him decisively.

Against his better judgment, he lifted the woman and carried her into the home. Father Man gently laid her body on a soft bearskin then closed his eyes for a moment. "She is fighting to live," he said when he opened his eyes. "That is a good sign."

"Corn Snake says The Red Wing, but there is something else," Quill said. The woman moaned in pain.

Before beginning a healing ceremony, Father Man sat quietly, weighing what to do. He knew that bringing a white woman into their home could cause trouble for the whole village. There were white settlers and soldiers in the mountains who might find her and retaliate even though it was not they who had taken her. But he also knew that his wife had already made up her mind or she would not have brought this woman to their home.

Cougar Two Foot, an apprentice of the couple since he was young, and now a shaman in his own right, heard about the woman and came into the tipi. He stood by her side looking over her injuries. This *One Who Knows The Way* was a tall and strong man with intense eyes. His cheekbones were high and his nose long. His head leaned forward when he walked, and he moved with a graceful gait that was even and sure like the cat for which he was named. Despite his age, about the same as the woman's, he held a youthful appearance.

"Her people will be looking for her," he said. "White people have spread into our land like water into a cloth. They have no right to come onto our mountains, yet they take our best hunting grounds and putrefy our waters. They kill more than they need, leaving good meat and bones behind, sometimes taking only the skin or tongue. And there are so many, the animals are forced to retreat up into the mountains, and now if we are to eat, we must spend the winter in the cold and snow." He spit at the fire. "To them, nothing is sacred."

"Her injuries will heal," Father Man interrupted, "but her spirit may choose to join the Sun. We will see if The Great Mother will take her body for herself or let her remain with us." Then he turned to look at Cougar Two Foot directly,

"What you say about the white man is true, but this one is a cub in our arms," he said glancing at his wife. Cougar Two Foot snorted, and left the enclosure.

While Father Man sat next to her and closed his eyes, the woman felt as if she were being gently lifted onto the fragrant smoke of the burning sage, floating on it into a wondrous expanse. The sound of his rattle brought her back, but then rocked her like a baby, and she drifted off into a deep sleep. While she slept, Quill cleansed her wounds, and put ointments on the tears in her skin, wrapping them tightly.

Later the old woman went back to the canyon to look for anything that could identify her patient. She found a hair comb lying in the dirt, and a sleeve from the shredded red and white checked gingham dress the woman had worn. Though she washed it in the river she could not remove all the blood. In the stained cloth she wrapped the wedding ring from the woman's injured hand, the comb, and a broken silver chain, which had been clutched in her fingers.

"Has she spoken?" Father Man asked looking over to the bearskin where the woman lay.

"No. Well, yes, she did say 'gare it'. What does that mean, 'gare it'?" Quill questioned. "And I found these," she said unwrapping the package to show him the articles she had collected.

He took them in his hands and closed his eyes. Instantly, he was in the midst of the laughter of a family. "A happy celebration of some kind," he told his wife. "Several young children. A big gathering with many encircling this woman." Then a swirl of fear and dark confusion filled his senses. He handed the items back to Quill. He nodded, "Comanche and white men did this."

The steep winding trail led down to the opening of a dark cavern. The light from it shone brightly, drawing the woman inward.

A man wearing a buckskin shirt trimmed with white wolf fur, and a hat with large black feathers began to walk in step. She could not see his face, but he felt familiar, calming and reassuring.

The opening was ahead, its soothing light just within reach, and for her the pull to it was strong.

"Not yet," he said halting her step. "It is not your time. Go back. Finish your journey. Back, my dear one," he said again, the feathers on his hat opening and closing like raven wings during a mating dance. "Your boy is waiting for you." But she did not want to turn around. "Go back, now," he insisted.

Shocked awake by the vision, the woman opened her eyes to unfamiliar surroundings. The enclosure was dark and smelled of dirt, herbs that were hanging from the tipi poles, smoke from the fire outside as well as drying meats and fish woven onto branches propped near the flames. But again a wave of terror flowed through her gut, and the instinct to run overwhelmed her. With a gentle hand, Quill kept her from sitting up. Her injured shoulder and hip had been tightly bound. And she now understood she was not to move, but in truth she could not have if she tried. The old shaman held a gourd to her mouth to help her drink a thick, strong smelling brew that tasted like dust.

"Where am I?" the woman asked in English.

Nothing seemed familiar. She did not remember the trappers who bound her, that she had fallen or that she had been cared for by these Indians. She did not remember what happened yesterday or even last week.

Suddenly, the walls closed in, and she became agitated. A surging need to weep overcame her, and the woman's chest heaved, but it hurt so much that she could not allow herself that release.

"Be still. You must rest," the shaman said in her own language. And as if she could understand what the woman was thinking, Quill shook her head and told her, "Who did this to you? Someone who knows no kindness." Then she continued to put strong smelling poultices of herbs and oil on the torn skin, re-bandaging the wounds.

2
MOUNTAIN CABIN
COLORADO TERRITORY

Winter, 1872

A blizzard raged outside the mountain cabin. Lieutenant Jahn Van Andusson finished his coffee laced with strong whiskey and relit his pipe. He was tall, slender, with a thick shock of auburn hair, and though it was winter, his face was dark from time spent in the saddle. His cavalry uniform was well worn, the coat having been repaired many times.

Someone knocked on the door. The lieutenant reached for his gun. When the door opened he saw it was Juniper Jack, a man who distilled liquor and sold it at trapper's fort. He was with his friend and business partner, Johnny Garry. Jahn had met the men before on his travels through the mountains. They were friendly enough, and it was nice to have company on such a blustery night.

While they sat in front of the fire, Juniper Jack regaled him with the stories of selling the watered down stock to the Indians. As in the past, they found that Van Andusson was not one to share his thoughts. He, on the other hand, barely heard them as he was deep in thought, remembering that summer day in 1852 with its cacophony of sounds, images and smells that often swirled through his dreams: dried corn husks, his father's shouts, screams from his mother, arrows hitting the house, and the cry of his little brother, James.

THE SUMNER RANCH

Summer, 1852

Sweating profusely, Jahn awoke with a start to see the old couple, family friends Sara and Henry Sumner, standing by his bed. Sara was leaning over him stroking his head. She hugged him, and he clung to her neck. "There, there. We are right here, Jahn, right here. It is all right, dear boy. We are here. Honey, bring him some water, will you please?" Henry went to the pump in the kitchen, filled a glass, and gave it to the boy.

"Do you think you can get back to sleep now, Jahn?" Sara said putting the glass down on the nightstand.

"I think so." The boy rolled over onto his stomach, and like she had done so many years ago with her own children to help them sleep, Sara rubbed his back. Then the old couple closed the door, leaving it slightly ajar so they could hear if they were needed again. The boy, his seven-year old sister, Holly, and fifteen-year old brother, Richard, were staying with the Sumners. With the death of their father and little brother James and the loss of their mother, none of them had been able to sleep through the night.

"I feel so for his distress," Sara told Henry, both of them also feeling acutely the loss of their friends. "Time will tell if there is any hope, but I fear there is not."

A posse of neighbors, David George, Sean Finnian with his son, Conor, and Gregory Rhyerson, all friends of the children's parents, gathered outside the Sumner's house, waiting while Richard saddled his horse.

"I'm coming!" Jahn called out to his brother as he ran to the barn.

"No, Jahn, you stay here." Richard said stopping him. "Help the Sumners take care of Holly."

"But I want to go with you!"

"Stay here, I said!"

Richard was not sure what they would find and did not want his brother to see anything that would upset him more. He knew that it was not merely rumor that these Comanche raiders were the most vicious and cruel of men, tearing the flesh of their victims in the most heinous fashion, not only out of revenge for killings in their villages, but also for the mere pleasure of it. He had seen the results on men who came into the saloon–those that had lived.

Jahn, though disappointed not to go, was sure that they would be able to find their mother because he knew that she was alive. He felt it in his bones.

Richard and the posse rode for several days following the trail left by the marauders. The first day they found a black circle from a fire where the thieves had camped. The third day Conor found a piece of red and white gingham cloth torn from a dress and blood stains on the rocks nearby.

Richard grabbed the shredded material and pressed it to his face inhaling its scent, then held it to his chest, but he could not contain the distress this find caused, and he emptied his stomach along the side of the trail.

Up until then they had easily followed the raiders' hoof prints through the aspen and pines, but when all the signs were washed out by rain, they had no choice but to return home.

Before the raid Holly had been a lively, talkative child, always asking questions and wanting to follow her brothers wherever they went. Now sitting by the fire, she sat silently holding her doll. Jahn had hardly been able to contain his concern. His brother had been gone for four days. What if he, too, had been killed or taken by the Indians? The thought made him crazy, and he paced the room like a caged animal.

Sara was making supper.

"Jahn, will you go to the barn and help Mr. Sumner finish up his chores?"

Glad to have something to do to burn off his energy, he ran out of the house to where Henry was cleaning out the stalls. He picked up a pitchfork full of soiled straw and threw it into the wheelbarrow. With each stab into the muck, he grew more and more agitated.

"Stop, son," Henry admonished in his slow and methodical way of talking. "You are going to hurt yourself."

"Where are they? They should have come home by now," Jahn said throwing down the pitchfork in frustration.

"Take a long breath, Jahn. If they can, they will bring her back."

The mountains were vast and the trails difficult to follow even in good weather, and Mr. Sumner, like his wife, was not confident that the posse would be able to find the children's mother in such a vast territory.

Henry put his hand on Jahn's shoulder. "All right, son. Let's coop up the chickens, and go see what Mrs. Sumner has for us for supper."

Throughout the week, Holly had not said one word, ate little and slept fitfully. Sara or Jahn bathed and dressed her, combed her hair and wiped the sweat from her face.

"I am worried about her, Henry," Sara said. "I wish the doctor was in town. I am not sure where he is now, but I have heard he is due back this way in a week or so."

"I will see what I can find out," Henry said getting ready for the long ride to the Dry Goods Store.

Sara sat down in front of the fire, pulled Holly onto her lap, opened a book and began to read to her.

Jahn came in with a basket of eggs.

"They are laying well," he said distractedly. "Have the pigs eaten yet?"

"No," Henry said, noticing that Jahn looked exhausted from sleeping badly. Jahn went to the swill bucket to take it out to the pen. But before he could get to the door, the Sumners' dog began to bark.

"Richard!" Jahn said, bursting out of the door, and racing up the road.

As the posse rode into the ranch, Jahn noticed five riders, not six.

"Where is she? Why didn't you bring her back? Where is Mama?" he said looking to each rider.

Richard pulled out the bit of dress. "This was all we found, Jahn. Then it rained and all the tracks were lost."

"You came home without looking more? This proves she was there. She is alive. I know it! You must go back!"

"Where? We have no idea where she is, Jahn," Richard said, physically drained and emotionally used up. Jahn tried to get onto Richard's horse, but his brother stopped him. Frustrated and not knowing what to do, the boy began pounding on his brother's chest.

"I know she is alive, I just know it!"

Richard grabbed his brother's wrists and then hugged him tightly. "We will go out again tomorrow, you and I, together."

3
QUILL AND FATHER MAN'S CAMP

Despite their advanced age, Quill and Father Man moved about the tipi surely and confidently, dancing around each other like birds, jockeying for a place at the woman's side, each plying their gifts toward her healing. Father Man sang chants, and often sat next to her with his eyes closed in meditation while Quill gently bathed her, fed her and helped her when she needed to evacuate her bowels. More than once the couple had wiped tears from the woman's eyes. But they could not know that they were from appreciation for the kindness and care she was being given.

Even with his initial aversion, when Cougar Two Foot came into the tipi, he could not keep from glancing at the injured woman, his eyes pulled to the red streaks in her hair, the blue in her eyes, and the way the fire outlined her cheeks.

"What does she say her name is?" he asked.

"She cannot tell us. Her memory is hiding out of reach," Quill answered.

"The clear sky matches her eyes," Cougar Two Foot noted offhandedly.

"And her mind," Father Man remarked.

"No cloud story," Quill said matter-of-factly.

"No Cloud Story," Father Man said. "We shall call her that for now."

"No," Cougar Two Foot said. "Clear Sky. I think it should be Clear Sky, for her eyes."

"All right then, Clear Sky," Father Man agreed.

The woman looked at the men quizzically. Cougar Two Foot looked away. Father Man pointed to her eyes and then to the heavens.

"Clear Sky," he repeated.

She attempted to say the words, not understanding that that had become her name.

That night Quill asked Cougar Two Foot to watch her while they tended to the ill in the village. Reluctantly, he came and sat down on the ground near the injured woman, and so as not to awaken her, began to chant a healing song inwardly. Deeper and deeper, he fell into himself till the walls of the enclosure and the ground all fell away, leaving him in the Vastness of Creation. Before him, enfolded in light, sitting on the back of a huge bear, was his wife holding their little child. She smiled at him, and his heart nearly exploded with joy. The baby reached out to touch his father, but when their fingers connected Cougar Two Foot jolted upright and his eyes flew open, and he was once again on the floor of the tipi. Soon the overwhelming ecstasy that he had felt faded into deep sadness as he was reminded that with that birth, the spirits of his wife and his child had gone to live in the Sun where there is always plenty of game to eat.

When he realized the injured woman was awake and had been watching him, he put a gourd of water to her lips. She was able to swallow a small amount.

4

Several more search parties made up of parishioners from their father's church had gone looking for their mother, but finding no sign of her, had given up.

"I am sorry, son," they told Jahn.

"You can't stop looking! She is out there somewhere!"

For weeks each night in his sleep, Jahn scoured the dense forest looking for his mother. Each night, in a morning mist, he would see the back of a female figure hidden in the trees. "Mama! Mama!" he would shout, running toward her. But it was not his mother, only an Indian woman who disappeared into the shadows before he could get to her. He would wake to find that either Henry or Sara had come in to comfort him.

Richard had tried to calm his siblings as best he could, but he was not doing much better, sleeping fitfully and eating little. Holly who still would not speak, nor seek any comfort, was like a rag doll that had to be carried everywhere. But Jahn, agitated and angry, paced about the house unable to settle down.

Mr. Sumner and his wife, who had lost their four boys to diphtheria many years before, were enjoying having children in the house once again. The children felt safe there. Even so after a month Richard wanted to go back to their home at Silver Leaf Ranch.

"It is not a good idea, young man. What if more Indians come? You are only fifteen, and you have young children to look after. Stay here with Sara and me. You are most welcome to do so."

Richard pushed, and finally got his way, so Holly, Jahn and Richard Van Andusson moved back to Silver Leaf Ranch.

Richard released Spider, the horse Mr. Sumner had lent them, into the paddock for the night and went into the house to begin to clean up. *I must keep moving. Keep doing something,* Richard thought, *anything not to remember.*

And when Jahn walked in the door, all he could hear were the screams from his mother and his little brother, and the pounding of horses' hooves. A serpent carrying all his fear, hatred and distrust of Indians had taken refuge in his chest.

Richard and Jahn put away the things that had been strewn on the floor and picked up the debris that had collected in the house from the door having been left open for so long. Several mice had made their home in Jahn's pillow and soiled it beyond use.

Richard swept the floor, and Jahn put the rug back in front of the fireplace. Even though the horses were gone, Richard ran to the barn to see what he could do to put it in order. While the boys worked, Holly sat in the rocker asleep clutching her doll.

Little by little, they got the house put back together as the boys thought their parents would have wanted it. Each night when the sun went down, Richard built a fire to warm the room, and then he would read to Holly.

To be safe, overnight the boys took turns guarding the house, sitting on the roof wrapped in a blanket, with a loaded gun in their lap. The days were long and hard to get through, but by nightfall Richard and Jahn were usually ready to rest and after a few weeks, they each slept through one or two nights.

Upon waking each morning both Jahn and Richard half expected to hear their mother singing or father chopping kindling, or James, little James, laughing, but when they did not, a weight of permanent disappointment set in. Jahn vowed to himself that he would find his mother, but he did not tell Richard his plans to scour the mountains.

"We must do something!" Jahn shouted at his brother. "What if someone has seen her? They would not know who she was or where she had come from!" The boys rode along the river in silence for a time. "The bank might print up a poster for us."

"The bank?" Richard queried.

"They have a printing press in the back. I saw it once when I went in with Pa."

Richard rode into the village that afternoon to speak to the bank manager. "Yes sir, Mr. Steadman, I know it is expensive for you, but how will anyone know about our mother if they do not see our poster?" he said.

Steadman stalled.

A man called out from the front door in a heavy French accent, "I will take care of it, Josiah."

"Mr. Brevier, that is very generous of you. Generous,

indeed," Steadman said, relieved that he would not have to put out the money for it.

"Glad to do it," Brevier said smiling.

"Sir, you do not know how much this means to us," Richard said.

"I can imagine," Brevier said taking the young man's hand in both of his. His wife and daughter had been taken many years ago. His daughter's body was found a few days after the raid, but he never knew what happened to his wife and had been inconsolable for years.

That evening the boys sat in front of the fireplace and composed what they wanted to say.

"Mr. Steadman told me if we have a drawing of her they are able to make a plate of it and put that on the poster. You draw better than me. Make a picture of her. Put those hair combs in it. She had them on that day."

"How about both of us drawing her, and we'll use the best one," Jahn said. The boys took out their pens and paper and labored over the images until they were satisfied. "At least they'll know what she looks like."

"We can only hope," Richard replied, secretly feeling it was wasted effort.

The next week as promised they had the stack of posters, and the boys took them to neighboring ranches, forts and settlements. Jahn anticipated that there would be a response right away. But even though there was not, he remained sure that he would be able to find her, and he never allowed his mind to rest on the possibility that she might be dead.

5

Like a gaggle of geese, Quill's four friends came into the hut quietly chattering with one another. They still felt disturbed by the presence of the white woman, and so did not speak of her outside the village, but as Quill was their friend, they did as she asked, one or all visiting each day while Quill or Father Man went about the business of caring for her injuries.

During the day, when others needed to be tended to by the Medicine couple, The Gaggle, as she called them to herself, came to keep her company. Clear Sky could feel their hesitancy, and it made her uneasy, and though she wanted to sleep, she almost never could while they were present. Eventually, though, she understood that they were there to help with the healing of her body. And she learned their names: Shy Girl was delicate and slim and tended to repeat herself and what others said, Petals was talkative and gregarious, Long Cedar Branch was stern and quiet and had a way of getting sharply to the point. But if Quill was the leader of this noisy clutch, then Stands In Front was the second in command. She made all the decisions for the group when Quill was not there.

"Like Quill's grandmother," Stands In Front said, nodding toward Clear Sky, raising her eyebrow disapprovingly.

"Pure Heart had the same color eyes," Shy Girl remembered. "Yes, she did. Same blue eyes."

"How is Clear Sky today?" Petals asked the woman.

The woman looked at them blankly.

"She does not understand us," Long Cedar Branch remarked. "White women are so stupid." She took a bearskin in her fist and held it up saying " *'we-da'*. "

Carefully, Clear Sky tried to repeat it.

Long Cedar Branch said " *'we-da'* " once again this time more slowly and louder.

"She is not deaf," Stands In Front chided.

The woman repeated it this time with more ease. Long Cedar Branch snorted and pointed to something else.

"She learns quickly, yes, learns quickly," Shy Girl said excitedly.

"We'll see," Long Cedar Branch disagreed.

"Maybe our tongue will be too hard for her," Shy Girl said, not wanting to contradict the other women.

No white men had come looking for her, had attacked their village or taken their horses in retribution, so in time the women began to accept her. At Quill's suggestion, her friends came to work with Clear Sky each day teaching her their language.

6

Over the next few weeks, Quill, first settling into the embrace of the fullness of the Infinite, would then apply the herbs and ointments to Clear Sky's wounds. As her fear, anger and rage melted into acceptance, the wounded woman's body responded, little by little, stitching together sinew and skin.

The shaman couple looked over Clear Sky's injuries. The bottoms of her feet had healed, and the puncture on her hip had closed nicely as well. They agreed that it was time for her to try out her legs. Cougar Two Foot ducked his head into the opening of the tipi just as they were trying to lift Clear Sky onto her feet.

"She is heavy for you," he said to his mentors. Stilling his own reluctance, Cougar Two Foot carefully put his hands under the small of the woman's back, raising her to standing. She took a few steps on her own, but then her knees quivered and let go. He caught her, but sharply pulled back his chest.

He did not like that he wanted to help this white woman, but despite these feelings, he came to the tipi every day to assist her to regain the strength in her legs. Clear Sky got stronger and looked forward to working with him, and even regained her appetite.

Cougar Two Foot, guiding her as they walked, escorted the white woman through the small village. But seeing the camp with its unfamiliar sights, sounds and smells filled her heart with terror once again, and her chest began to heave.

"No one here will harm you," he told her. "You are in Father Man's charge," but added under his breath, "if I were in your village, there would be a gun pointed at my head."

She did not understand all that he said and clutched his strong, steady arm.

"Hello, Clear Sky," shouted one woman.

"How is she today, Cougar Two Foot?" asked another.

Some looked at her with distrust and annoyance, some with fear, but most, if they looked up at all, soon went back to what they were doing. The children stared at her out of curiosity, especially the little girls.

This life was still so unfamiliar to her that each day felt like a challenge, and though she longed to feel the comfort of having a family, she felt unable to fit in. And there was the echo that nagged at her of what that faceless man said in her dream. *What son?* she wondered. She was only dimly aware that she had had a family, but she felt sure they were all dead.

"You remind me of my grandmother," Quill said to Clear Sky one day. "She was married to the masterful healer, Great Bull," Quill said, "my grandfather."

"Yes?" Clear Sky asked.

Quill looked deeply into Clear Sky's eyes and then said, "Another time." But Quill began to ruminate about her family.

She and Father Man had had two sons, Yellow Bark and Three Rocks. Both had married and moved away to live with their wives' families in different communities. The couple had tried to have more children, but Great Spirit had other plans for their two girls, taking them when they were but days old.

And then there was that terrible day many years ago that Father Man stood outside the tipi not knowing how he was going to tell his wife that their second son was gravely injured so soon after their eldest had been killed. The men brought Yellow Bark back from the hunt, laying him just outside the shelter.

"Where is my son?" Quill had asked when he came in. "Wasn't he with you?"

"My dear wife…" he started.

With rising concern seeing the grave look on Father Man's face, she asked, "Husband, where is Yellow Bark?"

"Outside." He looked away.

"Well, have him come in." She did not look up so as not to reveal her own unease.

"Come outside," he said with some effort. "He waits for you there."

Quill ducked through the skin at the door of their tipi, and looked down to see her son lying on a litter, barely breathing. He was bloody and broken from the hooves of the buffalo that had made their path across his body.

Quill ran to her son afraid to even touch him. "There is so much that needs to be healed. Where will I begin?" But when she looked up at her husband, he shook his head. "What happened?"

"We were burning out the field to force the bison our way," one of the men answered. "Yellow Bark turned to call to me when his horse caught his hoof in a badger hole, throwing both horse and rider to the ground. He did not have a chance to save himself. My brother rode in, but by then the buffalo had already passed over him."

Yellow Bark gazed at his mother with sad, blood-filled eyes, then his eyes changed to a stare of heart breaking stillness.

With Three Rocks already dead, she could not even fathom that her second son was gone as well. For weeks, Quill did not speak unless someone asked her something directly, and then she would have to rouse herself from a deep well of sadness. Father Man, needing the comfort as well, held her many times while she wept.

Since neither son had produced any offspring, Quill enjoyed the company of this white woman, and began to look on her as if she were a daughter.

7

1872

At the end of the day after riding long hours, the men had settled down for the night. Johnny Gary poured some whiskey in his own glass and then passed the bottle to Juniper Jack who then passed it along to Jahn. Jahn took a swallow, lit his pipe, then once again his thoughts fell onto those early days just after the raid:

After the day's work was done, he would reach under his parents' bed for the basket that contained his mother's journals. She had written in them sporadically through the years, and reading them was comforting, allowing him to feel her presence. Having read and reread passages almost daily, Jahn could recite them from memory.

She wrote of her marriage to his father, and how since his mother's mother had died of smallpox when his mother was six, Granny had been so kind stepping in as a surrogate parent during the preparations, fitting her dress and helping with her hair. She talked about how excited and nervous his father, Garritt, had been on their wedding day.

April 15th 1842

...Since Richard was born we have wanted to have more children, but God has seen otherwise, and I have lost two, a boy and a girl. Though I am pregnant once again, try as I may, instead of feeling jubilant, I do find, on occasion, I tumble down into an abyss of sadness. I fear that young Richard is not getting what he needs from me as I can hardly keep my mind at peace...

January 25th

...At last we have a child, a new baby boy. We have called him Jahn Wolf Van Andusson. His chortle makes me laugh so hard that I disturb his nursing. Richard adores his little brother, and helps me endlessly with his care...

March 21, 1849

...Our little girl is growing so fast. Seems like yesterday that Holly Virginia was born, but now James Wolf is almost three and Holly is nearly four. She is a delightful and intelligent child, full of fun. When she can walk she would rather run or gallop like the horses. She is interested in everything around her and has become quite a chatterbox. She follows after her brothers more than they would like, I fear. And James is the spitting image of his father. He even walks like him, and definitely is a papa's boy. If his father wipes the sweat from his brow, James follows wiping his tiny forehead. It is very cute to watch. They are dear children both of them...

Jahn remembered the day that his father decided they would move from Peidman's Landing in the San Luis Valley up into the mountains. It seemed exciting to him, but it was not for his mother.

February 25, 1848

When I was very young, eight years old, 1822, I think, my papa moved us from the city of New Orleans to a settlement in the San Luis Valley. He had read stories of trappers making a lot of money up in the White River area, and was convinced that he should go there to trap beaver.

We took one of the first steamships up the Mississippi River to St. Louis. Even though we slept on deck it was so exciting, so thrilling. Later we joined a wagon train. That was anything but fun. Long hours of riding and sometimes walking to where? Only God knew.

I couldn't sleep, my clothes were soiled and I felt filthy all the time. I complained bitterly to my father and mother, but they merely encouraged me to keep going. It took us several weeks to get to the base of the mountains, and what was there was not much.

In New Orleans, though the family spoke English at home, everywhere in town we spoke French. But in the settlement, almost everyone was Mexican. Few spoke English. And only when my father's trapper friends came to the house did I get to speak French.

Papa soon found the life of a trapper too hard. We wouldn't see him for months at a time, and when he came back he was so exhausted he could hardly get out of bed. After that, he helped at the trapper's fort, began to raise horses to sell, and of course, gave sermons on Sundays.

February 28

I enjoy my life here at the San Luis Valley Episcopal Church. San Luis Valley has turned into a well-established settlement. I feel safe here where many of the women have become my closest friends. But recently U.S. Soldiers have begun fighting with the Mexicans close to us, and now even though the United States has just signed a treaty with them making Colorado part of its territory, Garritt feels it would be safer up in the mountains. And truth be told, for some time he has had his eye on all that free land available for raising horses. But to me the idea of dropping myself into the wild mountains seems preposterous.

"Garritt, isn't there somewhere else we could go? Even the thought *of venturing off into the mountains with four children, having to build a house and start over is more than I can take! What about schooling, and what about our friends? We will be all alone out there. And you know how ruthless those Indians can be."*

Baby James lay in my arms while I rocked him to sleep. But my movement was too fast and agitated for my baby to drift off. Distressed, James began to cry. Garritt took him from my arms but did not have success at calming his young son and handed him back to me. "Honey, we will build new friendships as we build up our congregation," Garritt said flatly, avoiding the safety issue.

"It will be too hard on the children to leave all their playmates," I yelled futilely. "And besides they are too young!" But I knew I was talking about myself as well.

Normally, I can ease Garritt into a decision that suits us both, but in this instance I could not. And underneath the usual trepidations about moving, I feel an even deeper dread about the future he is planning for us and have had many nightmares of our family being torn apart.

Though I have never told anyone, there have been many times when I have been aware of what was to happen in our future, but perhaps this time it is just that I have heard stories about my Great Aunt Agnes who, as the tale goes, was taken from her family, husband and two boys by marauding Indian thieves. But we don't really know because no one ever saw her again.

I think it was retribution, for her husband had not been kind to the Indians and had treated the ones in the surrounding tribes very badly, sometimes cruelly. He never allowed them to hunt on his land or sell their wares at his store even when they were in desperate need of food and supplies, and he thought nothing of killing them to get them off his property.

I thought about taking the children and leaving, but it was only a momentary consideration. I love Garritt, and do not want to leave him. Besides as a lone woman how would I take care of myself, let alone my family?

"*I must go where I am called,*" *Garritt ended the conversation on the subject.*

Holly *is none too happy about leaving her friends.* "*I don't want to go,*" *she said, and cried most of the night when I told her of the move. Luckily James is too little to understand, but young Jahn told me that for him the idea of going up into the mountains was exciting, a big adventure. I wish I felt the same.*

April 27

...*Thank goodness there is a small Episcopal Church up there that is in need of a pastor. Of course, Garritt has neglected to tell me this before now.*

April 30

Garritt *and Richard were gone for several weeks to find the right place for our new home. When they returned, I could see that Garritt had hardened to the idea of the move. Even Richard tries to encourage me by telling me that the site for our ranch is beautiful. He and his father plan to go up there in a few weeks and begin the foundation for the house.*

I went to the Mercantile to ask Juan about our needs for this arduous journey, and made a list of the things he suggested: warmer clothing for the early fall, plus molasses, clarified butter, of course, and desiccated vegetables and meats for soup. I also gathered seeds for flowers and vegetables. It will be late to put in a garden, but we will need whatever we can grow for the long, cold winter.

"*Keep your gun handy,*" *he told me setting an extra box of shot on the counter.* "*Those savages up there won't think twice about killing you and taking your horses. My advice? If you see them, kill them. Best thing we could do is exterminate those varmints.*"

"*Now Juan,*" *I said in my best Spanish,* "*you must be*

exaggerating. The Indians here don't seem ruthless."

"Señora, it is worse than you can imagine. Those savages do not like that white settlers, or Mexican for that matter, have taken what they say is their land."

It sent a shiver down my spine, and now I was even angrier with Garritt for making us go.

June 16

...It was more than a week's travel up into the mountains. Our wagon lurched over the rocks, jumbling everything in the rig and everything in me. Torrential rains drenched our belongings, making them nearly impossible for our poor horses to pull, and the children complained with the compounding fatigue of the journey. Garritt kept his hand on his gun no matter where we were, pretending that it was to keep us safe, but I knew him, and I knew he was wondering what he had begun. Is this what we had to look forward to? A life where you are always looking over your shoulder?

One day he went into the woods to look for game. I heard shouting and several shots. I was terrified! When Garritt ran back to the wagon, he told me that several trappers had cornered an Indian and were about to attack the poor man. Garritt shot into the air startling the men. Who when they turned to look, released their grip, giving the Indian an opening to escape.

"Aw, you should have let us have him, Reverend," one said. "It would have been good sport to string him up by his heels then set a fire below. They truly squirm with that one."

"They all laughed remembering!" Garritt said in disbelief.

The thought of it made me ill.

That night on that mountainside when we made camp, with the bright blaze of our fire heating us as well as keeping away animals, with my children huddled against me warming themselves in my arms, I never felt so small in the world.

Thank goodness, without another incident, except for the rig wheel breaking, which Garritt fixed, and the weather, which he could not fix, we made our way to our land.

June 23

We are on the North Fork of the White River near Trapper's Lake...Facing east we have a view of the mountain ridge, and to the west a valley that spreads out below. Upstream from a tributary of the river that runs near the house is a tall waterfall with the glorious sound of the water cascading over huge boulders... Neighbors from all around have come to help build our house. And imagine my surprise when we arrived to find that these wonderful people had started a garden for us, even putting up a fence to keep the critters away from the starts...

Our neighbors have been so generous with their time and resources, I hardly know how to begin to thank them all, and I am thrilled to know that we will have friends to visit and company to entertain.

October 21

Near the center of our small town, hot water comes right out of the earth! It smells a bit like eggs that are too old, but apparently, it is a place the Utes use for healing.

Surprisingly, I have not seen as many of them as I had expected to, just a few women with their long black hair and cotton or animal skin clothing, trading goods for food at the Mercantile. I wish I could understand what they are saying. For the most part they keep to themselves, but occasionally I see them furtively looking my way.

The Indians in San Luis Valley had complained that since so many white men have come, game is scarce, so they come to the fort to trade for food. I guess it is the same up here. Apparently, they say we have moved onto their land. But there is so much land available, I do not understand their concern.

With all the talk of raiding parties making trouble nearby, stealing horses and burning down barns, the children and I have been told not to travel away from the ranch alone, but if we do, always with a man. It has left me feeling anxious and a little jumpy, especially in the night. And though Garritt has promised me that nothing will happen to us because God is protecting us, I make him keep a gun by the door in case God is busy with the many other things He has to do.

November 10

In a very short time, I have become fast friends with Sara Sumner, Bethany George, Martha Rhyerson, and Colbertha Finnian. I am particularly fond of Sara who makes me laugh and also feels like a rock I can lean on. We all join together for tea, sewing bees, canning and the like, and are the women's committee for children's church, each taking turns reading Bible stories while Garritt gives the sermon on Sundays. I am happy to see that the children have found friends in their offspring as well...

November 12

I just found this in one of the journals I wrote when I was fourteen years old:

"I woke up this morning knowing that my mother would be dead very soon. An angel came and told me not to worry, that my father would take good care of me. Though reassured, it was also a nightmare to say the least, but the strangest thing was that no one believed me. I told my father, our neighbor Mrs. Caldwell, and my best friend, Camila Peña. Camila took it the best. At least she did not call me crazy. Papa told me I was imagining things, and Mrs. Caldwell said the same thing only more harshly...

"...It has been two weeks since I had that dream of my mother's death. When my mama woke up this morning she had spots all over her face, and I am not allowed to go in to see her. Though Papa told me it

was not my fault, I am sure that I am the one who caused her to get sick by talking about it...

"...Mama has been sick for almost three weeks. She is not getting better...

"...Mama died today...Papa has reassured me that I could not know that Mama was going to die. He said it was just a coincidence, but even so in the future if I "know" something, I will just keep it to myself...

"...I borrowed a book that had all the cures for every disease known, from Doctor Vargas. He asked me why 'such a beautiful young child would be interested in all that,' particularly a señorita. 'That is not women's work,' he emphasized. I didn't tell Papa I had it.

When Papa was deep into snoring, I would relight my candle, and turned the pages as quietly as I could while I read. But one night I fell asleep, and in the morning Papa found me with my forehead pressed onto the book. 'What are you doing with this?' he yelled yanking the book out of my hands. Though he gave it back to Doc Vargas, I went and borrowed it again. This time I was sure not to fall asleep while reading it. At least, now I know that my Mama died of the small pox, a terrible disease..."

...I see now why I tell no one of those premonitions. People are afraid of them. They think that Satan is speaking through someone like me. But I do not think Satan or God is speaking through me. It isn't anything. I believe it is just like knowing that when the clouds above are thick and dark with water, it is likely to rain. But I keep quiet and don't even tell Garritt.

The Healings: I know that if I told anyone about my ability to heal people, they would be frightened by me and might call me a witch. I have read accounts of witches' lives in newspapers from the east. They have had terrible deaths, burned at the stake or drowned or hanged, so I never say anything to anyone, just make excuses to those I help, implying that they were not as injured or ill as they had supposed, and look with them in wonder and awe at how they have healed. I would talk about innocuous things as I worked on them, distracting them from what I was doing. But the truth is I don't think I am the one who heals them. It is God's love, and more importantly their willingness to take it in.

Jahn remembered that his mother sang songs to him and his siblings, hymns mostly, but no matter how bad the day had been he always felt better for having heard her sing.

December 20

…One time when I took my hand off Jahn's arm, not only had the bleeding stopped, but also the cut had closed up and was merely a pink line.

"You mustn't say anything to anyone about this, son. They will not understand. Not even to Pa," I warned. I patted the wound dry and placed a bandage over it.

"I don't need that," Jahn said.

"I know, but everyone will expect to see one. It's our secret, Jahn, all right?" I kissed him on his forehead, gave him a quick hug and told him to be careful when he went out to play.

Jahn ran his hand over the place on his arm that had been cut. He remembered that the children had not been the only ones who benefitted from her company. Congregants from their church, and even some from the Santa Maria Catholic Church, called on her all through the day because if they spent time with her, when they left they felt uplifted and relieved of their burdens. They would bring gifts and make excuses about 'just happening to be passing by'. She said she used her imagination to feel them being happy, and it seemed to alleviate their aches and pains.

It was only in her writings that she divulged the premonitions of what was to happen in the future.

Too bad she did not heed the one about us moving to the mountains, he thought.

8

While Clear Sky had been recuperating on the soft bearskin mat, she spent her days staring at the clean, white smoke swirling off the wood and watching as it curled up to the opening in the top of the tipi. To no avail, she had tried to force her memory to remind her who she was, and where she had come from, but eventually she would relent and go to sleep, which she found preferable to staring at that blank past.

When she was completely healed and could get up and move around on her own, Quill put Clear Sky to work. She taught her to skin the animals that Father Man killed, and to make clothing from their pelts. Staying close to the old woman, she helped with the chores of the day, fetching water, cooking meals, gathering wood for the fires, and mending moccasins. From Quill and her friends, she learned to use every part of the animals for either food or clothing. And when it came time to move to a warmer climate, Clear Sky would help to take down the shelter and work to build one in the new location.

Though she did not remember it now, her ability to see

what was coming was returning. But the way of life in the village was still so unfamiliar that when she began to see scenes in her mind, images that felt real, she did not know how to interpret them and tried to shake them off. Even when she attempted to think of something else, the scenes persisted, almost shouting for her to acknowledge them.

Then suddenly one day, she felt as if she were a young boy falling from his horse. The next day Father Man came into the tipi looking for his wife, his face wrinkled with concern.

"What is the matter?" Clear Sky asked.

"It is Yelping Dog," Father Man told her looking deeply into her eyes. "He has fallen from his horse." Sadly the boy died of his injury. Only then did she tell her benefactors what she had seen.

"I knew it," Quill hissed at Father Man. "I could see it in her eyes."

"Hush, Old Woman," Father Man retorted. "How do we know this is true?"

In the mornings, Clear Sky went with Quill into the woods to gather healing and cooking herbs, which they hung in the shelter to dry. They also dried meat, fish and berries and pounded desiccated tubers to a fine meal for winter food. In the evenings, when each day's work was done and she was beyond tired, Father Man, reluctantly and only at the insistence of his wife, began to encourage his charge to look into the smoke for answers.

"What do you see, Clear Sky?"

"Father Man, I am so tired I cannot see anything," she tried to explain, afraid her answer would not be well taken.

"Take a deep breath." He waited for a moment then resumed his questioning, "Now close your eyes, child, and tell me what you see." He was sure she would tire of the asking, and then his wife would stop nagging him about teaching her.

With her eyes closed, sometimes she would merely drift off to sleep and see nothing, but one day she told him, "Father Man, I do not *see* anything."

This does not surprise me, he thought, giving his wife a look as if to say, 'I told you so'.

"Do not worry," he said. "It takes special knowledge. You are not one of our people. You are not able to know the meaning of the smoke."

"I mean, Father Man, it is not that I *see* something," she said, "but I do *hear* a voice that speaks to me, and also it is as if I am the thing I hear," she said.

"Then tell me," he said with a sigh. "What do you hear?" Her understanding came more and more easily, one then another and another coming true, till the couple could no longer ignore the veracity of what she said she heard.

Every day was the same. Every day. The daily work was hard, but she got stronger and was better able to interpret what the smoke was telling her.

Though this life kept her busy and was satisfying, all along she kept hearing the man with the undulating feather-hat telling her, "*Your boy is waiting for you.*" Then she would become agitated and irritable and speak sharply to those around her.

"It is as though you have a stone in your shoe, and you refuse to stop and take it out. Whatever is bothering you...think of something else. Think about what you are doing. There is much work to do here. Put your mind on that," Quill would say, her temper flaring as well.

One day Quill sat down next to Clear Sky and unwrapped three things from within a swatch of stained gingham material. She looked at the ring, the comb and the broken silver chain that had been in the cloth.

"Do you know these?" the old woman asked, at once thinking she might remember, but hoping she would not.

"This is very pretty," Clear Sky said reaching for the comb, fingering the ring and the chain. "Should I?" she said as she gave them back.

"No matter. I will put them away for now," Quill said aloud to herself and rewrapped the jewelry in the cloth.

Quill wondered if the woman's memory would ever return. She settled into herself, into the Deep Knowing that is within all, and saw that when the woman knew her own strength, she would indeed be able to remember her life again. But that might be a long time in coming.

"We shall go pick herbs," Quill announced.

They gathered their baskets and headed for a favorite spot, a sunny patch on the side of the hill near the stream. When they got there, they saw several young boys playing in the water, each splashing the other with more and more force.

They are playing awfully rough, Clear Sky thought.

Sure enough, one boy fell and cut his arm on a rock. The boy shed no tears, but tightened his jaw. Without thinking, Clear Sky hurried over to help him. At first he pulled away, but then after looking into her eyes, he relaxed and let her touch him. "Well, let's see what you have done to yourself," she said in English as she washed the cuts. She spoke to him quietly and confidently, though not in his language, about what a fine boy he was, and how he was becoming such a strong warrior. When she finished, the wound had stopped bleeding, and he smiled a broad grin.

Quill watched with curiosity. *I knew it,* she thought. She would tell Father Man of the woman's gift. *Now, he might teach her.*

Even though her days were filled to capacity with all the chores to be done, Clear Sky often felt lost and despondent. Some days were so hard to get through, with depression weighing her down heavily, that more than once she had thought of ending her life.

One day she had been walking for an hour when she heard, "Where are you going, Clear Sky?"

"Nowhere," she answered absent-mindedly pulling her mind to the present. A young boy of about eight years was standing in front of her. "What is your name again, little boy?"

"Raccoon," the boy said proudly lifting his chest. "Come with me," he said. "Quill said you should come home now."

Raccoon, she thought. "Yes, of course. You are Long Cedar Branch's grandson." He smiled, and she followed him, only vaguely aware where they were going.

Heading back to their village, they traversed along one of the trading roads carved over centuries by the feet of ancient merchants traveling through the mountains taking their goods to barter for the produce and products of other villages.

A white family in their Conestoga wagon drove past. In it were seven children whose ages ranged from newborn to six. The wagon was packed to the hilt with their belongings. The father snapped the reins to hurry the exhausted oxen up the road. Next to him was a mother breastfeeding the newborn.

Clear Sky could not take her eyes off the mother, blond, young, wearing a gingham dress that was caked with dust. As the wagon passed, the women's eyes locked. Raccoon, not wanting to be seen by this white family, fearing he might be stolen, ran after her, grabbing a fold in her dress, and pulled her back into the woods.

"I am to take you home. Quill said so," he said wanting to get away from the white people as fast as he could.

As she lay sleeping in a dream state, Clear Sky saw a large vulture flapping its wings and picking at a carcass. It seemed as if the one became two, and the two, many, feeding on her body as she lay in the dirt, her arms flailing to get them off. She woke sweating, and sat up quickly. Above her stood a tall muscular man, one she did not know, who was lifting her hair from her face with his knife.

She gasped. "Who are you, and what do you want?"

He withdrew his weapon, and his mood shifted, becoming haughty and belligerent.

"White woman, you not one of us. I find you. You, all blood and torn cloth like pile of dirty leggings. You die without me," he spit out in broken English.

"What do you mean?"

Hearing voices from within the tipi, Quill pushed back the flap. "What do you want, Corn Snake?"

He said nothing, and bolted out of the door.

"He said he saved me. Is that true?"

"Yes, but he left you at my feet. I cared for your wounds, not him. Best to keep him on the opposite side of the river. That man bites like a snake in the grass."

Clear Sky asked Cougar Two Foot about the man as they went to gather tinder in the woods, "Who is that man, the one called Corn Snake?"

"I have known him since we were boys. He is not part of our family. He has walked a path filled with boulders, winter winds and terrible storms. Now he is the dog that bites first before he understands that it is safe."

"What happened to him? How is it that he speaks my language?"

"He was captured when he was ten summers, and taken through many forests and over many mountains, far from his people. He is Choctaw, from a place called Wide Muddy River, where it does not snow. He learned the white man's tongue when he lived with them. He has always talked of returning to find his family, but so far he has never left us. My wife's mother, The Silver Moon, took him into her family. If I go across the river, he goes across, stepping on the same stones. When I became an apprentice of Father Man and Quill, so did he."

"Is he a Shaman now?"

"No," he said swiftly.

He told her of the time when he was a young apprentice when Father Man had walked with him by the river's edge to pick up stones to skip across the water, and he had asked how to know when as an apprentice you are doing good and when you are not. He had seen Corn Snake try to harm with his medicine, and he did not wish to follow that path.

"You are learning quickly," Father Man said. "I am very proud of

you. You will make a fine Shaman one day."

"Father Man," he said, "I have seen Corn Snake mix herbs that will cure, and I have also seen him try to make the other kind."

"Luckily, his medicine is not strong enough to hurt anyone," his mentor told him. "But we must wait and see. He will make a fine Shaman if he can conquer his biggest enemy."

"Who is that?"

"The one inside of him who always finds that his arrows are never straight enough." Father Man took a long moment then told him, "Each flower is unique, each bird and each bear. Who is to say which one is better. When Corn Snake learns what it is that only he can bring in each moment, he will feel like a whole man."

He explained to Cougar Two Foot that even though Corn Snake had a difficult life for a boy so young, it was no excuse for his actions, but it does make clear why he struggles so.

As the two skipped rocks across the water, Father Man explained that there was a test he could give himself for knowing which path to take: He said, *"A bear lumbers across the trail and finds two pieces of meat. One has a strange smell, not like meat at all, but it is large and would satisfy his hunger for a long time. The other smells like the savory rabbit that it is, but it is very small, and he would soon need to find food. Which one should he eat?"*

Cougar Two Foot thought about what to say, but before he had a chance to answer, Father Man told him, "The large one will fill his stomach, but will make him ill, the small will give him strength to find more."

"Corn Snake keeps choosing the poisonous meat," Cougar Two Foot told Clear Sky.

She had seen him in the woods, churning like the river over the rocks during winter-melt, and at other times he was silent, sour and in a dark place. Whenever he saw her though, he got agitated, angrily scowling at her.

"Others in the village have told me they are afraid of him. I have to admit that he scares me a little as well."

"A storm rages in his heart, but I do not think you need worry about him," Cougar Two Foot said, having seen Corn Snake's anger many times.

9

December 1852

"Thank you, Mrs. Sumner," Richard said, handing Holly to Sara. "We will be back in a day or so." Richard stopped before going out of the door. "Mrs. Sumner, do you think Holly will ever get well?"

"She hasn't said a word since–since that day," Jahn added.

"I don't know, dear ones. I hope so."

"I wish you would let me come with you," Henry said. "I don't like the idea of your going alone and in this weather, but I mustn't leave the Missus by herself."

"Don't you worry, boys. Holly will be just fine with us here. Won't you, Sweetheart?" Holly clung to Mrs. Sumner's neck, but did not look at her brothers. Sara pushed a smile through her concern.

Jahn and Richard stopped for the night at a settlement midway to Fort Garland. In their satchel they carried posters that the bank had printed for them, which for months they had been hanging in every fort near Silver Leaf Ranch.

"Sure I don't mind puttin' it up, son, but I don't think it will do much good. I have heard a good many stories of family members bein' taken by them Injuns, but truth be told, I never heard a one where they came back. They was either sold to another tribe, was killed in tryin' to escape or disappeared into the woods never to be seen again." The shopkeeper saw the disappointment on the two boy's faces and relented. "All right. Let me see what you have. That her? She's pretty." He read it out loud:

Missing
Virginia 'Ginny' Van Andusson.
Taken, July 1852 near Trapper's Lake.
If seen, contact Richard and Jahn Van Andusson
at Silver Leaf Ranch or through the
Trapper's Lake Bank.

"Boys, don't get your hopes up. Like I said, I haven't heard no stories about folks gettin' back home again."

"That your mother?" a voice called from the back of the store. A soldier stood testing out the weight of the guns from the rack.

"Yes, sir. Might you have seen her?" Jahn asked. The soldier looked over the poster then shook his head.

"You know these mountains well, being in the cavalry?" Richard asked.

"Me and my regiment go all over trying to keep the peace. Yup, there isn't much I don't know about these hills."

"You can come and go as you please?" Jahn asked.

"With orders," he answered, "but pretty much, son." He gave Jahn a long look. "I'll keep my eye out for her."

10

"Keep your eye on your target, Jahn," Henry Sumner said. "Let your breathing be steady and smooth, and when you are about to shoot, let out your breath easily, and in the pause before the next breath, pull the trigger."

It was reassuring to hear this from Mr. Sumner because Jahn remembered his father telling him the same thing when he was first learning to fire a gun. Henry set the rocks on the branch and then stood behind the boy. Jahn aligned the stones in his gunsite and pulled the trigger. The bullet zinged the stone, sending it flying into the woods. The first solid hit of the day.

"Well done, son," he said patting the boy affectionately on the back. "The Mrs. will be looking for us. We'd best go in."

"You go on, sir. I am going to practice a little longer. Will you ring the bell when supper is ready?"

"Sure thing, Jahn."

Henry Sumner loved these moments with one or both of the boys. He had done the same with his own children and looked forward to working with Jahn or Richard whenever they came over for supper.

Jahn set up several more "Indians" as he called them, and practiced till he shot each one off the fence.

11

Spring 1853

At the end of winter hibernation, spring leaves filled the branches of the forest and early flowers were exploding open. The excitement had been growing in the village for some time. All the children had been talking about it. The women began to reminisce about past years, looking forward to seeing friends and family, and choosing stories they would exchange. The men boasted about the races they would win, and had been practicing on foot and on their best ponies since the snow melted. Throughout the winter, the singers had polished their songs, and the women had sewn the clothing for the dancers to wear. Soon all the bands of the northern mountains would gather to celebrate the annual Bear Dance, the sacred ceremony of the rebirth of spring, which was also an opportunity to socialize, for young people to meet, and for parents to arrange the marriages of their children.

But for Clear Sky, who had no experience of this joyful celebration, it meant not only moving the camp, setting up for the week of the gathering, but then packing up and moving it again. And knowing nothing about the sacred festivities, she felt apprehensive and uncertain about how she was to act or what she was to do there.

Father Man told her, "The men make a Cave Of Sticks, a large circle surrounded by a tall pine bough fence, like a bear cave, with the opening in the south or southwest so that the sun shines into it part of the day to warm the animal. We dance within the enclosure. Everyone inside must dance."

Then Quill told Clear Sky, "You will wear this dress and shawl I have made for you." The dress was a fine deerskin smock with wing-like sleeves, and a long fringe at the bottom that bounced with each step she took. Throwing the shawl around her own shoulders and prancing, Quill began playfully flicking its long fringe at her husband as she came near him.

"Keep them clean," she told Clear Sky. "Wrap them in this cloth so they will not be dusty till we get there."

"But I do not know how to dance this dance," Clear Sky complained.

"Easy. You can walk, can't you, and run, yes? Easy."

They left in the morning, traveling all day to where the gathering was held. Across the plains, a long way from the celebration, she could already hear the chanting of the men blending with the beating of drums, the shaking of rattles and the grating of the morache, wooden rasps. Even and intense, it sounded like a grunting, growling bear that was breathing heavily.

A huge crowd of men, women and children had gathered for the event, more Indians than she had ever seen before in one place. There were hundreds of people. With all the unfamiliar sights and sounds, Clear Sky stayed close to Quill, fighting the panic as it rose and fell in her chest. After they set up their tipi, Quill took Clear Sky with her to greet old friends.

"This is my daughter, Clear Sky," she said to all. "She does not know our customs yet, so we must help her."

A woman of Clear Sky's age came and stood next to her. She was tall and strong and had a big-hearted smile.

"I am Rain," she stated. "Come with me. I can show you everything you need to know." Rain took her hand, and dragged her from place to place.

First they went to watch the men wrestle. Quick and strong, each man jumped, grabbed and threw his opponents until one could not get up. Everyone whooped and hollered, calling out the names of the men in the match, culminating in an explosion of excited cheers for the winner. Then they went to watch the men throwing the lance through a rolling ring. The man with the most successful throws would win the game.

As they walked through the clusters of happy revelers, Clear Sky tried to understand what was being said, but found it difficult because with the excitement of the day, everyone spoke too quickly or in dialects she was not used to hearing.

Rain jumped into an ongoing game of cards. She bet outrageously, and was losing. "I'd better leave now. I will play again after the dance. Maybe my luck will be better then," she laughed. They went to find her husband, Eagle Hunter, who was brushing his pony, talking quietly to it to calm it down before the races. She introduced him to Clear Sky.

"You will be racing?" Clear Sky asked.

"I think he likes the races better than he does his family, certainly better than dancing," Rain quipped.

"She is hard on me." Then he boasted, "But I do love to race, and have won many over the years."

They stood next to the track waiting for Eagle Hunter's event while other races were held. The thundering of hooves and screeching cheers of the many onlookers set Clear Sky on edge, and her chest began to heave. Rain noticed.

"Let's go," she said. "I am hungry. The meat should be ready by now." The fire pit was blazing, and the smell of venison permeated the air. Rain took her knife, and sliced off two chunks. While they ate, she talked to Clear Sky about The Bear Dance. "Bear taught our people to be strong," she said, "to be patient, but also fierce when necessary. Our dance helps to rouse her after such a long sleep. When she wakes, she must find food right away so she forages for berries and nuts, then she looks for her mate. That is why the women choose their partners for the dance. Don't be afraid," she said. "It is all for fun." Rain smiled to ease her concerns.

Rain did not tell her of the sacredness of the wise and brave Bear, of its magic, what communications could be had with it or with the Shade Ones, those that have passed on. She knew Quill and Father Man would help her understand. If during the dance the white woman had questions about the ceremonies, she would answer them as best she could, but for now she wanted her to feel at ease.

"Are you married?" Rain asked to make conversation.

"I was, but not now." Clear Sky looked off into the dark, unattainable past for some inkling of a memory, then pulling her mind to the present, she asked, "Will you dance? You have a husband. I mean you are not looking for a mate."

"My husband does not mind if I choose another. He only likes the races." She shrugged. "I love the dance." The music and drumming reached a crescendo then came to an abrupt stop. "Come, we have missed the ceremony, but the dance will begin very soon." Rain took Clear Sky by the hand and pulled her through the entrance of the dance circle. "Go on. Choose someone. When you see the man you want to dance with, flick your shawl at him," she said going to one of the men. She flicked her shawl, and he stepped forward.

What was she to do? Rain would expect her to join in, and so would the others. Terrified, Clear Sky scanned the entire circle of men standing around the edge of the Bear Cave looking for Cougar Two Foot, but she did not see him. There were some she recognized from her village, but no one she felt comfortable selecting. Then out of the corner of her eye, she spotted the partner she would choose. He was smiling at her from along the side of the circle near the crowd of musicians. With renewed courage, she crossed. Awkwardly, she flicked her shawl, and he stepped forward.

"You will have to teach me," she said.

He nodded, and they stepped to the two lines.

Rain and her partner also joined the lines, the women on one side and the men on the other, each line holding hands. With the grunting rhythm of the music, the women stepped three steps forward while the men stepped back three steps, then the men stepped three steps forward while the women stepped back. They repeated this prancing step till the couples broke away to dance alone. Facing each other, with a loping, running step, the woman or the man charged forward while the other ran backward, and they began the dance as a couple.

This continued for the length of the dance circle then reversed course, the other partner stepping forward, again traversing its full distance, until the music stopped or the dancers became exhausted.

"This is your first Bear Dance?" her partner asked when they stopped to catch their breath.

"My first," she said.

"And I am your first partner," Raccoon said with a grin. He put his hands on her arms, and they began to dance once again.

Cougar Two Foot watched from outside the bear cave. When the music broke, he stepped into the circle.

12

Clear Sky and Cougar Two Foot's conversation was easy and affable, and at times they even laughed together. Unbeknownst to them though, through the cover of the forest branches, Corn Snake watched.

"Careful that white skin might rub onto you," Corn Snake hissed from the branches along the stream. "We have no cure for that poison," he snarled.

Cougar Two Foot whirled around, recognizing the voice immediately. "Go back into your hole, Corn Snake."

"Who was that?" Clear Sky asked hearing only the murmur of voices.

"An irritating mosquito," he reassured her, hurrying her back toward the camp.

But Cougar Two Foot knew that Corn Snake was always ready to pick a fight. The anger had been building between them ever since the two were young apprentices, and it became worse when he had married the oldest of Silver Moon's daughters and became his brother.

After many attempts to encourage the boy, even Father Man finally had to tell Corn Snake he would not mentor him any longer. Corn Snake had never been able to tame the jealous creature that resided in his chest.

Exhausted from the work of the day, Clear Sky had fallen asleep and was heavily into dreaming.

She stood in the middle of a river the water rushing past under her legs. Her right foot stood on one rock and her left on another. On one side of the river was a camp where she recognized members of her village as they went about their day, on the other was a ranch house. It seemed to be empty, but she wanted to go there, too. Distraught at having to choose which side of the river to go to, she stood helplessly immobilized, unable to make the decision.

She turned restlessly in her sleep, making disquieted sounds until Quill called her name and woke her. Quill gently but firmly shook her shoulder.

"What is it?"

"Quiet now. We must not be heard," she whispered. "We are moving camp."

"Now? In the middle of the night? We just got here," Clear Sky asked.

"We must leave before the army soldiers wake us with their guns." Father Man said. "Black Kettle saw them riding up the ravine."

He had told the chief that they had but a few hours to get the village on their feet and out of the area before army soldiers would try to take them to a reservation. They had standing orders to remove any Indians they saw. Those that resisted were killed and sometimes, most times, they were slaughtered whether they resisted or not. The villagers were already in the habit of moving their lodgings to follow the animals as they migrated through the forests and plains, but now to avoid capture, many of the villages in the mountains broke camp often.

"Come now. Pack everything," Quill urged.

The night was black as a cave. Clouds covered the stars, and there was not even a hint of a moon. Clear Sky roused herself enough to do as she was told.

Within minutes the women emptied the tipis then lashed the travois poles to their horses, folded up the skins and tied them onto the sled. The elderly and the very young sat on top of the mounds. The dogs were harnessed in the same manner carrying household items of pots, bags of grain, dried meats, metal for arrowheads, steel needles and sewing supplies. The men gathered the remaining horses and herded them away from the army thieves who would take their land. Clear Sky lifted her pack onto her back, and took the reins of the horse, leading it along with the others. Quill sat atop the tipi skins. They were at the back of the line.

Throughout the night, they walked in the darkness following their chief. The new camp was a half-day's walk to the northeast. No one talked, no babies cried, no dogs barked. The only sound was of the horse hooves and the drag of the travois posts on rocky terrain. People moved slowly, the cold air tightening their joints. Children sleepily shuffled onward clinging to each other's hands. This was not the first time the People had had to pack all their belongings and move in the middle of the night, but it was the first time for Clear Sky.

The night frost was cold and smelled musky. It made her hair damp, and her feet felt frozen, even in her warm moccasins. She put down her load to pull her shawl tighter around her shoulders.

"We must not stop," chided Quill from the travois. "We have been the last to leave, and are falling behind."

An eagle's call pierced sharply in the night. It was not an eagle though. It was a signal from one of the scouts. The shrill cry rang out again throughout the canyon. Two in a row. That meant the soldiers were close.

Quill got off and looked everywhere for a place to hide. "Over there," she told Clear Sky. They pulled the horse far off the road, into a thick grove of Juniper trees.

"Keep him still," Quill whispered.

Off in the distance from where they had just come, came the drumming of pounding hooves.

"Keep your eyes open, men! They are here somewhere," the soldier yelled in English as ten or twelve men raced by, their flaming torches breaking through the darkness. He pulled his horse up to a stop when something caught his eye. Holding his torch high above his head, he scanned the forest around him for signs of life. Off to his left he heard the crackle of breaking twigs. He whirled around, lifting his gun.

"You'd better come out now. Hands in the air. You won't get hurt if you come out on your own."

Quill stared through the thick branches of the trees, never letting her eyes off the soldier. Clear Sky clung to her. Both barely breathed.

He dismounted and carefully stepped into the trees. "Come out now, do you hear me? You don't want me comin' in after you. Bound to be bloodshed if I have to come in." Twigs and leaves crackled again. Slowly, he cocked his rifle. Out of the forest rumbled a large skunk. Suddenly, the animal's head jerked up, he lifted his tail, and turned his back to the soldier.

"Jesus!" the man swore, quickly mounting his horse and taking off.

"Skunk is our friend," Quill said with a wry smile.

Before long, Cougar Two Foot came through the trees.

"Are you all right?" he asked, his face sweating from running back to find them. "That was too close. You must keep up." He helped Quill back onto the travois. "Let me help you," he said taking the bundle that Clear Sky was carrying. He pulled the horse along the path.

She had not been sleeping well. Perhaps it was hiding from the soldiers and moving to yet another new location that was wearing her down. Suddenly, Clear Sky was inundated by an overwhelming sadness. It seemed as if the walls of the tipi closed in on her, so she ran out of it desperately trying to find relief.

She thought if she went up the mountain to the ledge that had a view of the valley below, she might find some peace. It was a steep climb, almost straight up. When her moccasins slipped on the crumbling boulders, she grabbed onto the branches of trees that miraculously grew from the rocks. Winded, exhausted, and feeling woozy from the exertion, she finally pulled herself up to the stone shelf then dropped down heavily onto it. But even this did not soften the heartache.

In the night, she had had a dream of her dead family. Though she did not remember the particulars, the sense of loss was so acute that now she considered throwing herself from the ledge.

She sat there for several hours staring out at the vista, but when the sun began to set, she made her way down again to return to the lodging.

"Where have you been?" Quill asked, intent on her beading. "Go gather acorns. Up on the hill," she said, waving her hand to indicate where to look.

It was late in the day and darkness came earlier than usual as the sky clouded for rain. Clear Sky still felt uneasy, but she did not want to disappoint her mentor, so she steeled herself and went to pick the nuts as well as herbs and mushrooms, filling the basket that was slung over her back. With the sun setting, she looked for the campfire lights flickering through the leaves to help guide her home. She had not been able to calm her mind, and she was agitated by sounds in the forest. Even the wind rustling the dry fall leaves unnerved her. The feeling of foreboding made her heart race. Each screech of an owl or snap of a twig tightened her stomach and throat.

Then she heard what sounded like footsteps crunching dry leaves. *What was that?* She turned to look. Only blackness. She stopped to listen, holding her breath. Silence. She could not help herself. Terror took over. Sweating with panic she crumpled to her knees unable to continue. *It is only the critters in the forest*, she tried to tell herself. *I need not be afraid.* Finally, she made herself breathe to calm her nerves and raised herself to standing to walk back to her tipi.

But now she heard the footsteps again, this time coming toward her. Terrified, she began to run wildly, knocking against branches, slipping on leaves and pine needles, and tumbling to the ground. When she looked up she saw a man standing in the trees, but in the night she could not make out his features.

"Who are you?" she yelled into the darkness. "What do you want?"

"So white woman, you alone," the man said in broken English. *A doe in the meadow*, he thought, feeling his loins beginning to throb.

Like lightning, fear ran through Clear Sky's body, leaving her frozen like a rabbit about to be devoured.

The man reached down, taking hold of her wrist and roughly pulled her close to him. She could feel his breath on her neck. His other hand began to caress her shoulders. She tried to get away, but could not loosen his grip. He pulled her toward him again.

"You *my* woman," he said with venom.

His hand reached down between her legs. Then he leaned forward onto her, forcing her back onto the ground. His grip was strong and the weight of him heavy. She could not cry out, nor kick her legs nor hit him with her free hand. Instead, her mind went somewhere else, and her body became limp.

Then a voice rang through the woods.

"Corn Snake," Cougar Two Foot yelled. "Let her go!"

"When I am through," he said continuing with his assault. "She is just a white woman. No one cares what happens to her."

Cougar Two Foot was surprised to hear himself shout, "I do."

He clasped his hands together, and brought them down hard across the back of Corn Snake's neck and threw him off Clear Sky. But Corn Snake was dazed for only a moment then dove for Cougar Two Foot, wrapping his leg around his waist, and toppling him to the ground. Adroitly, Cougar Two Foot rolled him off. The two men swung at each other, each landing hard punches. Corn Snake pulled his knife, but was immediately winded by a hard blow to the stomach. Cougar Two Foot yanked the weapon out of his hand, and threw it into the woods. Corn Snake lunged at him once more, but Cougar Two Foot was able to bring his fists up hard under

Corn Snake's chin. The man fell backwards unconscious.

"Are you all right?" he asked, gently lifting Clear Sky.

"Yes, I think so," she said. "How did you know I was here?"

"Quill was concerned that you had not come back. She sent me."

Clear Sky's knees buckled. Cougar Two Foot picked her up, and carried her back to camp. He put her on the sleeping pallet and sat with her for a while, then went to find his teachers.

In the darkness of the tipi, as the evening fire warmed the enclosure, Clear Sky lay waiting for them to return. But her mind raced, and she could not settle herself.

"*He is here,*" she heard.

The flap opened, but it was not her mentors who came in.

"Get away from me!" she yelled.

Terrified, she looked for something with which to defend herself, and grabbed a ladle.

Before she could strike, Corn Snake snatched it from her hand, tossing it aside.

"Not finished," he said in broken English, glaring at her.

Corn Snake lunged at Clear Sky, seizing her arm and pulling her pelvis close to his. This time she beat him with her fist. He swung and knocked her to the ground. But before she could defend herself again, he leapt at her, forcing himself upon her. Overcome by the muscular man, she was defenseless under his strength.

"No one here to help you. You mine now," he sneered in.

She struggled again to loose herself, but his grip was as tight as the bite of a wolverine.

She tried to call out, but no sound came from her mouth.

"White woman. You are just white woman," he hissed. "No one cares what happen to you," he said.

But with great effort, she was finally able to cry out for help, calling for Cougar Two Foot.

Corn Snake angrily pushed her aside, his loins flagged, and his self-esteem blanched. He pulled her up by her hair, spit at her, and swung his hand across her face, sending her sprawling across the dirt floor, and then he ran into the night.

When her mentors and Cougar Two Foot returned they found her lying on her pallet shivering.

"What has happened here?" Father Man asked.

"He came back," Clear Sky choked. "Corn Snake."

Quill took a cloth and gently wiped the blood and tears from her face.

Cougar Two Foot, his jaw set, stormed out of the tipi. He found where Corn Snake was hiding, and dragged him by his shirt into a clearing. The first crack of his fist sent the man flying. But Corn Snake jumped up, attacking Cougar Two Foot with both fists. Cougar Two Foot plowed into his midsection forcing him against a tree. He let his rage take over, pounding the man over and over until Corn Snake could no longer stand. He lifted him up by his shirt one more time, but then threw him back down onto the ground.

"You'd best keep to your snake hole under the rocks," Cougar Two Foot spit, "or I will not be generous with your life a second time."

He had chosen not to end Corn Snake's life as was tribal custom for this offense, but he was not sure that was a good decision.

The next night Father Man insisted that the Council meet. Cougar Two Foot with hands bruised, knuckles torn, and lip split, sat outside the chief's tipi, his face burning with intensity.

The men and women of the council gathered around the fire. Each took his turn to comment on the offense and make a suggestion as to what to do with the perpetrator. Under other circumstances, they would have dismissed the concerns; she was only white after all, but Clear Sky was living in the house of Quill and Father Man and they could not ignore their demands for justice.

"What will calm your heart, Father Man?" Chief Harold Little Crow said.

"The snake bites, and so is not to be trusted," he said. With a clear and calm demeanor, he made his judgment, "He must live on his own."

Banishment was a harsh punishment. No one would be allowed to speak to him or help him in any way for the rest of his life.

Harold Little Crow looked at the elders in the council. As his eyes met each one, they each pulled their blanket tighter around their shoulders indicating agreement. In honor of Father Man, all had concurred.

Corn Snake, whose face was also badly battered and bruised, was brought to the center of the gathering.

"The Council has decided. You are to leave at once and never return." With that Chief Harold Little Crow turned his back on the man, then one by one the council members turned their backs on him as well. Outside the rest jeered and threw sticks at him till he was forced to retreat.

His mother, The Silver Moon, was told of the decision, and she had gathered his things along with his horse and waited for him down by the river.

Even several months after the attack, Clear Sky could not feel at ease so she stayed close to the tipi, going away from it only if Quill, Father Man or Cougar Two Foot was with her.

"We need twigs to start the fire. Clear Sky, go bring us some," Quill challenged. Even though Clear Sky was still fearful of venturing out on her own, Quill pushed, so she was forced to test her resolve. She stood at the edge of the woods for a long time, but was still unable to take that step into the thickness of the trees by herself.

A young boy called to her. "Where are you going?"

"Hello, Raccoon. I am going to pick up some tinder." She stood still without taking another step.

"I am to pick some sage," the boy said. "I am not sure where to look," he lied. "Can you help me?" She took his hand, and they walked into the pinewood together.

13

Holly sat in a chair holding her doll, staring vacantly at the fire. Richard had just come in from the barn, and Jahn was busy in the kitchen.

"All right, dinner is ready," Jahn called.

"The roast smells great," Richard encouraged. "Look at those biscuits. Light as a feather!" he said picking one up and taking a bite. "You are getting better at it, brother."

Jahn smiled, "That's because Mrs. Sumner brought Mrs. George, Mrs. Rhyerson, and Mrs. Finnian to the house to teach me how to cook more things. They were very kind not to laugh at my mistakes, and by the way, thanks for never saying anything bad about what I serve. Hopefully, I can do this on my own next time."

"You do fine. I do wish Holly would eat more though. And I do not think it is your cooking she is avoiding."

Richard picked up his sister and set her at the table, serving a plate and cutting up her meat. "Open your mouth now, Holly. You will like what Jahn has made for us. Here are some potatoes with lots of butter just as you like it." Holly opened her mouth then dully chewed the food, but began to cough deeply.

"When you go into town to sell the mare tomorrow, can you get more of Holly's medicine?" Jahn asked. "Her cough sounds worse to me."

"Sure," he said. "Pull out your book now, Jahn. Let me hear you read. You want to sound intelligent when Mrs. Sumner comes over tomorrow for your lessons."

In the middle of the night, Jahn woke with a start, but it was not the usual nightmare that shook him out of sleep. It was the hacking coming from Holly's bed. Her little chest was thickly congested and she was barely able to breathe.

"Richard," Jahn called. His brother was deeply asleep because after supper, he had gone to the saloon in town. "Richard wake up!"

"What's the matter?" he slurred.

"It's Holly. She can't breathe," Jahn said. Richard woke himself as best he could and came over with a lamp. Holly's face was glistening with sweat, and she wheezed harshly with every breath.

Richard told him, "Mrs. Sumner said we should boil some water and let her breathe the steam." So Jahn ran for the kettle, relit the stove, and waited for the water to boil.

"I wish Ma was here," Jahn thought. *"She could make her well."*

After a few minutes of inhaling the steam, Holly was better able to take a breath. Richard sat at the edge of her bed till she fell asleep again. Jahn finally fell asleep, too, but only to revisit his usual nightmare.

In the paddock were two new horses, a dark bay and a chestnut. Richard was at the house sweeping the porch. To Jahn this was peculiar, since Richard never did chores of this nature without being pressed into it.

"Hey," Jahn said in greeting, climbing the hill to the house. "Where did you get those horses?"

"I bought them off a trapper. You should have seen the scar across his face! He said he'd had it since he was a young man." Richard winced. "I know. They have been worked hard, but with some rest and care they will be strong and useful again," Richard said, quickly regaining his enthusiasm. "They will be the beginning of our herd."

"Who is going to mind them? You will be off hunting, and I have Holly to take care of—"

"I will help you," Richard broke in. "You will see. It will be fine. If we build a herd, we can sell or rent some, and then I will not have to be away so much."

"Right," Jahn said annoyed with his brother. "Where is Holly?"

"Asleep."

"How is her breathing? Doc said we should make sure that it does not become labored."

"I checked a little while ago. She's ok," Richard answered.

Jahn bounded up the steps and into the house to look in on his little sister. She was sleeping, but there was still a rasp in her breathing that worried him, and he had been awake most of the night watching her.

"Do we have any money for the medicine? Or did you spend it all at the saloon last night."

Richard reached into his pocket and pulled out a few coins, which he counted out and handed to Jahn.

"Just barely enough, Richard! You can't keep doing that!"

"Doing what?"

"Spending all our money on drink."

"You have enough," Richard said in defense.

Frustrated, Jahn went to the barn to saddle up his horse. Later that day they were to go to the Sumners for supper.

"Holly, you think you can take the ride to the Sumners? I know they want to see you. Mrs. Sumner said she is making something special for dessert, cherry cobbler. That should make you feel better." But by the time they got to the Sumners, Holly could hardly breathe.

"Mr. Sumner! Henry!" Jahn called.

Henry came to the door and immediately lifted Holly into his arms.

"You boys going to stand in the door all night," Sara called from the pump at the back of the house, "or can we eat this excellent supper I have made, which is now on the table getting cold?"

"Sara, put on the kettle."

"Oh, my poor sweet thing," she said when she saw Holly's drenched cheeks. "Put her on the bed. We will take good care of you, little one."

"Oh, Mama what should we do?" Jahn worried.

Each night, after he tended to the horses at Silver Leaf, Richard came to the Sumner's for supper. Holly and Jahn stayed at the Sumner's for several days till Holly could breathe easily once again.

Jahn felt like a racehorse waiting for a race to begin. He was jumpy and could not keep still. In the privacy of his room at the Sumner's, spreading out a map, he would plan the route he would take through the mountains asking everyone and anyone if they had seen his mother.

14

Late fall 1853

The body of little Holly Van Andusson lay in a box that would soon go into the ground. At eight years old, she had succumbed to pneumonia. Friends and family surrounded the new grave at the top of the knoll. They cried for the loss of Holly, as well as for the losses from the year before.

Richard was beside himself with grief, feeling that her death was his fault for not taking better care of her. But Jahn's eyes were dry. He had tucked that pain somewhere down deep within his psyche next to the one that he held for his mother.

"Oh, Holy Father," the preacher had begun, "take this thy daughter into thy bosom, and keep her by your side always…"

Abruptly, Richard, now sixteen and nearly a man, turned and ran down the hill away from the burial.

"Where are you going?" Jahn whispered hoarsely, running after him.

"I have got to get out of here," Richard clipped, wiping the tears from his cheek.

"You cannot leave now. She is not even in the ground."

"Leave me alone!" he barked.

Richard grabbed a handful of cash from the kitchen table, took one of his horses and galloped into town. Jahn went back up the hill to join the other mourners in the final prayers for his little sister.

"Don't you worry now, Jahn," Sara Sumner told him putting her arm around his shoulders. "Everyone grieves in their own way. He will come home when he is ready," she said softly. "Besides, God already knows what is truly in his heart."

Jahn appreciated how Mrs. Sumner always said the right thing. She was not one to judge and he loved her for it. Besides he judged Richard enough for the both of them.

"Come for supper, Jahn, and spend the night if you like," Henry told the boy.

Jahn thanked Mr. Sumner and did go for supper, but went back to Silver Leaf to be home when Richard returned.

The day after Holly's funeral, Sara Sumner came by with freshly baked bread. She could not help herself. Ginny had been her best friend, and with her gone, she felt she was the only one to look after the remaining children. And Holly's death brought the death of her own family right to the surface, making her feel choked with emotion. That she could not save Holly was a heavy weight on her heart so she became more determined to be supportive of the boys.

"Anyone home?" she called.

Sara went down the hill to the barn, where she found Jahn mucking out stalls, his sleeves rolled up past his elbows, straw caught in his hair.

"Over here, Mrs. Sumner," Jahn yelled from the stall at the end of the barn. "Good morning." Avoiding her gaze, he told her Richard was still asleep.

"Have you had anything to eat?" she called.

"Some coffee," he answered. "Did you come here by yourself? You know you are not supposed to. What if the..."

"Come up to the house, and I will make you a proper breakfast," she cut in. "I have brought eggs the hens laid this morning, fresh as can be, and some of Henry's favorite pork sausages." She did not wait for Jahn, but marched up the hill and into the house, finding Richard asleep, his head on the table. "Morning, Richard," she said loudly letting the door bang shut. "Breakfast will be ready in just a few minutes. You have just enough time to wash your face and teeth."

"Morning," he said, lifting his head then squinting against the bright daylight. Very slowly he rose and with some effort went out to the pump to wash up.

Sara cleared the dirty glass, corked the half-drunk bottle of whiskey and put it on the shelf near the stove. She grabbed a rag from the washtub, took a whiff of it then picked up another and smelled it before wiping down the table. Jahn came in drying his hands on his pants. He went to the cupboard for plates and forks.

"Will you be joining us, Mrs. Sumner?"

"Thank you, Jahn, but I have already eaten," she replied, stirring the pan on the stove, "but kind of you to ask." She served the eggs, sausage and bread, and sat with the boys while they ate.

Jahn lifted the coffee pot. "Mrs. Sumner, another cup of coffee?"

"Sure will, Jahn," she answered.

"You, Richard?"

"Yes," he answered slowly so as not to jar his aching head.

At least Richard keeps his drinking to Saturday nights, she thought.

Sara Sumner's brother, Harland, had been a hardened drinker much worse than Richard, and she had learned that a drunk is always embarrassed about his drinking. But if you fought with him about it, his drinking became your fault. She found the best way to handle him when he was inebriated was to stay out of his way, and then feed him when he was clearheaded. She figured at least he might live longer that way.

Sara got up to leave. "If you do not mind, I am going to leave those pans for you boys to clean up. Henry will be waiting for me at the church. See you for supper?"

"Yes, ma'am," the boys said in unison.

"If I have a good day hunting I will bring something to add to the meal," Richard offered.

"That would be delightful," she said as she began to leave.

When his head was unclouded, she found Richard to be an intelligent and observant young fellow. Of course, she preferred him sober, but she was also determined not to lose faith in him when he was not.

Though Richard was hung-over, he could think clearly enough to know that he wanted to ride with Mrs. Sumner to the church to be sure that she got there safely.

15

For Jahn, twelve years old, the days seemed long and nights longer. With Holly gone, he had no focus, and his body felt heavy and slow, as much from lack of sleep as from worry. His life felt hopeless and unending. The only thing he truly wanted was to find his mother. He took the satchel from under his bed and stuffed a few things into the sack.

"Where are you going?" Richard asked, emptying the belongings back onto the bed.

Jahn did not answer, but began to fill the bag once again. Richard pulled it from his hands.

"She's out there somewhere!" Jahn yelled in desperation.

"It has been two years, Jahn! What do you expect to find? Surely, we would have gotten word about her by now if she were still alive." Jahn took back the bag and continued to pack. "Look, you cannot go out alone," Richard said. "I don't want to lose you, too." He waited for Jahn to stop what he was doing, but Jahn continued. "All right. I'll go with you."

The boys set out to search the countryside once again,

stopping in the same lodges and saloons where they had stopped before, and at the same Trappers forts where they had already placed posters, but the response was always the same. No one had seen or heard of her.

"We have already been all through this part of the mountain, and have found nothing. Let's go home."

"Just a little longer," Jahn pleaded.

"When are you going to accept that she is dead?"

"She is not," Jahn hissed through gritted teeth. "I know it! She is alive."

"There is a doctor coming through tomorrow," Sara Sumner told Jahn, "so I want you to take care of Lizbeth George while her mother and I go into town."

"You want me to do what?" he complained. "Couldn't Conor do it?" It was rare that he dug in his heels with her, but this was more than this twelve year old boy wanted to do. Jahn had planned to ride to a fort southeast of the ranch to put up another poster. "A doctor? Is she all right?"

"Jahn, dear, I would not ask you if there were someone else," Sara responded. "And yes, I think she is going to be fine, but she has been quite tired of late, so we thought we had better have someone look at her, someone who knows about women's bodies."

"All right," he responded embarrassed at having asked. "What am I going to do with a seven-year old girl for a whole day?"

"Well, to start with you could pick flowers for Sunday's service since the preacher is in town this week. The vases are in the back of the church, in the closet."

"That sounds–fun," he squirmed.

"Take her for a swim in the river after that."

Begrudgingly, he agreed.

"Good. Come by the Georges' in the morning first thing. We want to get an early start before half the town descends on the physician."

"Yes, ma'am," he pouted.

The next morning after chores, Jahn rode to the Georges' to pick up Lizbeth. She came skipping over to his side and took his hand. He shook it away. Kicking the dust in the road, Jahn said, "Mrs. Sumner says that we should pick flowers for the church service."

"Goody, I love flowers," Lizbeth giggled. "What is that?" she said pointing to the folded posters that he always carried in the satchel next to his gun. "Let me see!" She grabbed one and opened it. "Oh," she said. "I bet you miss your mama. I would if it were mine. My mama says you are never going to find her, so you'd best just give up trying. But I don't think you should ever give up looking. I never would." She folded the poster and replaced it in the sachel "You going somewhere to put these up? Can I come? I can help."

The mere mention of his mother stung him deeply.

"We are to start by gathering flowers from your mother's garden," he said pretending to ignore her comments.

"We have lots of flowers," Lizbeth said. "Mama planted a big flower garden this year. Do you like flowers?"

"Sure." Jahn picked up a stone and threw it as far as he could down the road, then picked up another, and tried to beat that one.

"What is your favorite?"

"I dunno. Yellow ones," he said throwing another rock.

"Me, too," she giggled again.

Lizbeth was missing her front tooth which gave her a

slight lisp. *All the more reason to ignore her*, he thought as the girl ran into the house for a knife to cut the stems.

"Here let me have that," he said taking the blade. "You might hurt yourself." They walked to the back of the house where Mrs. George had grown an expansive garden. He had never seen so many blossoms. The colors blanketed the hillside like a patchwork quilt. His mother, who loved to see this garden, had talked endlessly about how she wished hers looked as full.

"See I told you. Mama loves flowers. Over there! Yellow ones!" she squealed, skipping off to the row of roses. She scooped up a handful of colorful petals. "If you put these in a book they will dry and still keep their smell, at least for a little while. Here," she said, handing Jahn a handful.

"All right, sure." He stuffed them into his pocket.

Jahn took the basket of flowers, and then pulled the little girl up on to the horse behind him. Then after they went to the church to fill the vases Jahn said, "Swimming is fun. Can you swim?"

"Yup," she hesitated, "but not too well."

"I will help you," he stated confidently.

"Will you plait my hair for me so it does not get all tangled?"

"Sure," he smiled. She turned around handing him a piece of ribbon, and he gently lifted her hair to begin the braid like he had done so often for Holly.

After the swim, Lizbeth asked again to help Jahn hang his posters. Where he had planned to go was only a couple of hours away. *We could be back by supper*, he thought, *and Lizbeth's mother and Mrs. Sumner won't know where we have been.*

"All right," he said finely. "You had better be quiet while we ride. I have things to think about." Lizbeth promised she would, but could only keep that pledge for a short time.

Coming from deep within the woods, they heard hard laughter. Two men were riding down the trail.

"Isn't that Mr. McCreedy and Junior from the feed store?" Lizbeth asked peering through the trees.

"Ignorant savages," McCreedy spat, his heavy Scottish brogue ringing through the woods. "They think they can hunt game on my land anytime they want. This should teach the rest of them."

"How much are they givin' us for these Injun scalps, Pa? Same as for Irish scalps back home?"

"Don't much matter, laddie," he answered shifting on his horse then spitting tobacco juice through the opening in his teeth. McCreedy had two bleeding scalps in his hand, and his son had a dead deer on the back of his horse.

Jahn walked his horse in for a closer look. "Hello, Mr. McCreedy," he called so as not to surprise the man.

"Who's that there?" McCreedy called in return.

"Jahn, Jahn Van Andusson, sir," Jahn called.

"You better get on home, son. Nothing for you to see here."

Before Lizbeth could catch sight of the worst, Jahn pulled the horse around and galloped away. They rode back to her house in silence.

16

Despite her reluctance to tell anyone, word had gotten out that Clear Sky could see the future. She was surprised to find so many would come to a white woman, but they did. Their questions ranged from the mundane to the extraordinary. Mostly, they had to do with whether this boy and girl would make a good match, would food be plentiful during the winter, or how to get along with a spouse's mother.

"Quill," Clear Sky worried one day, "I cannot always hear the answer for every inquiry. What should I tell them?"

"A straight arrow is more useful than a broken one." She looked to see if Clear Sky understood. Stirring the contents of the vessel in the stone-lined hole in the dirt, and then placing several pieces of wood on top of the ceramic jug, she lit the fire. "Mixing bad meat with good, no one can eat."

So Clear Sky listened to the Inner Voice to help those who came, all the while staring into the smoke wafting off the burning wood. Soon the tipi was filled with baskets, blankets and food, combs and rawhide ribbons with colorful feathers for her hair. Some brought horses and others, knowing that the three of them were the only ones in the tipi, promised physical labor. She did not put honey on what came, nor did she make up an answer just to please them.

Her own future, though, she could not see, nor could she yet remember her past.

"Come now, let us take some of these things where they can get some use. We certainly do not need all of them," Quill told her.

"Do you think I will ever remember?"

"That is not important now. Only this day."

Quill took one basket filled with tubers and Clear Sky took another containing a blanket and some small metal pots. They carried them to the tipi of a family whose father had died in the winter and who as yet, had not filled his place with another man.

While they walked, Clear Sky asked Quill why she and Father Man had not taken slaves, like many in the village had done, or other wives, as was the custom. After all, their sons were gone, and they had no daughters to help.

"I do not need them. People pay for their healings with food, clothing or with their time," she stated, walking back to their tipi. "Besides, how can one person own another?" She hesitated before she spoke again, "One bear does not own another bear. One tree does not own another tree. I do not believe that one human should own another. We share this time and place working together, that is all. Besides, you complete the circle of our family."

"And wives?" she asked tentatively.

"Father Man wants to please only me."

Slavery was common in the villages. Along with owning many horses, it showed power and wealth, as well as adding manpower when family members were lost. And slaves made for good commerce no matter how mistreated they were, particularly the women and young children, and many wives meant more hands to help as well.

17

Every day Clear Sky watched as Quill picked and made medicine out of the healing herbs that grew near the summer camp. "Bring me peppermint, lavender, sage, milk-vetch, bear root and horsetail," she might tell her. She had told Cougar Two Foot that Clear Sky was still filled with the fear of the wolverine that she carried in her heart, since her abduction and the encounter with Corn Snake. She would send him to be her guide, and thus allow her to feel safe.

"Did we find all she wanted?" Clear Sky asked.

Cougar Two Foot looked into the container. "More lavender. There on that hillside," he said pointing to the sunny patch ahead of them. "Sage, lavender and peppermint like to have a lot of sun," he instructed. She knew this, but said nothing.

They picked in silence then she asked, "Tell me of your wife, if it is proper for me to ask."

The pain of the memory tumbled forward, furrowing his brow. Unused to sharing information about his life, he remained quiet. And even though she was curious to know more about this man, she did not press him. She knew how longing and pain could fill a heart. Her own ached for the unknown. She was white and knew that she had lived very differently from the way she was doing so now. If nothing else, she longed for a way of life that seemed familiar and comfortable. Each day she was challenged with learning something new, not only the language, but also each aspect of life in the village, all of which was unfamiliar. She found she became exhausted easily, and her dreams were filled with apprehension.

When their baskets were full, and they had also collected branches for the fire, Cougar Two Foot and Clear Sky began to walk to the tipi. Now with the setting of the sun, mosquitos began to swarm, and they had to run home.

"It is a good thing no one needed these herbs," Quill chastised. "Now that you are finally here," she said squinting her eyes, looking from one to the other more than once, "go grind the lavender and mix it with bear oil. Cougar Two Foot will show you how much of each to use."

"Yes, of course," he said, distracted by the firelight shining on Clear Sky's hair.

"This should be familiar to you."

"Yes, Quill. We have used this often," Clear Sky said.

"Indeed," she said looking at the both of them. "Then you remember, it can also ease the itching of those mosquito bites," she said as she ducked out of the tipi.

"I was married to The Silver Moon's daughter, Bright Star," Cougar Two Foot said quietly. "She died in childbirth, our baby, a son, as well."

"My heart is heavy for you." Then Clear Sky was quiet for a long time, and did not look at him when she asked, "You have not wanted to marry since?"

"I had two wives, but they each got tired of me and ran off to be with another man," he said staring off into the distance. "I could not stop thinking about Bright Star and my child," he explained.

They took the pungent herb, ground it to a paste then mixed it with the bear fat. The aroma of lavender filled the tipi. She dabbed some on the back of Cougar Two Foot's ears and neck, and he did the same for the bites on her face.

18

The band had to move again in the night. The camp was set up, and the day's work was done, but the darkness that more often brought instant sleep to Clear Sky did not do so this night. She lay on her pallet under a blanket and a thick bearskin, unable to sleep due to the aching in her once injured shoulder. She listened to the nighthawk's song, the call of an owl and yip of the coyotes at the riverbed. She watched the smoke from the fire curl upwards to the opening in the roof. The snows had not yet begun, but the nights were becoming damp and cold, so she wrapped her covers tightly around her neck, making a cocoon around her face.

She had been with this couple for two years, and more now than not, she felt like she was part of the village family. Still she felt a perplexing sense of loss and was acutely aware that she was white. But more disturbing was the wall that still stood between her and her past, the barrier that had no door or window to give a view to where she had come from or who she was. No matter how hard she tried, she could not break through it. As this filled her mind, she vowed to throw herself more into the life in the village in hopes of quelling the nagging questions.

"She is white," Father Man said. "She is not one of us. Her great-grandfather's grandfather did not teach her ancestors, like ours did. She is a goose in a pack of dogs. What does she know about our ways?"

Quill pretended not to hear him. She sat quietly remembering.

"Why is your skin pale, not dark like mine, and those dots what are they?"

Pure Heart answered her young granddaughter kindly. "I do not come from here. My mother and father came from a long way across a big ocean of water, and they brought me with them. The people of that place, called England, all have skin that is pale like mine. And those dots are called freckles. Many people where I came from have those dots. Some have them all over their body and not just on their arms like me."

Quill, then called Little Bull, thought for a long time about that, then told her grandmother, "I like your dots." The little girl stared at the ground. "I wish I had dots like you."

"Pure Heart was not one of us at first," Quill countered, "but she learned as easily as our own."

"As easily, dear woman? The crow has a better memory than you," he scoffed. "The campfire of my mother holds many stories of how she had not been able to fit in, how she longed for her sons and daughters from the white man. Our robes did not suit her for a very long time," Father Man reminded her.

"Clear Sky does not have those longings. She is not missing something she cannot remember. No matter what you say, I think she will carry the medicine bundle well, and you know she will, too. Don't be such a foolish old man. I am going to teach her. You do what you will."

"Now you are being foolish, Old Woman," Father Man said putting his arm around her shoulders. "Wait. Wait until we see if she is a garnet in the river or just another gray stone. And what will happen to you when she does remember? She will run to her old life, and not even take her belongings when she leaves."

This was a conversation they would have many times.

Even by firelight, Quill's gnarled fingers easily picked up the porcupine quills and colorful glass, stringing them onto the beading needle, applying them to the moccasin in her hands. Clear Sky watched the old woman sew the tiny beads she had gotten at the trapper's fort to clothing, shoes or bags. It was intricate work that required patience.

While she worked, it was comforting for Quill to reminisce about her dear grandmother, especially when memories of her children's deaths pushed forward as they tended to do even after all these years.

Little Bull sat between her grandmother's knees while Pure Heart taught her how to put beads on a stringing needle. While they talked the little girl played with the two gold bracelets on her grandmother's wrist. The old woman slid them off, leaving behind a white shadow left by the sun tanning her skin. She put them on her granddaughter's tiny arm.

"They are very large," the child said sliding them all the way up to her shoulder. "What stone is this?"

"The purple stone is called amethyst."

"And these clear ones?"

"Diamonds."

"Where did you get these?"

"From a land very far away. They belonged to my mother, and her mother before her," she told the child. "When you get married, I will give these to you."

Little Bull continued to fondle her beloved grandmother's hand. She poked her fingers at the dots on her arm. "What do you call these again?"

"Freckles, Little Bull," her grandmother told her in English.

"That is a funny word. Freckles."

Clear Sky reached for the comb to smooth her hair.

"Ay, Clear Sky, do not comb your hair at night. You will bring the trickster to our door."

Then Clear Sky inadvertently hit the bead tray.

"Ay, ya, Clear Sky! You move too quickly," Quill chided. "You will not like picking those out of the dirt," she said remembering having done the same thing herself. "Now look here," the teacher said. "You come from the back, pick up a bead on your needle and push the wire back down close to where the needle came up through the cloth. See? Close," Quill emphasized. "Too wide," she snorted, pointing to the stitch her student had just made. "Take it out."

Father Man whispered to Clear Sky, "Slow, like the turtle. She will not let you do it badly, and none of us will like it if you shake that hornet's nest."

Clear Sky had initially begun by beading small things, but today she had decided to decorate a dress. The work was laborious and slow, but when finished it would be bright and colorful, adding charm to the colorless skins and cloths of her garments.

"The beads are like shiny sparkles on a river, stars

twinkling at night, the flowers blooming in the forest. With your beads you tell a story. And how they are sewn on tells us who you are," Quill reminded her, quoting something her grandmother had told her. "If you care how you attach them, then your beads will bring harmony. If not, well, why bother to do it at all," she said shaking her head. Quill looked at the work in Clear Sky's hands. "You must learn to appreciate the placement of each bead. You are hopping like the rabbit, but you must move carefully like the turtle. Start over," she said frankly. Father Man covered his smile.

"You make beaded things to sell to white folks at the trapper's fort," Clear Sky challenged. "You want to bring harmony to them as well?"

Father Man's eyes opened wide as he waited for the response.

Quill's neck stiffened for a moment, then her shoulders eased, and so did Father Man's face.

"Yes, particularly since the white man does not understand how all things are a part of Senawahv. All they see is land to be taken, fences to be put up, animals to be slaughtered, and even then they take only the skins or the best part of the meat, leaving the rest to rot in the sun. They do not understand." She sat back for a moment looking into the distance. "The squirrel, the cougar, the eagle, even the grass on the plains sings the same song with the breath of the Creator. Perhaps when my beaded belt encircles their waist like a colorful snake, they feel something, something they have not known before, that the Creator dances in their heart," she said with a satisfied smile, then looking at the dress in Clear Sky's hand she said, "Pull out those stitches. Begin again."

Quill enjoyed teaching Clear Sky. She found she learned

quickly, and took criticism gracefully. Though if you asked Clear Sky, she was more likely to say she was afraid to counter anything Quill said. Even so, unspoken by either, affection had begun to grow between the two of them. For Clear Sky, each day left her feeling more at home with her new family, but in the night when ghosts played with her mind, the horrors from her past pushed hard against her unwillingness to see them, leaving her in a wakeful sweat.

Father Man, Cougar Two Foot and Clear Sky stood over Gerald Strong Arm looking at the swelling in his belly.

"Tell me what you see," Father Man asked. The two settled themselves and waited for an answer to come to the surface. Instead, Clear Sky fell into the empty feeling from not knowing her past and began to feel agitated.

But like flowers with the coming of spring some distant memories had begun to return: One day while she was attaching the colorful glass beads to her dress, instead of her own hands she saw the hands of a woman stitching a bit of clothing, a man's coat. Not on the buckskin she was used to seeing in the village, but cloth made of wool tweed, a coat whose buttons were made of leather. At the time she felt a strong feeling of love for a mother. And another time when she was walking among the horses in the paddock she found herself disoriented as if in a crowded throng of a busy street, but she could not identify anything more than this. She had always sensed that she had been married, and had had a family, but with that came an intense feeling of sadness. Without knowing how or why, she knew that they were all dead.

"Clear Sky? What can you tell me?"

"Nothing, Father Man, not today." He looked at her closely.

"Clear Sky, go and make this up for him to drink."

"Yes, Father Man," she said. She had been hoping she would be allowed to watch this time.

Quill scowled at him.

"Not now, wife."

After Quill, Father Man and Cougar Two Foot finished their ceremony Quill packed up their things. Clear Sky was waiting for them outside the tipi.

Ahead of him the trail led upward circling the mountain. Jahn had been here many times, as it was the way to a trapper's fort where he and Richard had hung one of the posters.

Three men and one boy all with arrows cocked in their bows crossed the path. The hunting party stopped when they saw him, waiting to see if he was going to cause trouble.

He opened his palms to face them.

"Do you speak English?" Jahn asked.

"What you want, boy?" one man asked in English keeping his bow cocked.

The Indian boy disappeared into the woods to relieve his bladder while Jahn described what had happened to his mother. The man who spoke English translated for his friends.

He reassured Jahn that they did not know of any Ginny. As Jahn went on to the trapper's fort, he wondered if they were telling him the truth.

Raccoon rejoined the men. "What did he want?"

"The young colt was lost," said one of the men.

Raccoon ran back to the village as fast as he could, terrified by what he had seen. He wanted to warn them, for on the high trail that led past the hot springs and down into the valley below, was a family from another village camped in a clearing, and almost all of them were dead, their faces, arms and legs blistered with oozing red bumps.

When he found Clear Sky he described what he had seen. "Where are Father Man and Quill? They must come," he said. She did not wait for Raccoon to find the Shamans, but ran to the camp. Sure enough there was an entire family—a husband, three wives, two daughters, and three sons, all with red spots all over their faces. Only one was alive, a girl of about ten years.

"What is the matter with them," he said breathing heavily, having run after her.

"Stay back, Raccoon, and tell everyone in the village to keep away from them. They will make you sick."

When Father Man and Quill came into the clearing she told them the same thing.

The girl became delirious with a fever as the poison found a way out through the red blotches on her skin. Clear Sky stayed with her, feeding her, giving her water and putting ointments on the welts. She spoke softly to the child, reassuring her that she would get well. After many days, the oozing and itchy spots on the child's skin began to disappear, and the girl sat up and asked for food.

Although her face and torso were badly scarred, she recovered from Measles. When she was well enough, Clear Sky took her back to the girl's village.

Clear Sky returned to her camp and went to lie on her

pallet exhausted. It was the middle of the afternoon when she closed her eyes hoping no one would come in to disturb her. The face of the girl continued to play across her mind. With stories that had circulated throughout the region, of white men's illnesses killing off whole tribes, she had been surprised that she had not gotten the disease, and had worried she might die trying to save the girl. Finally, she drifted off to sleep.

"Do not come near your mother," she heard her father say in her dream.

She wanted to run into her mother's arms, but her face–"What happened to her face?" Covered in bumps so much so that her eyes had closed.

"Can she see me, Papa?"

"No, Love, she cannot see you anymore. Let your Mama rest, Honey." As he spoke a dark cloth, black as night fell over her mother, and Clear Sky woke with a start.

"She did not get the white man's disease," Father Man noted.

"She could have–and died," Quill said. "Remember she would not let us anywhere near the girl. She was very brave on our behalf. And now the young girl will live to be a great grandmother."

Father Man thought back to when Quill was called Little Bull, snorting in frustration like a bull when she had been teased for being part white and scoffed at for wanting to become a Shaman. To him, behind her back, the villagers spoke of their concerns that because she was part white, she could not possibly know the ways of the People. But they had been wrong, and she had become a noted healer in the mountain tribes. And then he remembered Pure Heart, white through and through. She had married the fine healer, Great Bull and had joined him in his sacred ceremonies.

I will have to think more on this, Father Man told himself.

19

Richard had done his best to raise his siblings, but it was a weight he was not equipped to carry. When he spent nights in town at the saloon drinking, his moods became erratic, his temper volatile, and his hands clenched, ready for a fight. More than once Jahn had to drag his brother out of the bar and throw him onto his horse just to get him home.

Richard would fight him all the way, throwing out his fists in all directions. "Do not tell me what to do!" he would howl. Occasionally, Richard would hit the target, leaving Jahn with a black eye. Sometimes the only way to get his brother home was for Jahn to clip him in the jaw first.

Richard loved his brother and would not have harmed him intentionally, because he knew that without Jahn as his steadying post, he would have already ended his life by his own hand. He was grateful it had not come to that.

Selling Richard's pelts to pay for them, the boys had five horses now, and Richard had built additional stalls for the growing herd with room for that many more again. The fifth Richard had bought from that same trapper with the bad scar. The horse had been pretty worn out, but he gave it rest and care. Now it was strong and would be useful for endeavors less strenuous than carrying trapper's gear through the mountains.

Jahn walked the horses into the paddock so he and his brother could muck out the stalls. Excited by the heat and the smell of dung, the flies were relentless. Swatting them proved useless, so Jahn finally gave in to their merciless, unending buzzing.

"Do you want to get married?" Jahn asked Richard.

"Usually you have to have someone to get married to," he shot back.

"Yes, I know. I mean do you see yourself getting married and having children and all that?"

"I think so, but I do not think it will be this year," Richard scoffed. "What brought out that question?"

"Sean Finnian got married," Jahn said throwing the dirtied straw into the wheelbarrow.

"Like I said, you usually have to have someone to get married to—but when I do you can be sure that you will have to sleep in the shed."

"Funny."

"Besides who else would take care of you, you gangly, rangy varmint."

"I was just thinking that if you got married, you would not mind so much my looking for Ma."

"That is enough of that talk. You are chasing after a ghost," Richard said, thinking, *There, I have finally said it! Maybe he will listen this time.*

Richard threw a pitchfork of dirty straw at his brother.

"Eck! Come on. That smells."

"No more than your socks," Richard said laughing, dodging Jahn's attempt to heave fouled straw back at him.

Jahn jumped on his brother's back and put his head in an arm lock. "Say uncle!"

"Ow! Uncle, uncle!" Richard said rubbing his neck and laughing. "You are getting to be a pretty strong guy! What about you? Do you want to get married?" Richard asked, picking up the pitchfork again.

"No," he said, then pausing. "Well, maybe." He was concerned that a wife might want him home all the time, and he would not be free to scour the land for his mother.

"I think girls smell beautiful," Richard mused. "Sometimes when a pretty girl walks by it reminds me of Ma's flower garden in the summer."

They worked another hour or so freshening the straw and filling buckets with clean water and stacking the bins with hay. The sun was high and hot.

"Beat you down to the river!" Richard said, taking off at a hard run. Jahn, now almost as tall as Richard, had long legs, and even with a head start Richard could not win. Jahn dove in the water with all his clothes on.

Spinning around, spraying water in all directions with his cupped hands, he grinned, "Now I do not have to wash these!"

"Here let me scrub you clean," Richard joked making a scrubbing motion with two large round rocks.

Jahn dove under and pulled up Richard's feet by his pants leg. Both tumbled under the cold river water. The boys walked back up toward the house wet, but cooled off.

"Let's go see Mr. Sumner," Richard said awkwardly changing the subject. "He has a newborn filly. I think he may even give her to us," he said.

"Mr. Sumner is always so kind to us," Jahn said finally, grasping for any good feeling he could find, then adding,

"Richard, Ma is not dead."

"Jahn–"

"She is not. I know it!" he shouted.

20

Spring, 1857

It had been five years since Clear Sky had come to live with the People of the Mountain when Father Man declared that it was time for her to join with another. He said, "You have been without a man too long. Your heart is now ready. At the time of the Bear Dance, when the flowers are blooming, you will ask Cougar Two Foot to sleep in our tipi." As an afterthought, Father Man said, "It has taken him some time, but now his heart is ready as well."

"Yes, Father," she replied obediently. But at once she not only felt an abundance of joy and happiness, but also an impending sense of loss.

"The two of you will be very helpful to our people," Father Man told her, knowing that the bond between the two was already tight.

The spring evening was balmy, more so than it should have been at that time of year. Clear Sky sat outside the tipi looking up at the full moon and the blanket of stars through the tops of the pines thinking about Cougar Two Foot and their coming marriage. He was a talented healer and a kind man, but also a ferocious warrior when he needed to be, and she knew that he would jump in front of an arrow if it would save her. At the same time, he could be stubborn, overly cautious about her safety, and then there were those relentless questions about how she could know the future. But over time, she had come appreciate Cougar Two Foot's strengths and forgive his weaknesses. The sound of his footsteps was both familiar and reassuring.

A cold breeze began to blow, so she wrapped her blanket around her shoulders. Cougar Two Foot sat down beside her, and pulled the cloth even more tightly, tucking it up around her neck. When she sat next to him, she felt his strength, his loving warmth, and it melted her heart. He took her hand, his dark hand covering the whiteness of hers. Then he presented her with a pouch, a gift he had made from soft doeskin, trimmed in beaver, with a tie ending in beads and a fox's tail. Heavy and colorful beading helped to keep the pouch flap closed.

"Thank you," she said drawing the gift over her head and across her chest. She ran her hand over the soft fur. "It is very beautiful."

Clear Sky knew that Quill had already spoken with Cougar Two Foot about making a family, and she knew that was what Father Man expected of her as well. He had told Father Man that since he has been long in choosing another wife, he also wants a child right away. Though Clear Sky did not know why, she felt uneasy about having a child, fearing that it might perish. She got up brusquely and walked down the path.

"Wait for me," Cougar Two Foot called to her. They

headed toward the river and walked along its banks. Walking helped, and she settled down, finding his company made her feel at ease. "Do you want to join with me?"

Inexplicably, Clear Sky became shy and her stomach fluttered. She looked into his eyes and then she heard, *"You will learn to love each other deeply. You will have a son who will be a great hunter and a fine leader and will live a long life."* This gave her a feeling of relief that she would once again have a family.

"You have been my friend and my savior, Cougar Two Foot. Yes, that would please me very much."

Wrapping his arm around her shoulders, he asked, "Maybe you can teach me how to better hear the smoke?"

"And you will remind me what herbs to use?" she countered.

"Lift your arms," Quill said tenderly to Clear Sky on the day of her joining.

Clear Sky held her arms out at shoulder height while Quill wrapped the ornately beaded belt tightly around her waist, the one made for her by Stands In Front. With strands of the same colorful beads, Shy Girl and Petals had threaded her once auburn hair that had in the last few years turned completely white. Long Cedar Branch hung her gift around her neck, a large white medallion with a bright red center. Her dress was made of the softest deerskin, which the bride had fashioned herself. It had taken weeks to stitch the intricate design across the front. Quill made new moccasins for her that were heavily beaded with the same red and white colored glass that was on her dress.

"These belonged to my father's mother. She was white like you. Pure Heart told me they had belonged to her grandmother," Quill said, pulling from her wrist two gold bracelets and slipping them into Clear Sky's hand. They were of an English design, one holding an amethyst and the other three diamonds.

Though she had never spoken about her after the day Quill suggested that Clear Sky reminded her of her relative, she had heard stories about Pure Heart from the village women.

Long Cedar Branch could not contain her joy, but as usual her thoughts came with sharpness. "Now that he is taking Clear Sky for a wife, he can marry my daughter as well."

"Hush," Petals said. "That is for Cougar Two Foot to decide."

From his little finger, Father Man took his ornate silver ring—a large turquoise flecked with gold, and slid it onto her middle finger. "This belonged to my mother," he said. "I would like you to have it."

Soon Clear Sky stood before her mentors and their friends. Both looked at her with parental approval and appreciation, and The Gaggle grinned.

"Daughter, you are ready?" Father Man smiled affectionately.

"Yes, father. Cougar Two Foot is a good man, a fine healer and an excellent hunter. He will provide well for us," she said as if it were part of a ceremony.

The ritual was simple. Cougar Two Foot would be asked to remain overnight with the family in their home. Clear Sky was more than ready to fall into the embrace of this man for her wedding day.

Some in the village believed that the marriage was not sacred, and many had mixed feelings about whether this couple should join. They had known Cougar Two Foot's wives and some thought he should partner with another but not with this white woman, yet others thought highly of this couple. Even so, nothing was held back in preparation for their union, and the entire community gathered to celebrate.

Chief Harold Little Crow, a very fine hunter, maybe the best of the People of the Mountain, a confident and proud man and a fine leader, wore his feathered headdress and best shirt for the festivities. He stood in the center of the gathering waiting for the husband-to-be.

Cougar Two Foot entered the clearing in front of the wedding tipi, and the gathering sang their pleasure with a lively chant. His beaded shirt hung so well on his strong frame that many of the women giggled with excitement when they saw him.

"We are very proud of you, Cougar Two Foot. You are a fine healer, and we honor you on this day of your joining," Chief Harold Little Crow said, presenting the new husband with a heavy necklace made of Jasper and bone. Cougar Two Foot's shy smile expressed his joy.

"Thank you, Harold Little Crow. May I give you this gift?" He handed the chief a pouch full of new arrowheads. "They are of strong metal, very sharp," he said.

"It is a fine day to join," the chief said, accepting the gift graciously.

Clear Sky stepped out of the opening of the tipi looking as happy as any bride could be. Cougar Two Foot stepped to her side.

"You look beautiful," he whispered in her ear. "What does the smoke say for us today?"

"That I will not hesitate," she whispered back to him.

Cougar Two Foot looked over the faces of his friends

and beamed.

The celebration was long and loud. The men played games of strength and agility, while the women cooked. The smell of roasting game, fish, baked squashes and fried corn meal wafted through the air.

After a time, when all were occupied with the revelry, Cougar Two Foot took his bride into the wedding tipi. In the morning, as was the custom, the couple would gather his things from The Silver Moon and her husband's tipi, and make a place for them in the home of Father Man and Quill.

She did not want to be nervous, and she had thought of their joining often, but now that she was in the midst of the celebration, Clear Sky couldn't help but shiver nervously at the prospect of intimacy with her new husband. She undressed slowly, holding her dress over her till she could feel the tender look in her husband's eyes wash across her body.

He was cautious and hesitant, wanting to surrender to the love he had for her, but remembering the loss of his first wife and their little boy had made him unsure as well. Quill had made him aware that Clear Sky might find it awkward because of what had happened to her five years ago, so he was patient and tender with his bride. They lay naked on the bearskin bed holding each other, talking softly.

Finally, she took his hand and placed it on her breast. Soon she told him what to do to give her pleasure, and he did the same. And with all the noisy festivities outside, neither felt they had to hush the ecstacy they felt with the other's touch. Afterwards, they lay content in each other's arms. Their wedding night proved fruitful. From that first night of sharing love, Clear Sky became pregnant.

Her pregnancy was easy. She was sick for only a short while, then enjoyed feeling the growing child within her belly.

Excited to become a father again, Cougar Two Foot was most attentive and supportive of his wife. Any worries or concerns they may have had regarding the birth of this child they kept deeply buried.

In the fall months when the People of the Mountain moved to the valley on the warm side of the hill, Clear Sky would give birth to their child.

21

The sky was clear for the first time in days. A fresh layer of snow covered the ground, and walking the paths was not easy. Clear Sky's belly was large, and her body felt cumbersome as she negotiated over slippery rocks and roots.

"Surely you must want to come out soon, little one!" she said out loud, tired of carrying the extra weight.

The cooking pot, filled with its herbal mixture, seemed particularly heavy. Bluebird, who was feeling poorly, was expecting her with the remedy Quill had mixed. When she began to pour the hot brew into a smaller container, there was a pop, and the warm liquid from her womb trickled down the inside of her thighs.

Just then The Gaggle, chatting like a babbling brook, came down the pathway toward her fire.

"How are you today, Clear Sky?" Stands In Front asked.

"Ah, ha!" Petals said giggling and pointing at the wet stain on her dress. "It is your time!"

Stands In Front asked, "Where is Quill?"

"She is with Bluebird," Clear Sky answered.

"Shy Girl, go tell the old woman her grandchild is on the way," directed Stands In Front. "Long Cedar Branch, you help me walk her. Petals, you go and prepare the birthing tent."

"Wait, Shy Girl. Take the tea with you. Quill is expecting it," Clear Sky said. "And someone get Cougar Two Foot," she shouted. "He is with Father Man down by the rock bluff."

"I will go. I will go," Shy Girl called out, trundling off toward the river on her old legs, a container of tea in her hands.

It was comforting to Clear Sky that they had come just as her water broke. All four women had had children and were now doting on their grandchildren, and some even had great-grandchildren.

"Get up now," Stands In Front directed. "Get up. You must walk." She and Long Cedar Branch stood by her side.

Clear Sky walked uncomfortably. It felt as if the three of them had been walking for miles when the first contraction hit. She crumpled to her knees. Long Cedar Branch looked between her legs to see how open she was.

"Very soon," she stated.

"Looks like the child is coming out faster than a fox running for a mouse. Breathe, my dear," Stands In Front said sympathetically.

I remember this, Clear Sky thought. She inhaled deeply and then exhaled a longer slower breath as she had been taught by these ladies. By the time they got back to the tribal camp, and she squatted in the birthing tent, her contractions were close together and the little child was well on its way.

Cougar Two Foot ran from the river.

"You stay out here," Long Cedar Branch instructed him, so he stood outside the tent pacing back and forth, stopping with each loud moan or scream, then pacing some more. Finally, there was a long silence. Just as he started to step inside the enclosure, Long Cedar Branch's head broke out of the opening with a big grin on her face. From within the dark tent came the nasal cry of his newborn son.

"Your wife says his name is Swift Fox because he was in such a hurry to get here," Petals told him as she looked at the wailing child who had just been bathed. Petals wrapped him in a soft cloth, the baby calmed down, and was now cooing softly.

"She has named him? It is too soon to give a name. Tell her that he must be on the earth for six summers before a proper name can be given," Cougar Two Foot said.

"We told her that, but she did not care. His name is Swift Fox."

When Cougar Two Foot looked into his baby's eyes, the deep hole, the empty chasm of sadness that had followed him since his family's death, filled in with joy, and he beamed.

"Swift Fox. That is a good name. He will be a swift and sure hunter," he said hearing something within and speaking it aloud.

"You are a father, son?" Father Man called gasping for air, his old legs carrying him from the river as fast as they could.

"I am," Cougar Two Foot said coming out of the birthing tent. "A boy!"

Father Man laid their catch on the rocks, then took a bit of dried ceremonial herb from the pouch he kept at his waist. Passing the flame over the long stone pipe, he inhaled, drawing in the air slowly, and with several puffs he was able to light it into a glowing red ball. Then he handed the pipe to Cougar Two Foot, who took in the smoke with satisfaction.

"What use are you two standing here?" Quill scoffed, scurrying up the path toward the birthing tent, with Shy Girl close behind. "Go home, Cougar Two Foot. Prepare the bed for your wife and new child. Old Man, you go help him."

"You heard her," Father Man winked.

Quill pushed her head into the opening of the enclosure. "How are you, daughter?"

"We have a son," she said tiredly.

"A handsome and strong body," the old woman said, "and quite a voice! I could hear him from Bluebird's."

Petals lay the newborn in Quill's arms. She cradled her grandson for a moment, cooing before giving him over to his mother.

"I will go to see if your husband has made enough preparations for your return." She disappeared out the door, surreptitiously wiping the tears from her cheeks.

"Those blue eyes are going to cause him trouble, and that brown in his hair." Long Cedar Branch said flatly to Petals.

"We have to wait and see if they turn. And what a thing to say to our new mother," Stands In Front hissed under her breath. "As if she could do anything about that. Keep a more careful tongue, Long Cedar Branch!"

"What did I say but the truth? And we can see clearly that she is no new mother!"

"Quiet now. Let us leave the truth for another time," she retorted.

"I do have ears, Long Cedar Branch," Clear Sky said, her eyes filling. "I have had other children, but they are all dead."

Clear Sky held her son with tenderness, but with a feeling of confusion, an unclear picture of a past birth. *Never mind*, she told herself. *This little man needs me now. Look how strong his legs are.* Swift Fox, though just out of the womb, seemed to be sprinting already, his little legs kicking sharply. He let out a muffled, nasal wail, and his mother gave him her breast.

Cougar Two Foot called from outside, "Wife, are you and my son ready to come home? I have clean clothes for you here—old ones that you ask for," he said as he stepped in, but was speechless at seeing his newborn son.

"Wait over there." Stands In Front said grabbing the clothes out of his hand. "She will be ready in a minute."

"Yes, of course," he said excitedly then backed up and waited, cradling his son in his arms.

When Clear Sky saw Cougar Two Foot her heart welled up with joy. She was tired, but deliriously happy.

The ladies helped the new mother stand. They dressed her in the worn clothing, carefully packing moss between her legs to catch the blood that was slowly draining from her womb after the birth. Cougar Two Foot put his arm around his spouse's shoulder, and walked her home.

"I am tired, my dear husband. Do you mind if I lie down for a few minutes?" she asked, dropping down onto the soft bearskin.

"Yes. I mean, no, of course, rest," he answered.

The new mother had already closed her eyes and was drifting off to sleep. When he saw her and the baby sleeping together, the new father's heart swelled with delight. In his mind he was already making plans to teach his son to ride, hunt, shoot a bow and arrow, fish, and to throw a knife and hatchet. His revery was broken when Father Man came through the tipi door.

"Come," he said. "We will go to the Quiet Place, and sing the praises of your wife and your new son so that the Creator of All knows we appreciate their good health and the safe birth of your child."

Quill came in with a handful of herbs and bark to make a tea and a piece of strengthening Yampa root for the new mother to chew. "You will feel better after you have this," she said.

After a few hours, Quill and Long Cedar Branch returned with some dried meat and wild blueberries. At the tipi of Long Cedar Branch, Quill had made another potion of the healing herbs and brought that as well. The new mother sat up easily, though her body still felt the exertion of the birth. She smelled the wonderful aromas, ate the food with relish, and drank the tea. "I will be ready in just a few minutes."

"Now," Quill said decidedly. "Up you go." She and Long Cedar Branch took her under the arms and lifted her to standing. They wrapped the newborn baby securely in a soft deer skin, setting him on the moss-covered cradle board, then helped the new mother thread her arms through the straps and tighten them onto her shoulders. "Come little man," Quill said chucking the newborn under the chin. "We shall gather some more flowers for your mother's tea."

That afternoon Shy Girl and Petals sent over their young granddaughters to help care for little Swift Fox so Clear Sky could rest.

22

The time for Jahn to leave home was fast approaching. He was seventeen and Richard knew that he would have already joined the cavalry had they allowed him to do so.

"But what will I do if you are not here?" Richard worried. "I cannot run this ranch all by myself."

"You can do it, Richard. If you need help, hire someone," Jahn reminded him. "The horse trade is good and you certainly are making enough money from it to take on a hired hand."

"You cannot go. I will not let you," Richard yelled.

Having help was not what was worrying Richard. Ever since Jahn said he would be signing up when he turned eighteen, Richard had become irritated whenever they spoke about it. And Jahn had learned that when his brother became agitated, things went better if he left him alone. And besides, he was not asking for permission. His mind was already set.

"I am going hunting," Jahn said. "Do you want to come along?"

"Sure," Richard said, his mood lightening slightly.

The boys gathered their rifles and shot and went into the

woods. Leaves and twigs crunched under their feet. This was Jahn's favorite time of year, the crispness of the air infused with the musty smell of rotting foliage.

"Where do you think you would be posted?" Richard asked as they walked.

"I do not know, but surely not far from here," Jahn said not convinced this was the truth.

"Do the Sumners know?"

"Yes, we have talked about it."

"What did Sara say?"

"What could she? At first, she was upset that I would be leaving home," Jahn said understating what had happened. "She cried a little, but Henry seemed to understand. I know they will miss having me near, and I will miss them both, too, but Richard, I must go," Jahn said.

"Look!" Richard whispered. "A rabbit."

"Let it go. There is something better ahead, and we don't want it to run from the sound of your shot. Keep on walking." Within a few minutes Jahn pointed, "See?" Prints from a bighorn sheep in the soft, moist ground, led up the mountain.

"How did you know that?" asked Richard gaining interest in the hunt.

"How did I know what?" Jahn said.

"How did you know there would be something better?"

"I don't know. Sometimes I know things before they happen."

"That's spooky," Richard teased. "You see dead spirits, too?" he said elbowing his brother in the ribs.

"Be quiet now or you will scare away dinner."

This was the first time Jahn had told anyone of this. It was something that he was just learning about himself, and he was not sure what to think about it, and his mother was not there to help him understand.

A week after Jahn's eighteenth birthday, Richard and Jahn rode side by side to the church. Jahn had wanted to see the inside of it one more time before he left to join his dragoon. Richard carried Jahn's satchel, a last gesture of brotherly care before Jahn left for his post at Fort Garland, on Ute Creek, very near where they had lived before moving to the mountains. The Sumners and several other friends were waiting to say goodbye. Jahn and Mrs. Sumner walked into the old church where his father had preached. There was still no regular minister, only an itinerant preacher who came every couple of weeks.

Jahn stood stiffly in his new starched and pressed uniform. His highly polished boots made a crunching sound as he walked over the dust and dirt that had accumulated on the floor. He took up the broom and swept the dirt out of the door, returned the broom to its place then looked around the empty sanctuary. It had been eight years since the raid on his family, and the loss of his sister a year later. As he looked around the church, he felt nostalgic for times when he loved having fun and was easily pleased.

"You look very handsome, Jahn," Mrs. Sumner said. "You *will* come back and visit us often, won't you?" she said, squeezing his arm, her eyes filling with tears.

"Yes, ma'am, and I will write to you," he said as he hugged her. "I love you," he said.

"I love you, too, Jahn. And I will look forward to getting your letters."

They held each other for a long moment then went outside to join the others.

Conor and Adam Finnian and their parents stood outside.

Each took their turn to wish him well and say goodbye.

"You take care of yourself," Adam said.

"Come back and tell us what you are doing," urged Conor.

"I will," Jahn replied.

"Now, you watch over your shoulder, Son. We want you safe. And of course," Henry said, "you always have a place here with us, but you know that."

"Yes, sir. You have been very kind to Richard and me. I will always remember that," Jahn said. Henry reached out for Jahn's hand, but overcome with emotion, he threw his other arm around the young man's shoulders. He reached into his pocket and pulled out a silver watch on a fob and handed it to the new soldier.

"This was my father's. It's from England, one of the few things that survived the trip across the plains to get here. I would like for you to have it."

Jahn took the watch, opened it and looked at the face. On the inside of the lid was inscribed, "For my dear son, from his loving Father."

"You tuck the watch into your vest pocket, and attached the chain through the buttonhole," Henry said, almost unable to hold back his tears.

"Thank you, sir. I will carry it always."

Even though Jahn wanted to go, it was hard for him to tear himself away from his friends and their families, all the people who had been his lifeline over the years. But he also knew that in the cavalry, he might have more freedom to go where he wanted, though he had not told anyone that this was the reason for his joining.

Lizbeth George ran to him, handing the new recruit a bunch of yellow roses.

"Thank you, Lizbeth" Jahn said looking down at the sweet thirteen year old.

"I am going to, I mean...we are all going to miss you, Jahn." She burst into tears, and ran back to her mother.

He broke off the flowers, and stuffed them into his pocket. Later Jahn would put the petals into the leather folder, which he would carry with him wherever he went, the one that held the drawing of his mother.

"I am going to miss you all as well," Jahn said slowly looking around at all their faces.

Henry held the reins of a stallion, a big gray, the horse that Richard had given Jahn, while Jahn tied his satchel to the back of his saddle. Grey Boy danced in anticipation. There was a tearing in Jahn's heart as he rode away from all that he had known, and he was grateful that Richard rode with him half the day before turning back.

"Listen, Squirt," Richard teased. "You keep your head on, and shoot straight."

It was going to be hard on Richard not having his little brother there to pick him up when he fell. When they parted ways, and Jahn rode on toward Fort Garland, where he was due to report in a week, he worried that he might never see Richard again.

23

"Now come here young man, and sit on an old man's knee." Father Man lifted Swift Fox, his two year old grandson and the darling of his life, onto his lap. "I believe he has grown," he said looking at Cougar Two Foot.

"He certainly eats enough," Clear Sky grinned. "I believe he will be tall like his father."

Cougar Two Foot laughed, and picked up his child, holding him high above his head. "How do we look from there, little pup?" Swift Fox giggled with delight as he always did when being picked up in this way. Then his father handed him back to Father Man.

Father Man looked into the boy's eyes and then closed his. After he took a deep breath he said, "He will be a great leader and a fine hunter. But he will need to learn to share his mother. This will be hard on him."

"Father Man," Clear Sky chided, "at this age he needs his mother to live." But she did wonder what Father Man had seen, as he did not elaborate.

Father Man tickled the little boy, who giggled uncontrollably.

"Old Man, you are going to make him sick to his stomach," Quill said. She took the boy from Father Man's knee and cuddled him, kissing his neck, making him chortle with delight.

"You just want the baby for yourself," Father Man laughed.

After a few minutes, the youngster began to fuss. "Eat, little one," Quill said, giving him over to his mother who held a piece of broth-soaked corn mush to the baby's mouth. "We have much to teach you. You must grow to be big and strong and have a mind as sharp as an arrow."

The snow season came and went twice. Now the days were filled with warm sun and an occasional rain storm. As was the custom for a grandfather, Father Man took four-year old Swift Fox outside and watched while he ran after bugs or pounced on leaves. Neither looked happier than when in each other's company.

"Grandfather," Swift Fox asked. "May I hold that?" he said pointing to his grandfather's healing rattle.

"This?" he said picking it up and shaking it. "You know I use this to scare away the snake spirits that get into a man and make him sick. Snakes are afraid of its noise," he said whispering as if telling a secret.

"May I shake it?" the boy asked, his speech clearer than you would expect from a child his age.

"Just this once," Father Man answered. "When you are older I will teach you how to make it work for you."

The boy took the rattle in his small hand, and shook it timidly at first, then again and again with growing confidence.

Father Man was pleased that he could feel the boy in the

sound. "Shall we go down to the river and look for fish for our meal? Go and tell your mother where we are going."

Then they walked together toward the Yampa River, in the lush valley where the families lived during the warm months. "We must be very quiet when we look for them. The fish have big ears that you cannot see."

"Yes, Grandfather. Very quiet."

The young boy was not sure what that meant, but he knew his Grandfather would teach him. The two walked hand in hand toward the water, the older one stepping slowly and carefully over tree roots and rocks, and the younger skipping over them, his feet barely touching the ground.

Jahn rode off the trail through the woods toward the smoke he saw coming from within the trees. Up ahead was a village of about fifty tipis. So as not to alarm the community, he dismounted and walked into the clearing, leaving his rifle in its holster.

To his right were several children playing with a young puppy, one young boy holding a stick while the canine, playfully growling, pulled at it with its teeth. To his left was a group of six women circled around the fire, working and chattering like hens. Though they all had years on them, only one of the women had hair that showed her age. Shining brilliantly in the sun the white hair flowed down the woman's back like a sparkling river. She ran her hand through it showing a large turquoise ring on her middle finger. But when he took a step toward that tipi, an arrow landed at his feet.

"What do you want, soldier?" Corn Snake asked from deep within the woods.

"No call for alarm. I was just wondering if you might

have seen this woman?" he said holding out the picture of his mother. But Corn Snake did not move, forcing the lieutenant to walk away from the encampment.

He took hold of the drawing and stared at it. Hiding his recognition of the woman in the picture, he answered, "No, I do not know this woman. Who is she?"

"My mother," the lieutenant answered.

Corn Snake chuckled inwardly debating whether to kill this man or laugh at him out loud. "Do not bother my people with this. She is not with us."

"Perhaps someone in the tribe might have seen her?" Jahn said turning to the village.

Corn Snake pulled an arrow from his quiver, and set it on the bowstring. "You are wasting your time here, soldier."

"I am at Fort Garland. If you happen to see her, can someone let me know?" He knew that no one would tell him if they did, but he could not help but ask. Jahn got back on his horse, and headed back to the trail.

I will come another time, he thought, *when this Indian is not pointing an arrow at me.*

Clear Sky sat talking with The Gaggle outside the tipi, shucking late summer corn. Across the way, Swift Fox and the other children, back from a soak in the hot springs, were playing with a dog, throwing it a stick.

A breeze blew so she smoothed her white hair, which was loose, flowing down her back. She looked at the faces of Quill's friends, and realized they had become her family, her aunts, all extending hands of care and affection. It was a good feeling, one of fullness. But suddenly something unsettled her, something she had not felt for a long time, a feeling of being a stranger, a white woman, having no Indian brothers or sisters, father or mother, of being separate. At the same time she felt a deep longing, though she did not know for what. This feeling of separation had been hard for her, and only with the birth of her son had it abated. But as quickly as that feeling flowed in, it washed out, and she shook off the unhappiness, once again melding into the joyfulness of this talkative group.

Several weeks later, Jahn came back to where the village had been, but the field was empty. The camp had moved on, leaving only dark circles from where their fires had been. The weather was cooling, so the families would go to where tipis could be protected from the harsh winter winds—or army raiders. There could be no way of knowing where they had gone.

25

"Come quickly!" The Silver Moon said, breathless from running up the path to where Clear Sky was walking. "He is like a bent branch–can't stand. Please. Please come!" She ran back into the woods, not knowing if Clear Sky would follow.

Clear Sky found Father Man, who called to his wife, but she was not within hearing.

"Tell Cougar Two Foot to go and see what is the matter," Father Man said.

"Yes, Father," she said with a sense of foreboding. "Are you sure you should not go?"

"You go as well," he said without looking up.

Reluctantly, Clear Sky went to look for Cougar Two Foot.

She called for him then saw him through the trees in a field near the camp. "The Silver Moon needs us now."

"The Silver Moon? Who is ill?" Cougar Two Foot asked without looking at her, stuffing a handful of green leaves into his basket.

"She did not say."

Cougar Two Foot and Clear Sky went deep into the woods to an encampment not far from the village. There they found the man on his knees, doubled over in pain. As they suspected, it was Corn Snake.

"Where does it hurt? Can you describe the pain?" Cougar Two Foot asked with reservation.

"Like a knife in my belly," he said in too much pain to fight. "Here," he said pointing to the middle of his stomach.

"Sharp?" Cougar Two Foot asked. "Or like an old vine squeezing a branch?"

"Old vine," he answered with difficulty.

It took all his will and strength, but Cougar Two Foot looked past the cloak of fear, anger and hatred that covered Corn Snake's true nature, and the fear and anger that covered his own, to the place that they shared in common. From there he spoke to the man.

"I am going to touch you gently," Cougar Two Foot said, placing his hand on the abdomen. "You tell me where it hurts the most." With his fingers, he pressed lightly, looking for a response. When he came to the place in the center below the rib cage, Corn Snake moaned.

"It is here?" he asked to confirm what he knew.

"Yes."

"Any blood in your mouth or when you defecate?"

"No," Corn Snake answered.

"If you eat is it better or does the vine twist more?" he asked.

"It loosens," he grunted.

Cougar Two Foot took his bag of herbs, and began to set aside the ones to be made into a tea.

Clear Sky took them and prepared the mixture that he requested. Before she could stop its stampede, the memory of

Corn Snake's attack came back, and she felt fully the horror of that night. Cougar Two Foot, too, remembered that night as well. He waited for some time for those disquieting feelings to dissipate. When he was able to find a feeling of safety for Clear Sky, he began his chant.

"Drink this everyday till the pain is no longer," Cougar Two Foot told him. "Let me know if he needs more," he told The Silver Moon.

By the time he finished the healing ceremony, Corn Snake was able to stretch out on the sleeping pallet. He lay intently watching Clear Sky as they packed up their things. When she passed him, he grabbed her wrist. For a moment, he thought he would tell her about the soldier who had come to the village, the soldier that was her son, but instead he decided to enjoy the fact that she did not know of him.

A feeling of fear and panic over took Clear Sky once again, but she was able to calm herself, and when she became filled with compassion, he jerked his hand away.

The next day The Silver Moon, came to them with her payment.

"Thank you," she said quietly handing Cougar Two Foot a sharp, metal hunting knife, and for Clear Sky a woven basket.

"My son is not a bad man," she said before leaving.

26

1864

Quill was stooped over the grinding stone, pulverizing tubers, placing the meal into sacks, and Clear Sky was mashing summer berries into a paste, when Father Man called out to his six-year-old grandson, "Come. Bring your bow and arrows."

The boy slung his prized weapons over his shoulder and they walked together toward the practice tree in the field. Furtively, Clear Sky watched while Father Man tied a sack of grass to one of its branches. One side of the leather bag had a red mark on it the size of Father Man's fist. Father Man swung the pouch so that it rocked back and forth. He took a shot, and hit the target square in the center. Swift Fox raised his bow, pulled back the arrow and loosed the dart. It missed. The boy pulled another arrow from his quiver, and put its notch on the bowstring. He pulled back again, and let the arrow fly, but it missed once more. He shot his arrows over and over, each time missing the mark.

"That is too hard for a boy so young," Clear Sky said as she got up to toss the seeds roasting over the fire.

"Father Man will teach our young pup to learn quickly,"

Quill replied continuing to grind the meal. While Father Man taught his grandson and the women worked, the sun made its path across the afternoon sky.

Quill was not one to talk about her own family except to say that she had adored her grandmother. But she did tell Clear Sky, "Pure Heart was always snarling at my father, like a mean wolf. I once asked her about it. I was very young then and did not know better. She only said that she had had other sons, and that this one reminded her that they were lost to her." There was a long silence then Quill added, "Your child is a star in your eye. That is good."

By the end of the afternoon, when the women had finished their work and supper was cooked and ready to eat, Swift Fox shot the final arrows. The bow snapped, the arrow hitting the target. He again pulled back the string of his bow. With the arrow between his young fingers, he stood watching the target sway. Once released, his arrow sped directly into the bag once more. He missed the next three, but made the next two. It was only when he truly felt the arrow in the target before he shot did he hit the mark.

"You see, the little fox learns quickly," Quill said under her breath, grabbing the last of the corn they had gotten from the fort.

Father Man walked over to the tree, took the bag, and this time spun it as he let it go. The bag rocked back and forth as it unwound. The mark on the bag flashed blinking red with each rotation. He told the boy to hit the mark.

The boy pulled back his arrow and loosed it, missing the bag altogether. Another arrow missed, then another, then five more. The two walked over to the tree to pick up the darts. Swift Fox, less sure now, began to feel ashamed.

They walked back to the quiver. Father Man handed him

another arrow and instructed the boy once more, "Feel the flicker of the red mark. When you can dance with it, let your arrow go."

Many of Swift Fox's arrows hit the ground or the tree, but not the target, let alone the red mark.

"Become the target," Father Man said patiently.

Swift Fox pulled back the string on his bow. He watched. When he felt the bag rocking back and forth, and then felt the rhythm of the blinking color on the pouch, he launched his arrow. To him it flew slowly, arching toward the target, hitting dead center into the red mark. The boy stood motionless for sometime taking in what he had experienced. Father Man patted his grandson's shoulder proudly.

"We shall go home now."

When they walked back to the camp, the boy's arms were quivering from the exercise.

"Grandfather, why does it seem like the arrow flies slowly?"

"When you are one with another, there is no time," he said putting his large hand on the boy's head. "If you practice every day, when your legs hang long on the side of your horse, you will be able to hit the mark from a gallop."

27

1865

Jahn dismounted Gray Boy to look more carefully at the ground. For about three days, he had been following three men he suspected of raiding settlers in the area. As they had not expected to be followed, their horses hoof prints were easy to see.

Normally, he would not go without his men, but he had been sent to Steamboat Springs at the Commander's request, and his men were on patrol elsewhere.

The sky was getting dark so he chose a place to make camp for the night. No fire though, because below was the camp of the raiders. He waited, pulling his blanket tightly around his shoulders, futilely trying to stay warm and get some rest.

The shadows were long and the light in the woods was spare as the setting sun sent out its last light of the day. Unbeknownst to the boys, who had been practicing shooting their arrows, watching from a distance were four sets of eyes.

"Your mother is going to be angry with us," Swift Fox told Tall Stalk.

"Not only my mother! Your mother has a very loud voice when she gets mad," he countered. "We had better hurry and pick up our arrows."

The seven-year old Swift Fox and his friends, Tall Stalk and Wind, two brothers, seven years and six, were supposed to have been home by now.

"Will you reach my arrows?" Wind asked his older brother.

"No, you get them," Tall Stalk replied teasing him with a tap on the back of the head.

"I will help you," Swift Fox said.

Then the three ran toward the tree they had used as a target.

Silently The Red Wing and his men, their faces painted black, moved through the forest loosening their ropes, readying them to capture the children who would become good barter or slaves. Slinking through the darkness in the woods, the men surrounded the boys.

These men were the pride of their tribe, always bringing back something of value. Mostly they stole horses, but when circumstances were right they also brought home human prizes. The men could almost hear the cheers when their people saw them bringing back three young boys.

Suddenly, Swift Fox stopped what he was doing, and listened. He felt an ominous cloud form all around him and his friends, but he noticed too late. The small boys, easily overwhelmed by the men's strength, were tied up and put onto horses.

Swift Fox was placed behind the raider who rode at the back of the line. The boy tried to get free, but could not loosen the grip of the rope that bound his upper arms, though he was able to inch it higher, allowing his forearms and hands to be of use. As they rode along, he took the feather from his hair, and let that go. It floated to a bush and caught at eye level. He untied the scarf at his neck, and let it slip down to the ground. Next he dropped his headband. He tried to untie his braided wristband, but it was too secure and would have been too obvious to the man who held him tightly. When he could, he also broke branches to leave a trail.

"Where is my son?" Clear Sky asked, stirring the pot on the fire. "Husband, go tell the children it is time to eat, and send the brothers home."

"They are in the woods," he called back. *They have just gotten preoccupied*, he thought as he went into the trees to find them. But when he came to the place where they had been, their bows lay on the ground, their arrows were scattered, and the ground looked chewed up. He ran back to the camp calling out for Two Rivers, father of Tall Stalk and Wind. Clear Sky heard him, and ran out to see what was the matter.

"Something is wrong," he told her.

Clear Sky felt a chill run through her veins, and her heart began to flutter like a fearful bird. She ran to the boys' mother, hoping they might be at their home, but Summer told her they had not returned.

"Something has happened," Clear Sky said. Summer looked stricken.

Cougar Two Foot got the horses, while Two Rivers, his bow across his back and a spear in his hand, began looking closely at the area. They saw hoof prints of four horses heading down the trail southward. Two Rivers plucked the feather from the tree branch.

The path went straight ahead, then split to the east. By this time it was so dark that clues were difficult to see. Two Rivers did spot something though–the cloth Swift Fox had dropped.

The boys were bound to a tree tightly, like flies caught in a web. Tall Stalk began to cry, and Wind choked back tears as well.

"Make sure they don't get away. If they cause you any trouble kill one of them," The Red Wing barked as he mounted his horse to ride back to the band's camp.

"Badger Tail, check their bindings and give them a drink," said The Night Hawk.

"You want some water?" the short and stocky brave asked. Though their language was similar, the boys could not truly understand. "Water. You want some?" he said again this time holding out the gourd cup. The boys nodded.

Swift Fox's fear turned to anger, but he resisted the desire to spit at him. To calm himself, he breathed slowly and deeply as his grandfather had taught him.

The braves boasted to each other about their exploits, and what good fortune would come from it. The Night Hawk remarked that the half-white's arrows flew straight into the target. As he turned the rabbit over the fire, another noted that the youngest one would be perfect for his kin.

Once the men had had their fill of meat, they played a game. Badger Tail drew a small circle on the ground. The three men took turns throwing their knives into it, and with each successive round they stepped farther away from their target. This contest went on for a long time with The Night

Hawk winning most of the rounds.

While the men became distracted with the amusement, Swift Fox's eyes darted in every direction looking for something to use for their escape. He knew they had to get away before they traveled even a day, or he might never see his family again.

There it is, he thought. Just a few inches from his foot was a stone with one edge that was long and sharp. He stretched his legs as far as he could, taking the rock between his feet, pulling it toward his groin. When he could reach it with his hand, he grabbed it, and slid it under his leg.

The boys tried to work their hands free from the rope, but it was too tight, and was hurting their wrists.

"Never mind," Swift Fox said. "We shall be long gone before they wake. But for now close your eyes, and pretend to sleep like the possum," he whispered.

Tall Stalk leaned against the tree, and Wind let his head fall onto his brother's shoulder. Swift Fox curled his body as best he could, so he was able to watch the men more closely.

The Night Hawk called out, "Red Shirt, see if those boys are up to anything."

Badger Tail threw his knife once more into the ring and missed. *The ghost of my brother must be pushing my knife. He always had to win everything,* he thought.

The fire had begun to die out. Red Shirt threw on another log while Badger Tail went to the tree where the boys were tied. He tugged at the rope to be sure it was tight, making the boys squirm at its pinching.

It was getting so dark that Cougar Two Foot and Two Rivers could hardly see the hoof marks along the water, but as they went over the hill, they saw a fire. Leaving their horses tied to a tree they crept on foot toward the light.

Summer followed Clear Sky back to her tipi where she stood outside watching for the return of her husband and two sons.

"What is the matter?" Father Man asked.

"The boys are missing! Cougar Two Foot went to fetch them for supper, and found their bows and arrows scattered on the ground," Clear Sky said barely able to speak another word.

Father Man threw piece of wood on the fire, and settled his mind. Inwardly, he spoke to Swift Fox as if he were standing right in front of him. *My grandson, you and Senawahv are one. This has always been so. You are a fine young man, and very smart. You know you are free to come home when you wish. We greet you with open and loving arms.*

He held him in this mental embrace for sometime then got up to stir the pot on the fire.

A surge of calm and clarity came over Swift Fox. He waited, pretending to sleep, till the captors nodded off. Before long, the sound of heavy breathing rose from the men. Very quietly, the boy brought out the sharp stone. He rubbed and rubbed it across the rope at his wrist. With great effort, he was able to cut its bind. Then he undid the knot on Tall Stalk's hands, and quietly moved to Wind to free him. Once his friends were loose, Swift Fox instructed them to slip into the woods.

"Do not run. Pretend you are trying to sneak up on a mouse," he told them.

He waited till the brothers were in the depth of the trees then made his way to where the horses were tethered. Slowly, he loosened their ties and jumped upon the back of one still holding the ropes of the others. Lying down on top of his horse, he let it walk freely into the trees. The others followed. When he was out of sight, he picked up the boys and kicked the horses to a run.

The braves woke as one.

With hooves and hearts pounding like drums at a war chant, Swift Fox wove in and out of the trees, picking up the path to the west. The men ran across the angle to cut them off. Kicking his horse even harder, Swift Fox and his charges tried to get ahead of them, but they got caught in the tree branches, and the men quickly encircled the boys.

"You are too smart for your own good, Blue Eyes," The Night Hawk snarled.

Surrounding the children, the three men closed in on their prey. Swift Fox kicked his horse, but Badger Tail stepped in front of it, and the stud bucked, dropping Wind onto the ground. Badger Tail grabbed the fallen boy around the waist lifting him high into the air. Wind kicked and screamed trying to get away, but Badger Tail was strong, and held him tight.

The Night Hawk ran in and grabbed the horse, and pulled Tall Stalk off. Red Shirt took that boy, and twisted his young arm behind his back. The boy screamed in pain. The Night Hawk grabbed Swift Fox.

Two Rivers wanted to run in, but Cougar Two Foot caught him by the shoulder before he was seen. Cougar Two Foot whistled a bird's call, one that Swift Fox knew from hunting with his father. Carefully drawing his bow, he watched for just the right moment.

Swift Fox bolted to the side, pulling The Night Hawk around, giving his father a clear shot. Cougar Two Foot released his bow, and the arrow shot directly into the thief's back. As the other men turned to see what happened, both fathers let loose arrows into each of the captors.

"Take the children to our horses," Cougar Two Foot told him. Then he began to gather the horses left by the thieves.

As if from the dead, suddenly with renewed strength, The Night Hawk rose behind him, his knife high, ready to bury it deep into Cougar Two Foot's neck. But Cougar Two Foot caught the bandit's arm, and wrestled him to take away the blade. With the knife just an inch from his skin, and his arm tiring from the struggle, he drew up a surge of power from deep within, and with all his physical strength, rolled the raider onto his back. As he fell onto him, the arrow pierced deeper into the man's body. Crying out in pain, The Night Hawk's eyes widened, then he fell limp to the ground.

Drawing a clear breath, Cougar Two Foot stood up. Inexplicably, he looked up the hill where a soldier stood, gun aimed at the renegades. For a moment their eyes met, but when the soldier saw that the fight was over, he lifted his gun, and un-cocked it, got on his big gray horse, and rode into the darkness of the forest.

Swift Fox flew into his mother's arms. She hugged him tightly, and longer than he wanted.

The story would be told and retold over many campfires, and when the annual Tribal Gathering was held, Swift Fox would tell all of his capture, his escape and the bravery of his father.

28

The Captain sat at his desk going over orders.

"Take a few men with you," he said to his twenty-two year old lieutenant. "Jahn, I appreciate your enthusiasm, but try not to risk your life or your men's."

"Sir, I can handle this one alone."

"Take Smythe, Berenson and Tadwater with you," the Captain said ignoring Jahn's comment. He reminded Jahn that the Comanche raiding parties had come a long way to get what they want, of how treacherous they were, and how vicious they could be if they took a prisoner. "If you get caught, we would not be able to save your life."

Comanche raiders were treacherous, but Jahn had seen how the settlers treated the local Utes, and though he could not tolerate being in the same room with one, and even though extermination was part of their orders, he could not condone the cruel and wretched treatment he had seen some of his own soldiers give them. The ranchers were not any better, killing women and babies and burning homes, even taking their children as slaves.

The three soldiers stood outside the Captain's office.

"Great," said Smythe, listening through the door. "Now we have to look after him. Last time we went on patrol he took off by himself. Nearly got myself killed trying to find him."

"We had better take care of ourselves with this one," added Berenson.

"–And him," Tadwater broke in. "The Captain will say it is our fault if the fool gets hurt."

"At least, we might get some good scalps," Smitty laughed, knowing that each one brought a monetary reward from the government.

The Captain told Jahn raiders had been hitting hard in the northeast, Arapaho country, pointing to that section of the map. "Take your men, and see what you can do to help the settlers."

"Now we are in for it," Berenson whispered loudly outside the door. "What is it with him anyway? He's on a mission to save every kidnapped white person out there. I don't want to be the one caught in some snare because of it."

"Jahn," the Captain said not looking up from the map. "Be careful, and do not endanger my men or yourself unnecessarily."

"Yes, sir," he said snapping a salute and leaving the room.

"Saddle up, Gentlemen," Van Andusson told his men. "We leave within the hour."

The men gathered at the livery at noon, checking over their gear as they waited for their leader.

"As you know," Van Andusson said, an official air hiding his personal interests, "Comanche raiding parties have been attacking settlers in the northeast. The Arapaho who live in that area will attack us if they think they are in danger, so we must be respectful. It is up to me, to us," he corrected, "to ensure the safety of the settlers. Also keep your ears open for any talk of white men, women or children being carried off by raiders."

"Sir?" Tadwater asked.

"Just tell me if you hear anything, Sergeant," he barked.

The soldiers traveled north toward Ridgewater Bluff, then went south to a saloon at the settlement at Great Fork, where a general town meeting was called.

"They come in fast, in the middle of the night, Lieutenant," a distraught rancher complained. "How can we signal anyone for help?"

"Those dang Injuns are good at hiding themselves," a farmer called out.

"Not only that," one of the ladies cried, "When the men have gone looking for them, others sneak back and demand we cook them meals."

Jahn looked over the distressed crowd who could not know that his disquiet was equal to theirs. With the continuous stream of white families moving from the east, the Indians were seeing this encroachment as hostile, so Jahn knew that nothing was going to keep the settlers from being attacked, or the settlers from attacking the Indian villages.

Like two animals fighting over the same piece of meat, he thought. *Even though the one made the kill, the other wants it for itself.*

The meeting broke and the crowd filed out the door.

A redheaded boy of about twelve pulled at his arm. "Excuse me, sir?" The boy clutched his sleeve. "Jeremy Wellis, sir. Four days ago my sister and mother—they were taken." The boy held the lieutenant's gaze. "You must help me find them. Please. My mother is Virginia and my sister is Jane."

"Do they call your mother Ginny, by any chance?" he asked.

"No, sir, Ginger on account of her hair being red."

"Red like yours?"

"We all have red hair."

"And how old is Jane?"

"We're twelve. She's my twin."

"All right, Jeremy. We will see what we can do."

The young boy shook and shook the lieutenant's hand.

The soldiers mounted up and headed south. All were feeling disgruntled and nervous about searching for the woman and her daughter.

"Now how we supposed to do that?" Berenson muttered under his breath. Then he shouted to the other men, "Oh, bloody hell!"

"Not our job to go find 'em, is it?" Smythe chimed in. "Did Captain say, and while you are at it go find any white women and child taken by the natives? No, he said help the settlers fend off raiders which we can't do much about anyway."

"They may have heard something at the trapper's fort," Van Andusson broke in disregarding his men's grumblings. "That they have red hair should help. And Berenson. If it were your mother, what would you do?"

"I'd be lookin' under every branch or twig for some sign, Sir," he said embarrassed at his outburst.

"And if you were twelve?"

Smythe answered stiffly. "I'd be askin' for help from soldiers that came to town, Sir," he admitted.

"Right then."

The next day they pulled up to one of the Rocky Mountain Fur Trading stores. Jahn went in to talk with the owner, Frederick R. Wilkes, who had hung one of his posters in the store many years before. "Hello, Jahn, nice to see you. You've not been by in a long time," Wilkes reached out his hand.

"Mr. Wilkes, I trust you have been well. And Mrs. Wilkes?"

"Very fine. Thank you for asking. You made lieutenant? Congratulations. What can I get you and your men today?"

"Young man, who is that?" he had asked looking at the poster so many years before.

"My mother, sir. She was taken."

"Sad thing for sure," Wilkes said shaking his head.

"If you hear anything will you tell us?"

"Sure thing. Did hear of a woman taken by that black-faced scavenger, The Red Wing. You heard of him? The story goes she caused him so much trouble he beat her then sold her. She's dead no doubt. Don't know if it be your mother, son. Hope not."

Since then Jahn had made a point of stopping by periodically.

"I am not only here for provisions this time. We are tracking Indians who have been raiding the homesteads. They took a redheaded woman and her daughter, three or four days ago. You heard anything?"

Mr. Wilkes thought for a moment.

"Red hair, you say? I did hear of a redheaded woman,

don't know about a child though," he sighed. "Heard talk they was headin' south, was about two or three days ago. No one wants to mess with 'em, you know. Mean as they come," he said. "Take the horse right out from under your pants if you are not paying attention, and then cut off your ears for the fun of it. Jahn, you ever find your–"

"No," Jahn cut in. "Thank you, Mr. Wilkes," Jahn said. "Please give my best to your family."

The men continued riding south till night coolness filled the air. They pulled their gear off the horses and settled in for the night. In the center of the four men's bedrolls, the fire raged, crackling and spitting embers that then floated up with the smoke. Jahn stared through the branches at the dark star-filled sky, listening to the sounds of the night. An owl screeched as he dropped off.

The head of the nocturnal bird swirled around sharply toward a large crow that flew above the edge of a river. His black wings, opened wide, rested upon the updraft from the canyon below, where a redheaded woman and her child, their hands tied, were on their knees at the edge of the water. A renegade beat the mother, and she screamed for help.

From within the brush of the woods a wolf jumped onto the back of that man. The crow flew down, catching the woman by the back of her dress and pulled her straight up into the air, then set her down a safe distance away. The child called out. Several wolves ran in from different directions, growling loudly. Jahn jolted awake. It was daybreak.

His men lay on their bedrolls looking like wilted grass on a hot day, one snoring louder than the next.

"Get ready men," Jahn called kicking Tadwater's boot,

"We are going toward the river."

"Wha-what?" Tadwater struggled to open his eyes. Smythe and Berenson groaned and rolled over. Finally, they all rose, sleepily, pulling up their suspenders, putting on coats, hats and guns. Van Andusson pulled out the map to see where the closest river was.

"Here," he said. "This is where they are."

"Now how do you suppose he knows that?" Smythe whispered to Tadwater.

"Smitty, you and Berenson cross the river here, keep your wits about you, and be quick about it," he said pointing to a place on the map. "Tad and I will stay on this side. Follow the riverbank."

The men looked at their commanding officer dubiously, then at each other before pulling their horses in the direction of the river.

They rode till late afternoon when Berenson pulled up short. "Good thing the ground is wet and holds a print. Makes 'em easy to spot. There," he whispered, pointing. "Five horses with riders," he said leaning down the side of his mount. "Deeper here," he said indicating the mark. "At least one horse with two riders."

The lieutenant waved to the two soldiers on the other side to come back over.

"Are you sure, Lieutenant? " asked Tadwater. "This is just a stream. You said river."

"I'm sure," he answered.

The clacking of the horse's hooves on the stony bottom of the stream echoed against the hills as they crossed the shallow part of the waterway. Following it straight ahead for about a mile, they stopped when it turned.

"Smitty, go up that hill, and tell me what you see."

Outside the trapper's cabin where the lieutenant, Juniper Jack, and Johnny Garry were spending the night, a snowstorm raged. Suddenly, the door blew open sending in a heavy swirl of snow. Johnny Garry jumped up and set his shoulder against the door pushing as hard as he could to close it against the ferocious wind. The fire had almost been extinguished by the blast of cold air. Juniper Jack shook the snow off their blankets.

"Where was I?" Johnny asked. "Oh yeah, the chief wanted the whole barrel. That's half a barrel of whiskey, the rest filled up with water." He laughed throwing another log on the fire.

Jahn was paying no attention to the story as he relit his pipe and fell back into his memories while Johnny droned on:

Smythe scrambled up the incline, pulled out his spyglass, looked and then ran back down.

"Three men swimming. She's there. The redheaded woman's at the river's edge splashing water to clean a cut on her leg. Little girl's with her," Smythe said.

The soldiers pulled back into the brush. Van Andusson looked in all directions to be sure they had not been detected.

"What do you want us to do, Lieutenant?" Smythe asked in a low voice.

"Looks like they have made camp. We'll wait till nightfall," he said looking up at the sky. "It should be dark in about an hour or so."

Berenson took the watch. They would not be able to make a fire to cook or they might be seen, so Smythe pulled out pieces of jerky and handed them around to the men.

Once darkness filled the trees, Van Andusson gave his orders.

"Berenson, Smitty, you go back up stream and cross over, then come down even with us. We will come at them from four directions. When I whistle, ride into the camp. We will do the same on this side. Make as much noise as you can. Guns blazing. We want them to think there are more of us than just four. Be ready."

"Be ready?" Tadwater asked.

"To ride like hell," Jahn answered.

Jahn and his men camouflaged with leafy branches tucked in the brim of their hats stole quietly toward the campsite. The weather was in their favor as rain began to fall noisily on the leaves.

"How many do you count, Tad?" Jahn asked.

"I see four," Tadwater said with the spyglass pressed against his eye.

"Where are the woman and the girl?"

"Near the fire. Hands and feet bound." He handed the lens to the lieutenant. Jahn looked, then folded up the spyglass and handed it back.

"Our luck. They are drinkin' whiskey. We'll wait till the liquor has knocked them senseless," Jahn remarked.

Each man took his turn on watch until the middle of the night.

"Ready men? Make every shot count," Jahn said.

The lieutenant, quiet as a puma, moved to the tree on the hill nearest the sentry. As the guard's head bobbed trying to stay awake, he grabbed the man, and with relish slit his throat before he could utter a sound. Holding him from falling, Van Andusson quietly laid the body onto the ground. He took his pistol from its holster. The click of the hammer woke another brave, but as he tried to jump up, he was blasted from behind by Tadwater's gun. Smythe and Berenson rode into the scene shooting and screaming, killing the two remaining braves.

"Well, done, men!" Jahn said.

Jahn ran to the stump where the terrified woman and the girl lay huddled together.

"You are safe now. Ginger Wellis?" She nodded yes. "Are you all right?" *What a question,* he thought to himself. *Who could be?* "Jane, your brother, Jeremy, sent us to find you."

Ginger glanced behind Jahn and screamed. He turned to see one of the injured raiders raise his hatchet high, ready to smash it down on his head. He dove for the middle of the man's body forcing him to the ground. The raider kicked him hard with his heels and flipped Jahn over onto his back. With his hatchet poised to slam down on Jahn's face, Jahn held the man's arm, and punched his kidneys with his other fist. Just as Jahn's strength wore out, Tadwater jumped behind them, and wrenched the man's neck killing him instantly.

"Lucky for us the whiskey made it go easy," Berenson said.

"Lucky for me Tadwater got that one first," Jahn agreed. "Let's go. Best not stick around to see if they have any friends."

Smitty and Tadwater pulled out their knives and gathered scalps, hanging the bloody hair on their belts.

"One for each of us," Smitty called, handing one to the lieutenant then wiping his knife on one of the blankets at the site.

"Keep it," Jahn said handing it back.

They took Ginger and Jane and the horses stolen from the settlers, and rode back as fast as they could. Jahn knew there had to be more raiders than just those four.

"Be sure to double your efforts," he told the settlers.

"They will be angry about the death of their kin and the loss of the horses."

Jahn walked into the Captain's office, saluted, then pulled a tomahawk from his belt and slammed it down on his desk. Some the raiders had been killed, and frankly, he did not care to keep any of them alive.

"Four less thieves," he stated proudly.

"So I hear, Lieutenant. I am sure the Wellis's are very grateful to you."

"I was happy to be able to help them—sir."

"Do I need to remind you that you could have been killed or taken prisoner?"

"No–sir," he said stiffly. "But we were not—sir."

"Leave me your report by tomorrow." The Captain went to his desk and pulled out a sheet of paper. "Here is your next assignment. Tell your men they have two days leave, and to report to you Thursday. I do not suppose it would do any good to tell you that you must be careful."

"No, sir."

"Go on then."

He knew his men would be happy to have time off, and so was he. That evening, Jahn went into the saloon for a whiskey.

One soldier yelled, "Lieutenant Van Andusson, Hurrah!" Then another and another called out, "Well done, Jahn!" "Good for you, Van Andusson!" "Mighty great job, sir."

Jahn raised his glass in thanks, but it only served to strengthen his resolve. When he brought the glass to his mouth and drank, the familiar heaviness set over him again. He did not feel satisfied. He had returned loved ones to their families, but it had been someone else's mother, not his. It was never his, and it left him feeling wretched and empty.

29

Summer, 1865

Walking toward Clear Sky from within the woods, wearing a hat whose feathers opened and closed like a bird's wing, was the man she had met in her dream those many years ago when she was first injured. Billowing around his body was golden smoke, whose light came not from the nearby fire but from deep within his heart.

"Awake, my child. It is time for you to go up the mountain. Go to the overhang, the one carved out by time."

"Why?" she asked.

"Do as I tell you. Sit and be still. Watch and listen. Only that. Light your fire when the sun is sleeping," he said.

"Won't my family worry? I want to let them know where I am."

"There is no need. Leave a bird wing at your husband's arrows. He will understand."

Clear Sky awoke with the urgent feeling that she should go to the ridge. Without waking the others, she placed a bird wing as she was told, and prepared herself taking only a bearskin to protect her from the cold.

Father Man stirred, but said nothing. Once Clear Sky had left the tipi, he closed his eyes again. Quill had also heard the commotion, smiled and kicked him under their blankets.

Up on the mountain, high above the river, was an overhang of gray granite where she would set up her things. She gathered wood and set a fire for the night. She had always had the smoke to tell her what she needed to know, but now she would have to wait till night for that, when she would light her fire for warmth.

The rocks were still covered with frost, the sun had yet to highlight the leaves of the trees that surrounded her, and it was bitterly cold. She sat at the spot on the bluff, covered in the bear hide to help cut the bite of the morning air. Once dawn spread its warming rays across the earth, she closed her eyes.

"Do not leave this place," she heard the man within her heart say. *"Listen and watch. That is all."*

At first, time passed slowly, questions rattling in her mind incessantly: *What am I expected to do here? What will I eat? What if an animal comes and threatens my life? Will my son be worried when I am not there when he wakes?*

Throughout the hours she sat still. The sounds of the forest heightened: the screeching of an owl, small creatures skittering over dry leaves and twigs, all pulling her attention. Then she became acutely aware of the aches and pains in her body: the shoulder that had been injured, the knees that had been held in one position so long. She opened her eyes and stretched her legs, then settled down once more dropping into the Silence.

She went deep, but instead of experiencing the comforting Quiet That Has No Boundary as she had come to expect, horror shot through her.

Suddenly, encircling her like a torrential flood were hundreds of bats, flying in waves, funneling up to the sky nearly pulling all the air out of her lungs. Just as she regained her breath, she heard a horrific sound coming from behind. She turned to see a gigantic black horse rear up onto its muscular back legs, snorting and roaring, blasting fire from its nose and mouth, hammering its heavy hooves down close to her, shaking the earth. Each time it lifted its huge body, flames shot from its nostrils, burning everything in its path. The trees, the creatures in the woods, large and small were all scorched. In a large circle in front of her, the forest became nothing but smoldering shafts and smoking carcasses.

Just as the horse retreated, a huge snake with large, sun-bright yellow eyes began to slither around her waist and up her torso, its forked tongue darting in and out as it went. She felt her skin began to peel back, leaving the cast-off shell at her feet. As the snake reached the top of her head, a visceral, cathartic scream welled up from within her belly, the sound seeming to pour out of her throat, echoing throughout the canyon. By this time, Clear Sky could barely take air into her lungs for the fear that engulfed her.

In desperation, she grabbed sticks from the fire mound, and began to beat the earth with them, at first in hard frustration, attempting to pull her mind away from the frightening horse. But as she continued, the rhythm became more even, and her body began to vibrate with its sound. A voice rose deep from within, and she sang to the rhythm of the beating. The sound was comforting and soothing, quieting her restlessness. It took a long time for her to settle enough so that her thoughts stilled, but when they did, she experienced something that she had never been able to before this. She was finally able to sit quietly allowing whatever came to her mind to pass through without making an assessment of what it meant. It was as if ancient wounds became like smoke that drifted up into the clouds. Then she felt herself fall like a droplet from a waterfall into the unfathomable immensity of Creation, ripples spreading throughout all existence. For most of the day, she was in and out of this joyous experience.

When it came time for sleep, she brought her bearskin under the overhang. Rolling up in it, then pulling it tightly under her chin, she slept soundly till morning hunger tightened her stomach, but she was not to eat or drink for her time here. The man had been very specific about that. So she sat up and closed her eyes, expecting the delicious Quiet.

Instead, *the black monster reappeared, and charged, rearing its head, snorting flames, but this time she pulled herself to standing grabbing a blazing branch from her fire. She swung at the beast hitting its chest. It reared again, and again she hit it with her stick. Each time the giant black horse lifted his huge body she swung at it. The horse backed up, preparing to charge. Exhausted, she raised her lance waiting for the beast. The horse ran toward her, then turned and knocked her weapon from her hands with his tail. From deep within an angry growl formed, exploding as if she too could make flames. In a burst of power, she grabbed a short, sharp piece of wood to stab it with, but at that moment the horse disappeared and with it went her fear and rage.*

With her eyes still closed, Clear Sky took a long breath as all that had transpired washed out of her mind. This time when she dropped into The Unbounded, she became a star in the heavens, her brilliance crackling in harmony with all the other stars. Her days and nights became one until she became aware that she was constantly vibrating with the energy of All That Is. This was the first time that she had experienced what Quill had meant by the love of Senawahv, the Creator of All. She could find no edges, no walls to this Love. Everything that exists, even the space between, was made of it.

When Clear Sky realized she had lost track of the number of days she had been beating the stick, singing her chants or sitting quietly, she became anxious. And as if he could hear her thoughts, the man came to her in a dream. *"Be still, gentle woman. You need only watch and listen,"* he said. *"Only that. Watch and listen."*

The next night as Clear Sky sat in silence a profound Peace came over her. She felt as if she filled the sky, weightless in its expansive darkness. At once she was everywhere and everything, but at the same time she was only a small part of a magnificent whole. That night, even though she slept, she was also alert to everything happening around her.

In the early afternoon on the fourth day, when she opened her eyes, to her surprise, right near her was a mother puma nursing her three young. One of the cubs stumbled over to where Clear Sky was sitting, and sniffed at her arm. Another jumped upon the first one's back play-fighting, making young snarling sounds, the third lay down against her leg. After a time the mother Puma got up, ambled over to her, sniffed her breath, then turned, and walked into the woods. She called her cubs and they followed her into the trees.

Clear Sky had not felt fear. Instead, she had had an unwavering sense of calm. The only thing she had been aware of was the motherly attention the big cat showed her young.

At nightfall she gathered her bearskin, and descended the mountain toward her tipi. Father Man saw her coming.

"Tell me of your journey," he said.

And she told him of all that had occurred.

It is not the way our people would recount this experience, he thought. *Perhaps it is the way the whites would speak of it though.*

Then he looked at her intensely reading her face for her truth. "What have you learned, child?"

Mentally reviewing all that she had encountered, she summed it up for him, "That there is great peace to be found within All That Is."

"You will need a new name. Let us sit together." She looked at him quizzically. "You are not the same battered and bruised woman who came to us. You are not even the same woman who was here four days ago, is that not correct? You need a name that bespeaks of who you have become."

They both settled into the Love of Senawahv. There she heard a voice speak. *"White Smoke."* Startled, she opened her eyes, and told him what she heard.

Father Man closed his eyes briefly. "Yes," he smiled. "It signifies your talent. A fine name," he said. "From now on you will be called White Smoke."

Then she asked, "How long have I known you, Father Man?"

"Forever, child."

"But I have been living with you and Quill for eleven summers, is that right?"

He looked at her face for a long time then asked if she was beginning to remember her life.

"Not very much of it," she said. "Mostly, my life here."

"I believe Quill has our supper ready," he said. "She will be looking for us, also your husband and son." They walked back to the village.

Quill was stooped over the cooking pot stirring its contents.

"Go find your family, Clear Sky," she said.

"She is no longer Clear Sky," Father Man announced. "She is White Smoke."

"New name?" Quill stood up to look at her. "Tell me what has transpired." When White Smoke finished, Quill said, "It is a good name."

White Smoke went to find her family to bring them to supper.

"Now, Husband?" Quill asked.

"Yes, now," he said. From that day forward he taught White Smoke all he knew about healing.

Together Father Man, Quill and Cougar Two Foot worked to help the members of their village with their physical and spiritual needs. Clear Sky, now known throughout the village as White Smoke, had finally become their apprentice. As the years passed, Father Man and Quill grew older and more infirm, so the younger couple took over for them. Their abilities became well known throughout the area, and many came from far villages seeking their help.

And Jahn? He had never heard anyone speak of a woman named Ginny nor of anyone who matched her description.

The rain let up for a moment while White Smoke waited

within the trees at the side of the road for the parade of wagons to pass her by. There were so many white settlers moving into the mountains that it was like storm water washing down a hillside loosening boulders, taking with it anything in its way, everything in their path being disrupted or destroyed by the intrusion.

Husbands looked at her furtively with concern, guns ready, until they realized she was white. Wives noting that fact, having heard the stories of midnight raids, in horror pulled their little ones closer to their chest.

Out of their sight, she walked behind them for a while before turning off toward home.

Just after White Smoke had bedded down, Father Man went into the woods to relieve his bladder. In the fire's glow Quill folded an object into a piece of cloth, and hid it under her sleeping pallet. Only when Father Man was snoring loudly did she pull it out again.

Pretending to sleep, pulling her blanket up even closer to her face, White Smoke observed Quill with curiosity.

In front of the fire, the old woman unwrapped the bundle, carefully uncovering the object, a small book. Quill did not know how to read, but even so, she turned each page trying to understand what was written on it. In the fire's glow, she lingered over the pictures, taking in all that she could. Confused, she rewrapped the book, and slid it under her mat, then lay down carefully next to Father Man so as not to wake him.

In the morning, when the men had left the tipi, Quill slid the bundle out from under her blanket, and pressed the package into White Smoke's hands.

"What is this?" she asked.

"A white man's book," Quill said looking away. "Big Hands got it at the fort. Traded a beaver pelt for it."

"Why did she do that? She can not read what is on its pages."

"She thought it had good magic. When she could not make it do anything, she gave it to me. You will tell me what it says." she said emphatically.

White Smoke carefully unwrapped the book, and turned it over. She feared that she would not remember how to read English, and was surprised when she could. "*Book of Common Prayer,*" she said with a half-smile. "White man's religion uses different words. This is a book of songs to The Creator Of All," she told her mentor.

"White men sing songs to Senawahv?" Quill asked.

"In their way," she answered. White Smoke opened the book, and read the English words, then translated some of the pages, which seemed oddly familiar to her.

"Why did you stop? Go on. More." Quill said, eagerly leaning over the book. "How do you know what it says?"

"These are words," White Smoke pointed to what was written on the leaves of paper.

"Yes, words. I know that," Quill said proudly.

"The letters have sounds," she explained, "that together make up the same words that we use when we speak."

"Yes, yes." Quill looked over the writing. "My grandmother spoke English, but my grandfather would not let her teach me. What is that one?" she said pointing to the page.

"That says 'God'," she translated. "It is what the White Man calls Senawahv, The Creator of All Things. Your grandmother spoke English?" White Smoke looked up at

Quill whose gaze was intent on her.

"She was white like you," she said as a matter of fact. "White men write down their stories? We tell them at gatherings," she snorted with satisfaction. Quill pointed to the page again, "What does that one say?"

"You never told me she was white." Though she already knew the story, as The Gaggle had told her how Pure Heart had been taken from her family and was married to Great Bull, how she had longed for her lost family till the day she died, and had only been kind to her young granddaughter, and never to her own son.

"It is not important," she snorted again.

"Would you like to be able to read this book?"

"My husband would not like it." She shifted in her seat, and looked away, then picked up her beading needle again, and worked on the intricate design for the top of a shirt for Father Man. A few minutes passed in silence. "You can teach me to know the words?" she asked.

"If you like. Perhaps we could tell Father Man once you have learned. It could be useful when you trade at the fort."

So the lessons began for the old woman to learn English. Doggedly determined to grasp the language she had heard when she was young, Quill practiced reading aloud while White Smoke did chores in the tipi. The old woman began slowly, sounding out each word then once she got it she would read the whole passage again with more ease. White Smoke would look through the book for passages she thought her mentor would understand according to her beliefs, knowing she might be inclined to quit if she thought the ideas were ridiculous. She would take time later to have a conversation with her about their differences, but for now she wanted the reading to be easy and understandable. Quill was quick to learn, and did not get frustrated easily.

"This is the day which the Lord hath made; we will rejoice and be glad in it," she read haltingly. "P-salm. What is a p-salm? And those?" she asked pointing to the numbers.

"Psalm, oddly with this word you do not speak the "P". A *psalm* is a prayer, a poem or song. There is another book called the Holy Bible," White Smoke told her. "Those numbers tell you where to find this passage in that book."

"White man needs to write everything down?" She shook her head. "They do not let their prayers sing from their heart?"

"This makes it easier for everyone to say the same prayer, at the same time," White Smoke said knowing this was not going to be a good answer for her mentor.

"Every heart is different," Quill countered. "Why would they all say the same prayer at the same time?"

"It is what the white man does. Now try this one," she said, pointing to one on another page.

With her finger on the page, Quill began slowly sounding out each word as White Smoke spoke it,

> *O all ye fowls of the air, bless ye the Lord;*
> *O all ye beasts and cattle, bless ye the Lord;*
> *O ye children of men, bless ye the Lord;*
> *Praise him and magnify him forever.*

"This one I like," Quill smiled. "All the wild creatures appreciate The Creator Of All. Maybe the white man does not know how. They must practice with these prayers?"

"I suppose so," White Smoke said amused at her answer. "You are doing very well, Quill."

She snuffed, "Let me look at your beading."

30

1866

In his old hands, Father Man clutched a long and sharp fishing spear as he ambled toward the river. His gait was more labored now, with a hitch in his walk from stiffness in his knee that had come on gradually as again and again the seasons changed.

The children would return soon from foraging for herbs, and he wanted to bring home some sweet fish for the night's meal. Quill and Swift Fox had gone with them in their hunt for the best plants and had been gone most of the afternoon. All would be tired when they returned, so the old man wanted to have their food ready when they arrived. He would boil some tubers and steam the fish on the fire.

Father Man enjoyed making meals when he could. When he was younger the other men of the village laughed at him for cooking. "That is women's work," they had teased. *It brings me satisfaction to provide for my family in any way I can*, he thought to himself as he sauntered down the path.

In the orange glow of the setting summer sun, a blue-eyed soldier rode his large gray stallion into the village. He came into the camp slowly, his gun still in the holster and his rifle remaining in its case, so as not to arouse undue concern.

Father Man watched as the soldier approached. *What does that white man want?* Several men stepped forward with their knives and bows readied. Others looked up, but soon went back to what they were doing when they saw Father Man stop to take in the man's countenance.

"Good afternoon," the soldier said politely, dismounting. "I am looking for your Holy Man."

His accent is good for a white man, Father Man thought, as he continued walking toward the water, leading the soldier away from the village.

"What would you want with our Holy Man?" he asked. "You are in need of healing?"

"I am looking for someone. I was told that he might know something about where I could find–?"

"Who spoke of our Holy Man, soldier?"

"At the trapper's fort south of here a half day, the gentleman there. Excuse me. I did not introduce myself. I am Lieutenant Jahn Van Andusson. What is your name, if I may ask?"

"I am the shaman you seek." he said.

"Your name?"

"I am called Father Man."

"He said you may know of my mother," Jahn said with rising excitement. "Robbers kidnapped her fourteen years ago." The lieutenant pulled out the drawing from his saddlebag and handed it to the Father Man. "She is now fifty-one, auburn hair with red streaks and blue eyes like mine. Have you seen anyone of this description or heard any stories?" the young lieutenant asked earnestly, but with great deference.

Instantly, Father Man not only recognized the woman in

the drawing, but the configuration of the soldier's face was familiar as well. "Where are you from soldier?" he asked.

"Fort Garland," the lieutenant answered. "But I grew up near the trapper's fort at North Fork, southeast of here," he continued.

"How many summers are you?"

"Twenty-four."

"Young for a lieutenant," Father Man commented, continuing to walk down toward the bend in the river where the fish always hid. "You like to fish, soldier?"

"Yes, I used to fish with my father, Garritt Van Andusson," he said hoping the name would be familiar to him.

Gare...it, the shaman remembered. "Do you use a line or a spear?"

"A line," Jahn confessed.

"A spear takes patience, steadiness and quick reflexes," he said jabbing the water and bringing out a fish. Father Man stood at the edge of the river looking into the crevices then handed the spear to the lieutenant.

"You try it." Jahn took aim. "The fish looks like he is there," Father Man said indicating a near rock, "but he is here," he said. "A trick of the coyote" he smiled. "The water makes it look so."

Jahn looked at the fish for a moment then jabbed where the shaman had suggested. He missed, but tried again.

"They will not wait for you to aim correctly," the old man said.

Van Andusson looked into the flowing water for another.

"There," Father Man pointed. "He is not where he seems."

Jahn aimed once more then struck again, and this time he

pulled up a flapping fish.

"Soldier, you learn quickly."

Jahn started to hand over the catch.

"You keep it. Have it for your dinner."

"Thank you. I was wondering about the woman?"

"Hmm, yes, the woman. Let me see that again. What is her name, this woman who was taken ten years ago?"

"Fourteen. Virginia Van Andusson, but her friends called her Ginny."

"No, I do not know her," Father Man said flatly. "The man at the trapper's fort is playing a game with you."

He was disappointed in the man's answer, and also felt uneasy about the truth of it, but he knew it was useless to press.

"I am sorry to have bothered you."

"No bother. Always agreeable to speak with a nice young man." Father Man turned his back to the soldier, feigning attention to the stream. Reluctantly, the lieutenant rode off toward the west.

A moment later, eight year old Swift Fox tore into the clearing by his Grandfather's favorite fishing place.

"Hello, Grandfather."

"Hello, Boy," he said looking to see if the soldier was still in view, but the gray stallion had gone into the trees. "Were you successful in your hunt for herbs?" he asked.

"Oh, yes, Grandfather, I found very many. You would be proud of me."

"I am always proud of you," the old man said looking past the boy to where the soldier had ridden out of sight. "Where is your mother?"

"She and Father are at the tipi hanging herbs."

"Come, Grandson. Let us join them. Here are some fine

fish for our dinner."

He handed the string of fish to his grandson, and they walked together back to the encampment. The young lieutenant's eyes haunted him for sometime, and he was tempted to talk about it with his wife, but decided that he would never tell anyone of the encounter with the young soldier. That night, in his sleep, Quill heard him tell the story of a Jahn Van Andusson, but he would not tell her what had caused him to have this dream.

31
A TOWN NEAR FORT GARLAND

1869

The lieutenant sat up, rubbed his face, ran his fingers through his auburn hair, and then pulled on his pants. The beast trapped in his chest, the one that had been there since childhood, squirmed in its usual manner. No matter where he was or what he was doing this inner skirmish with feelings of sadness, disappointment and anguish churned, and along with that his nights were filled with dreams of the occurrences of that wrenching day.

Digging into his satchel, he pulled out a few bills and threw them onto the top of the table. He took his shirt and jacket off the floor where they had landed the night before, shook them and put them on. Still silent, he sat down on the bed again, pulling on his socks and military boots.

The room was small with only a bed, a table and some torn lace curtains at the tiny window. Clothes were strewn all over the floor and looked like they had been there for days. A half bottle of whiskey and a couple of dirty glasses sat alongside his hat, gun and holster.

"Where are you going?" his companion asked sleepily turning over in the bed. "Honey, stay for a while. You do not have to go just yet, do you?"

She reached for him, but he pulled away. The young mulatto was too thin, and her curly red hair was a ragged knot.

"Come on, Love, we can have some more fun before you leave." But he did not respond. "Wait for me, Jahn." She sat up quickly, looking for something to put on. "I will get dressed, and we can get some breakfast." Ignoring her, he continued dressing. "Will I see you next week then?" she asked.

"I put some money on the dresser," he said gruffly.

The girl looked disappointed and more than a little hurt. The lieutenant did not look back as he closed the door. Then he walked down the street to pick up his horse from the livery where it was being shod.

"Beckman!" the soldier called into the barn.

"Jahn. Good morning."

Jack Beckman, happy to hear the voice of his friend, hurried from somewhere in the back of the livery, coming to the entrance with a cup of coffee in his hand while still chewing a piece of sweet bread. For years, whenever Van Andusson was in need, he brought his horse to Beckman who was considered the best farrier in town.

"Gray Boy is in good shape, Lieutenant, but he is getting old. That ankle seems to be healing just fine, though you'd better go easy on him for another week. You have been riding him hard. Let him graze in the field a few more days before you take him out on patrol again."

Jahn looked off into the distance. To Jack, Jahn often seemed distracted so he was never sure if he actually heard him or not.

"Thanks, Jack. Best to your wife. Oh, and I brought this back for your daughter." Jahn pulled out a beaded bracelet, and handed it to his friend.

"She will love this," he said taking it. "She always likes those Indian things you bring her."

"Jahn," Jack said calling him back. "Yesterday a trapper came by here who was talking about a white woman living in a village near Black Forest. Thought you would want to know."

The lieutenant turned.

Jack looked out toward the street, and took another gulp of his coffee. He was one of the few who really knew Van Andusson.

"He still around?" the lieutenant asked.

"I don't know, but he went into the saloon when he left here. You might find him there, or at least someone may know where he was headed."

"His name?" Jahn asked trying not to seem excited. "What did he look like?"

"Tall," Beckman started as he thought back, "blond hair, nice looking, with a scar across his cheek where a bear clawed him. Around his neck, he wears a silver bear with a star on its back. His name, his name, his name," he repeated quickly rubbing his chin, "Josephson, that's it. Myron Josephson, but they call him Bear."

"Thanks, Jack."

Jahn swung open the doors of the saloon, and scanned the

dark smoke-filled room. Several customers who were barely awake sat at the bar with drinks in their hands. The bartender was wiping glasses and replacing them on the shelf. The old dog sitting at his feet got up walked in a circle then flopped down heavily.

"Morning, Jonas," Jahn said.

"To you as well, Lieutenant," the barkeep answered.

"You see a trapper in here yesterday?" the lieutenant asked.

"Does my dog here have spots?" he jested. "The one you are looking for, does he have a name?"

"Josephson, blond, tall," Jahn replied. "And a bear got him on the face," he said making a clawing motion at his cheek.

"Yup, I know him. Nasty scar," he said wincing. "Comes through here every so often. Was near Black Forest this time, heading northwest now toward Steamboat Springs. I seem to remember he was going to stay in town for another night. Ask over at the hotel. They might know him." The bartender swung his cloth over his shoulder. "You want a drink, Lieutenant?"

"Maybe later."

Van Andusson walked past the livery toward the hotel, his mind racing. He had joined the cavalry because it allowed him to search where he pleased. Over the years, he had gone many miles and had developed a reputation for being able to return prisoners back to their families–men, women and children–all kidnapped by raiders.

The hotel lobby was crowded with men looking for a bed and a bath.

"Simon, you have a trapper here by the name of Josephson, got a bad scar on his face, wears a bear with a star 'round his neck?"

"I don't know. I was not on duty last night, Lieutenant. Let me look at the register."

Simon turned the book and ran his finger down the page of names from the night before. "Miller, Scott, St. Joseph, no, Sanderman, hmm," the desk clerk said studying the register. "Josephson. Here it is. Josephson, Myron Josephson, yup. Upstairs in number 3." Jahn started for the steps. "Wait. I believe I saw him go across the street to Jessie's."

"Thanks," Jahn said as he pushed open the door to the busy street crowded with horses, buggies, and soldiers from the fort.

Jessie's Place was a noisy eatery filled with locals as well as travelers, where the room smelled like its specialty: meat goulash with onions and potatoes. The tables were crowded, and smoke filled the air from the fireplace, the kitchen and the cigars shared by the men.

Jahn was hungry so he sat down in an empty chair and scooped out a large bowl of the mixture from the pot in the center of the table. While he ate a few bites, he looked over the crowd for Josephson. A loud "hurrah" and then a burst of laughter came from a table behind him. The tall, blond trapper with the bear claw scar was standing, smiling his crooked smile, arms outstretched.

"She was white, and a little more than crazy in the head she was, but sure was a wild one in bed," he boasted. The trapper's friends laughed uproariously. But Jahn shot out of his chair to where Josephson stood, ready to pound the trapper with his fists.

"What do you want there, soldier?" the trapper asked, his eyes glazed with drink, his hand moving to his knife.

Holding himself firm, Lieutenant Van Andusson took a

calming breath before he spoke. "You are Josephson?"

"I am," he slurred. "And who is askin'?"

"Lieutenant Jahn Van Andusson," he replied. "Where did you just come from?"

"Few miles north of Black Forest. What's it to you?"

"That woman you were speaking of. How old was she?"

"I'd say about thirty. Poor thing was taken when she was young," he said to the crowd, then turning back to Jahn. "Sit down, Soldier. Have a drink on me," Josephson said with an amalgam of curiosity and caution. No one seemed to notice there was an Indian sitting at his table. He had seen Jahn's disappointment. He looked him over, and then put his hand on the polished horn talisman that he wore at his neck as if it were going to tell him whether or not to trust this soldier. Then he slowly slid over to one side of the bench. With some reservation, his stomach tightening, Van Andusson sat down.

"This is my friend Elk Horn. Sometimes he tracks for the army, but mostly we trap together," Josephson said still feeling cautious. "I am called Bear. Indians gave me that name on account of–" he said indicating the scar on his face.

"Where are you headed?" Elk Horn asked.

"Steamboat Springs," Jahn replied speaking only to the white man. "And you?"

"The same. I hear there are plenty of animals there," Bear said watching the soldier carefully.

Steamboat Springs at Big Bend was where the lieutenant was to find Captain George Wentworth, and make a report on him for his Commander.

Bear leaned over to Elk Horn, and whispered in his ear. Elk Horn looked at Jahn with a hard eye, then shrugged his shoulders.

"You want to ride with us?" Bear asked. "Leavin' in the

morning if you want to come along."

Jahn wrestled with the upset about thinking the white woman might be his mother, the need to be on his own and travel where he might, and wanting company after spending too many days in the mountains alone. And besides they may have heard of a white woman living with Indians who would be the age his mother is now. With effort, he set his upset aside.

"In front of the hotel at daybreak, if that suits you?" Jahn said.

"Might as well get somethin' to eat before we go," Bear told him indicating they would meet him at the eatery.

The lieutenant slid off the bench and got up to leave. "In the morning then."

Jahn unhitched his horse and walked him back to the livery. He called for Jack, toying with his gun while he waited for him to appear.

"I am heading up to Steamboat Springs. Do you have a good horse I can take, and will you keep Gray Boy till I get back? That should give him the rest he needs."

"Sure, Jahn, but you know Gray Boy needs to retire. He's worked hard all his life, and those legs are not what they used to be." Jahn knew he was right, but because it had been a gift from his brother so many years ago, he was hesitant about letting him go. "Look in the paddock. Any of those horses will be fine. The paint has strong legs."

Jahn went back to the fort for the night. The next morning he walked over to Jessie's Place to get a bite to eat and wait for Josephson. Even at that hour the establishment was noisy. Myron Josephson, known as "Bear", and his friend, Elk Horn, arrived only somewhat sober, both smelling heavily of whiskey.

"Mornin', Soldier," Bear said in a gregarious, loud slap-on-the-back way, his tongue thickened by the alcohol consumed the night before. "You remember my friend, Elk Horn. We always trap together," he repeated.

Elk Horn tapped his hat in response. Despite the obnoxious bravado of the previous evening, Jahn found he liked Bear, but he was not as keen on the Indian, any Indian. And though he wished it were not true, he could not help but feel his hackles rise; but for now since he was going to be riding with them, he pushed those feelings back under.

"What's in Steamboat Springs, Soldier?" Bear asked.

"Duties," he said. "Captain George Wentworth has his dragoon up there. I make contact with him every so often so he does not feel alone."

"Gambling," he heard Elk Horn mumble to Bear.

As he had become fluent in several native dialects, the lieutenant understood his comment. "You know him?"

"I know him. Dare say he knows me, too. He knows my money anyway. Son-of-a-snake took all of mine last time we met. He sure has *luck* with the cards," Bear said looking for confirmation from Jahn that the man was actually a cheat.

"I learned that the hard way myself," Jahn laughed. "I'll not play him anymore."

Just as they were about to leave, the lieutenant's lady friend came into the eatery. At first she looked pleased to see Jahn, then pretended to be annoyed, turning away while throwing her shawl tightly around her shoulders. Before he walked out of the door, Jahn stood behind her, and put his hands on her shoulders whispering in her ear, "See you when I get back." Though he did not necessarily mean it, saying so seemed to placate her for the moment, and she leaned back into his chest.

"Goodbye, Jahn," she said and smiled coyly as the men went out the door.

"She is a looker," Bear said. "That your girl?"

"No. Just someone I see occasionally," he answered. "She only likes my money."

"Looks to me like she has a soft spot for more than your cash," Elk Horn said in his language.

"Maybe she does," he answered. "But I don't really think so." His face darkened and his mood shifted. "Anyway, I have too much on my mind right now."

"What is her name," Bear enquired, "if you do not mind my askin'?"

"Sylvia. Sylvia Walters."

"Mind if I look her up when I come through?"

"Suit yourself," Jahn answered.

"Come on, Molly, now is no time to be stubborn," Bear chided. The mule wheezed and snorted, and rearranged the cargo on her back as best she could. Elk Horn checked the bindings and tightened the strap under her belly.

"All set there, Elk Horn?" Bear called loudly.

With their heavily laden mules in tow, the three men rode out of town.

32

It had been a long day. The horses and mules were tired, and so were the lieutenant and his two trapper companions. It was slow going through the wet forest, but they had been able to travel several miles before stopping for the night.

Now that the campfire was ablaze and warming, for their dinner Bear took a handful of desiccated vegetables and dried meat from the sack and threw them into the pot of boiling water. The smell of the soup and the aroma of strong coffee filled the air.

"This will warm you right up," Bear announced offering Jahn a bottle of whiskey.

Jahn downed a large swallow, expecting it to burn his throat. It didn't. He looked at Bear.

"I get the watered kind they gives the Indians—for Elk Horn," he whispered. Jahn took one more swig for good measure before handing the bottle back. "Remind me, Lieutenant, where are you from?" Bear asked making conversation.

"I was born down near the edge of the mountains in the

San Luis Valley. When I was six, we moved to North Fork near Trapper's Lake where we had a ranch."

"You ever been over to Black Forest?" Bear queried. "You seemed mighty on edge about my encounter with that white Indian they call Crazy Bird."

"A long time ago," he said hesitating before he spoke again. "White people living with Indians are usually taken against their will."

"This one was, too, but she was young when it happened, four or five," Bear lifted the bottle to his mouth again.

"And Indian children are taken to white schools against their will," Elk Horn shot back under his breath.

"Why so interested?" Bear asked.

"Not important," Jahn said then added, "It is an unfortunate story that presently has no happy ending."

"Well, let us drink to happy endings then. Or sad ones for that matter," Bear said hoisting the bottle to his lips once more. "Let us drink to friendship," and he threw back his head, filling his mouth, before passing it along.

The next day was like the last. An endless squeal of leather against leather singing out with each step of their horses and mules. After many hours, Bear and his associate had ceased talking, and all rode silently in the quiet of the forest. Up ahead, Jahn saw a patch of dry ground where he hoped they would camp.

"How about over there?" Jahn said pointing to the clearing. "It looks dry and we could get a fire started for coffee," he called to his companions. "Sure could use a rest. What do you say, Bear?"

"All right, if you feel you must," Bear teased. "Dang, this damp cold is getting' to my bones. I must be gettin' old," Bear bellowed.

"Old? Not you," Jahn called out. "You have more energy than ten men put together," he said. "How old are you anyway?"

"A couple of days over sixty," Bear grinned.

"Like me," Elk Horn corrected. "Forty-three summers."

"Now you are taking away all the fun, Elk Horn. I was just waitin' to hear him say–'Gee Old Man, you do not look sixty.'" Bear's infectious roar-laugh spilled out over the canyon then came back at them like a river bubbling a chorus of joy.

"It is well that you told me, Elk Horn. I was going to say Bear did not look a day over seventy-five," Jahn teased, and they all laughed. Jahn's mind went to his mother as it often did. How old would she be now? *If I am twenty-seven, she would be fifty-four.*

After scouting ahead for a better place to camp, Bear found a good place to stop for the night.

"We will be out of the wind," Elk Horn said. He pulled the mules hard, and tied them off, then unloaded the supplies and covered their backs with blankets.

Ahead was a grassy field. Once the animals cooled down they let them graze. Meanwhile, Elk Horn and Jahn went deep into the trees to gather dry wood.

"Feel chilled to the bone," Jahn said continuing to pick up kindling.

Elk Horn put his finger to his lips. "A hunting party. Two, three men. They won't like seeing your military stripes, Soldier."

From within the darkness of the far trees a buck, munching leaves and bits of grass, wandered into view. A hunting party of three men appeared with arrows cocked in their bows. The buck stopped and raised his head, his nostrils flaring as he smelled the air. In recognition of danger, his eyes bulged. One stalker pulled on his bow, releasing his arrow into the target. It went straight into the kidney, killing the animal instantly.

"I know him," Elk Horn said in English, relaxing his grip on his knife. "He is a friend," Elk Horn whispered. "Hello, Harold Little Crow," he yelled out.

The chief lifted his hand to them.

"Elk Horn, where is that no good scar-faced Bear?" the chief said amiably, but stopped short seeing Jahn.

"We are just setting up camp over that hill," Elk Horn grinned. "You will join us for the meal?" They agreed, but looked at the soldier suspiciously. "How have you been? And you, Two Lakes?"

"Deer Medicine has been good to us," the Chief answered.

"I am well, brother," Two Lakes responded.

Then turning toward Jahn, Elk Horn began, "This is—"

"I am Lieutenant Jahn Van Andusson," Jahn offered in the chief's language.

"And where are you headed, Lieutenant," the chief asked with caution.

"To the fort in Steamboat Springs."

Soldiers had been searching the mountains for Indians, taking prisoners, even killing off whole villages. Jahn knew this, and did his best to appear unconcerned about being in the presence of these men. No matter what he thought of the Indian, he knew he would never find his mother if they distrusted him.

"You travel with a bear and an elk, bad traveling companions," he said. "You would do well to—"

"Is that Broken Bow?" Bear bellowed. "Is he here beggin'

for food?"

Bear opened his arms wide to welcome his friends.

"Come and have some of this fine meat."

"Hello, Claw," the chief teased back. "It has been too long since we shared a meal. I suppose I will have to cook it for you?"

"It is good to see you my friend. I see your huntin' has improved." Bear laughed.

"When I saw Elk Horn I was wondering if you were planning to eat the sticks these men brought back? But I see you have a couple of big rabbits. They die of fright?" he teased.

Inwardly, Bear sighed. As much as he enjoyed his whiskey, there would be none served tonight, for except with Elk Horn he would not drink with Indians. He had seen that Indians and whiskey did not mix well, and he considered Harold Little Crow and his brother friends. Even watered down whiskey made Elk Horn tipsy.

Elk Horn cut up the meat, pierced it with sticks, and rammed them into the ground at the fire. The aroma of the cooking meat made Jahn's mouth water and his stomach growl. Bear scraped the back of the small skins talking with Harold Little Crow all the while.

"Our holy man, Father Man, do you know him?" Harold Little Crow asked Bear.

"No, I have not had the pleasure," Bear responded.

"He tells us it will be a cold winter, and to be careful of Coyote Medicine. The Trickster will make things not as they seem."

Father Man, Jahn said to himself pulling from his memory the name from one of his patrols. Jahn jerking his awareness to the present said, "I met him. Is he well?"

"Yes, more tired and a bit slower, but still wise," the Chief answered.

"Please give him my regards. He taught me how to fish with a spear," Jahn remembered.

Once the rabbit was cooked, the hunters sat around the fire, and ate while exchanging stories of their exploits, and making bets on cards. Meanwhile, Jahn remembered dinners at home with his family when his mother would ask each child what they had done that day that was special to them. Holly might say, *I saw a butterfly,* or James, *I threw rocks.* Jahn would look up at the mountains and wonder what was up there. He had a longing to explore, so when they moved he felt as if his wish had been granted.

"My arrow flew right to the top of that mountain," Harold Little Crow said pointing to the shadow several miles away. Everyone laughed.

He had learned to expect embellishment from Bear, but found Harold Little Crow loved to play in this manner as well. It was one of the most entertaining and enjoyable nights that he could remember.

33

The ground was hard and the air numbing. An assault of cold, wet, and wind made Jahn pull his blanket tightly up around his face and put his hat over his head before drifting off to sleep:

He was inside the house with Holly and Richard when he heard, "Yip, yip, yip!" *The high-pitched trilling and the thundering sound of galloping horses shattering the serenity of the ranch.*

"Indians!" his father yelled. Gunshots rang out, arrows swished, hitting a target, and a body fell hard onto the porch. Jan woke with a start.

Surreptitiously, he wiped his brow hoping that neither Bear nor Elk Horn had noticed it. Elk Horn had, but said nothing. So had Bear, but he also pretended he had not.

"Slept like a log!" Bear yawned stretching his arms out wide.

"We had better be on our way. The weather may turn," Elk Horn said in his language.

Jahn packed his things, and went to load them onto his horse.

"Wonder what worries him?" Bear said.

"The pod will open when it is ready," Elk Horn advised.

Jahn came back to the fire and began to spread out the ashes, then threw more dirt than was needed over the blackened spot where the fire had been.

"Fire's out," Elk Horn commented all the while watching Jahn's expression. "The ground is wet."

In time, the pounding in Jahn's heart quieted.

Jahn packed his pipe and lit it. He leaned against a log, staring up into the trees thinking of his brother, Richard. He had not seen him in a long while and noted that it was time for him to go to the ranch.

"I was sleeping on the bench on the porch when Mrs. Sumner came by," Richard had told him during his last visit.

Sara looked around the property, and saw that the horses still needed feeding and the barn cleaning. The empty whiskey bottle, having fallen off his lap, lay broken on the ground...

"Morning, Richard," she said.

"Morning, Mrs. Sumner," he sputtered sitting up. "Does Mr. Sumner know you came by yourself?"

"Henry was busy in the barn."

"It isn't safe from Indians, Mrs. Sumner. You know that," he said chastising her.

"I just need you to take a look at my horse, back right hoof," she said.

"All right." Richard rubbed his eyes.

Sara walked up the steps and sat down next to him. As she had done so often over the years, she put her arm around his shoulder, held him to her, and kissed the top of his head. She loved Ginny's two boys. With their parents gone, she had slipped into the mothering role easily, careful, all the while, not to tell them how to live. "You boys are getting older now, and need to make decisions on your own," she had said. Only when she saw their missteps did she encourage them to take a different road.

"Where is Jahn?"

"He went to town to collect payment on some of our horses," Richard said passing his hand across his chin, blinking his eyes to get a clear head.

"I suppose you will be wanting to feed the ones in the barn. I should let you get to it." She started to leave, but stopped. "How old are you now, Richard?"

"Twenty, ma'am. You remember, we had my birthday gathering at your house two weeks ago?"

"Yes, of course," she hesitated trying to picture the party again. Richard had told Jahn that he thought Sara's memory was going. "Richard, you are a man now, and need to make adult decisions."

"Ma'am?"

"Well, you will be wanting to get married, and have a family I expect. Hard to do if you are always sleeping off a night's fun."

She knew she could not change Richard, but she thought if she put a goal in front of him it might help to redirect his path.

"Yes, ma'am," he said rubbing his eyes.

"You are a fine young man. Do not forget that." She waited a moment then added, "The Spring Dance is next Saturday. You going? That nice girl, Melina, I think that is her name, the school teacher, you know her?" Sara asked not too subtly. "She needs an escort, if you are looking for someone to take." Without pausing to hear his reply she said, "We will be seeing you at Sunday dinner?"

"Sure will," he said. "Jahn and I will both be there. We will bring

some elk steak if that is all right."

"Wonderful." She got up to leave, "So what do you think about that hoof?"

He jumped off the porch, and walked around the horse, lifting all four legs.

"I think that you made that up so you could come by," he said. "Mrs. Sumner, you know you are welcome here anytime." He looked at her with eyes that said please do not think badly of me. "Sorry you caught me napping. It will not happen again."

"See you on Sunday, and bring Melina!" she called behind her as she left.

"Wait a moment," he called and took his gun off the porch. "I will ride you back to your ranch."

Jahn took a draw on his pipe enjoying the respite from the long day's ride.

"Dutch, you awake over there? You look like you have gone from this world, not dead, but maybe angels was talkin' to you," Bear teased, "or was it the devil?"

"No, I am here now. Just remembering something from way back. Did you need me for something?"

"Tie off that mule, and go find us our supper, while Elk Horn helps me get this fur scraped."

"Sure thing."

Jahn took his rifle and went in search of their meal, but he could not keep his mind on the hunt.

The next day Bear tried to get him to talk about his past by speaking of his own.

"My Pa could be an ornery old man," Bear said shifting his seat in the saddle. "Drank a lot, and gambled the same. Best to stay out of his way when the cards kissed another. But deep down I know he cared about me, though often I had to scrape away at the meanness to find it. What did your father do? What was his name again?"

Jahn explained that his father, Garritt Wolf Van Andusson, had been an assistant minister in Peidman's Landing in San Luis Valley, where he had shared the pulpit with his mother's father, Seider Spellman. His family had raised horses. They had a good-sized Episcopalian parish of about thirty families. After they moved to Trapper's Lake, his father had a smaller, close-knit group who looked after each other.

"You got family, wife, kids, Lieutenant?"

"No wife," Jahn said. "Just a brother left."

"What happened?" Elk Horn asked.

"Pa and one brother were killed in a raid. My sister died later."

"And your Ma?" Bear asked.

It was unlike him, but Jahn found he could not keep from telling the trappers about the raid.

"Rough luck, Lieutenant." Bear rubbed his face and shook his head. "Really rough luck. Once heard of an Indian grabbin' a woman, but she caused him so much trouble, he beat her. Sold her at the first opportunity. Those buggers can be mean as can be. Sorry, Lieutenant. My mouth has run away from me."

"No offense taken," Jahn said having heard that story before. "I know she is somewhere in these mountains," he divulged. "I will keep looking," he said under his breath.

"What's her name and what does she look like?" Elk Horn asked.

"Ginny, Virginia. Pretty, auburn hair that picks up red streaks when the sun gets to it. Eyes the color of mine."

Bear replied, "We'll keep a look out for her, Lieutenant."

The Aspen leaves had already turned from yellow to brown, most lay on the ground, and there was a sharp winter bite in the air. The cold rain, coming down hard in the growing darkness, was turning to sleet and then snow as the temperature dropped. Jahn and his trapper companions made their way up and down the long steep, winding paths with some difficulty. It would be a week of riding through the mountains to get to Steamboat Springs, and Jahn was looking forward to sitting in the steaming hot water that flowed out of the rocks from deep within the earth, the springs that the natives used for healing.

Elk Horn said in English, "The shack is up ahead. We will stop there for the night."

"My Pa, he was a trapper," Bear started as if they had been telling each other stories all along. "He and my Mama hunted together till I was born, then we did not see Pa much. Mama made a home for us at the base of the mountains near Shining Ridge. We lived in a tent for a while till Mama made enough money gamblin' with the local trappers and army folk to build us a house."

Bear was gregarious, and liked to talk. Elk Horn spoke very little, but listened to Bear's stories attentively. From the knowing look Elk Horn gave Jahn though, Jahn thought he probably had all of them memorized by now.

The shack, built by trappers who frequented the area, was a small lean-to with walls. Inside there was a stone stove, a pot for cooking and one for water. *And dry beds*, Jahn thought. It was not much, but it kept off the rain.

All three were wet right down to the skin. Once the fire

was stoked, they laid their wet coats near the heat, and before long steam began to rise from their dampness. Wrapped in dry blankets, the men began to feel warm again.

The three shared a dinner of dried meat, portable soup reconstituted in the pot left on the stove, and miner's coffee thick enough to set up a spoon, laced with Bear's whiskey.

"Snow's coming down heavy," Elk Horn said in his language as he came back inside with an arm full of wood. "Best to get a good night's sleep if we are to make many miles tomorrow."

"You never married, Bear? Most of you trapper men have families in one of the tribes," Jahn said.

"I never wanted to be tied down, but I have to say, now that I am getting older, having a warm bed to come home to sounds inviting." Bear looked over at Elk Horn who was staring into the fire. "Right now though, there are many pelts to be gotten, and Indian lasses to kiss," he laughed.

34

With all the rain, crossing the rivers was treacherous at best. Jahn took his billfold from the saddlebag and put it into his coat above where he thought the water line would be, then waited as Bear went in, his horse heavy with pelts and supplies. The river did not appear to be as deep as it actually was, and before he knew it Bear's horse had lost its footing, toppling it into the rushing current, throwing him into the freezing water. Sputtering, he came up for air and reached out for his fallen horse. But the animal was still struggling to get a secure foothold, so both horse and rider were being carried down stream in the torrent of freezing winter water.

There was no path, just thick woods. Elk Horn quickly tied the mules, then he and Jahn raced along the side of the waterway in an effort to get ahead of Bear. Jahn kept his head down as his horse broke through branches that blocked its way.

As they rode to get ahead of their comrade, the sound of falling water swelled to a deafening roar. When they came to the bend in the river, the horses stopped short, almost catapulting them both over the rocks. The river water fell about twenty feet, churning into a circle of large boulders. If Bear and his horse went over the falls into the ravine they would surely die.

Jahn jumped off his horse, took out his ropes, attaching one to a sturdy branch, and tied the other end around his waist. After securing his rope to a tree, Elk Horn threw Jahn the line. With two ropes in hand, Jahn waded out into the water as far as he could, waiting for them to come downstream, his feet lurching on the rocky bottom.

The horse, neighing in panic, came up first, struggling to keep its head above the icy churn. Jahn grabbed its bridle and tied Elk Horn's rope to it. The Indian pulled hard and brought the animal to safety along the shore.

The winter water was numbingly cold. Jahn could not feel his feet, and his fingers became stiff and almost useless. Shivering, he wrapped the rope around his arm and shoulder, and waited for Bear to pass by him.

Desperately reaching for Jahn, Bear flailed in the icy flow, but went under. Jahn dove into the frigid water, swimming out toward the middle. When Bear came up his lips had turned completely blue and his face ashen. He coughed and sputtered, gasping for air, but was still out of reach. Jahn stretched his long arms toward the man, barely grasping the trapper's fingers, but he was able to pull him closer.

"You are not going to let this cold river get you, are you, Bear?" Jahn wrapped the stiffened rope around Bear's nearly frozen body.

"Pull, you lazy bastard!" Bear shouted between stiff lips. "Your Dutch charm is not goin' to do me no good now. Pull!"

"What do you think you are, a fish? Quit trying to swim

away." By this time Jahn had hooked him tightly under his arm. Looking back at Elk Horn, he yelled, "All right!"

Elk Horn pulled with all his might while the men struggled to swim toward the shore. Exhausted and cold, they now lay on the icy bank, both shivering and panting. Elk Horn secured the horses and mules and made a fire. Wrapped in blankets, the two men drank hot coffee mixed with whiskey, and waited to regain feeling in their limbs.

"Not a good time to take a swim, Bear," Elk Horn commented.

"Needed a bath," Bear retorted. Bear became quiet, then turned to his friends. "Thanks, Dutch," he said to Jahn. Then he slapped Elk Horn on the back and poured another round of whiskey.

Jahn's hand automatically reached to his pocket. It was empty. He jumped up searching the land around him.

"What is it, Lieutenant?" Bear asked.

"My billfold. It was in my pocket." Panic hit Jahn like a bolt of lightening. He looked out into the icy water then searched the shore.

"There!" Elk Horn said pointing to where the water tumbled over the precipice. The wallet was bobbing at the edge of the falls. Jahn started for the ledge.

"You wait," Elk Horn said. "You are too cold, and might fall."

Carefully Elk Horn made his way along the ridge of boulders, his moccasins grabbing onto the dry stones securely, but the wet ones were slick with moss and ice. The leather billet bobbed as it inched closer to the falls. Standing on an icy rock, Elk Horn reached out his fingers, barely touching the prize, and with one last stretch he grabbed it, almost tumbling into the ravine.

Jahn held the wallet, almost afraid to open it. Soggy but intact was the likeness he had drawn of his mother.

"Much obliged," Jahn said to Elk Horn.

"Who is that?" Bear asked.

"My mother," Jahn replied. Both men took a look at the image.

"She is a pretty woman," Bear said and Elk Horn agreed.

"She is beautiful," Jahn told them as he set the picture on a rock near the fire to dry.

Once they had warmed up some, they spread their clothes, blankets and hides around the fire to dry. Then the men made plans for the next day.

"There is a fort not far from here," Bear said. "We can sell some of our pelts and get dry clothes and provisions."

They finished off the bottle of whiskey and ate some hot soup. Sleep did not come easily for any of the men, but when it did finally take him, Jahn was once again looking for his mother amongst the Indians.

The next night Bear brought out his last bottle of whiskey.

"Here, Dutch, have a swig."

"Not tonight," Jahn said, cleaning the dishes after supper and sitting down for a smoke on his pipe. "How long have you had that scar?"

Never one to let what he considered a good story go untold, Bear began his rendition enthusiastically.

"My Pa and me, we was huntin' beaver. Pa had gone off up river to see if his traps were sprung. I was makin' supper. Smellin' the food, the bear came my way. He was growlin' an' snappin' twigs as he lumbered through the forest, but he was already up on his hind legs by the time I saw him. Bad luck my gun was leanin' against a tree on the other side of the bear. But luckily, I had my huntin' knife in my hand…"

As much as he was hoping that listening to Bear's recounting would put his mind somewhere else, the memory of that day twenty years ago played out in Jahn's mind once again:

"What are we going to do, Richard?"

"Be quiet," Richard hissed. "Now get back in the corner, and keep your mouth shut. You, too, Holly." Richard pushed the corn baskets tightly around them, throwing a blanket over their heads. Then Richard peered out of the window at the raid happening outside. Next thing Jahn knew, Richard had squeezed in with them and was shivering all over.

"I've got to help them. Let me out," Jahn said.

"Be still, Jahn, unless you want to be dead, too."

Bear continued, "Pa lifted my bloody head onto his lap. 'Good Lord, Son, I thought you were dead!' Then he stitched me up. And this hat," Bear said holding up the well-worn, torn-up piece of skin he wore to cover his head, which he slapped on his noggin with a grin, "I made it from his pelt. We ate that bear for a good long time," he laughed.

"The scar makes you look quite distinguished," Jahn teased, coming back to the moment. But Elk Horn had been watching the lieutenant, and knew his mind was elsewhere.

Bear picked up his bottle and took a long draw of the inebriating liquid.

"We had better get some rest," the lieutenant suggested. "It will be another hard day of riding if it snows again."

Jahn unrolled his bedroll, but tossed and turned unable to settle his mind, which always reached out for that day. The longing for his parents, the ache of it, constantly sat on his chest like a heavy stone.

The next morning was bitterly cold. Elk Horn looked at the sky and furrowed his brow.

"Snow. We had better go."

The snow began falling in early morning, and by that afternoon had become quite deep, making the trails difficult to see, let alone traverse.

Jahn was deep in thought, remembering swimming in the icy river and Bear almost drowning. Juniper Jack looked out at the heavily falling snow and suggested that they stay in the cabin another day to rest up.

Johnny went out to check on the animals one more time before turning in. Luckily, the trapper's cabin had a protected corral for the horses and mules or they would not have faired well against the turbulent wind and snow.

Johnny melted snow and poured it into the trough, then gave them more grain. By the time he returned the men had fallen asleep where they sat. He threw another log on the fire, covered the men with their blankets then slid under his own. The next morning they parted ways.

"It's been nice spendin' time with you, Lieutenant," Juniper Jack said. "Maybe our paths will cross again someday."

"Maybe," Jahn said.

"Till then," Johnny called.

Jahn bid them farewell and turned off to the north toward Steamboat Springs.

"He sure is a broodin' kind of man, ain't he," Juniper Jack said under his breath.

35

Winter 1872

Firelights dotted the darkness through the swirling snow as White Smoke made her way back to her tipi from a meeting with Man Who Stands To Watch, one of the elders. He knew his time was coming to an end and wanted to know what he should do to take care of his family. Speaking with him had unsettled her, bringing to mind her concerns about the aged Father Man. She wished that her husband and fourteen-year-old son were home, but they had gone with the hunting party and would be away for several days. As she walked back to her tipi, those that were out by their fires greeted her, some wishing to engage her in conversation, others just giving a friendly nod.

When she stepped into the tipi, Father Man was preparing for sleep.

"What can I do for you, Father?" she asked.

"I am fine, Child," he said as he lay down for the night. "It has been a good day. I am ready to wake in the arms of Senawahv if that is what The Mother/Father wants," he said then closed his eyes. He had repeated this for several days.

Her mentor had been more winded than usual and was weaker than she had ever seen him. It weighed on her, knowing that this great man might be finishing his life. She was not ready to have him go now, and truthfully, she felt she would never be ready.

Quill did not look up from her beading, but White Smoke saw the tears in her eyes, and could not help but feel compassion for the woman who had been this shaman's partner for more than sixty years.

Even Quill was so withered now that she needed assistance getting up and down, preparing meals, and generally getting her own needs met, let alone having enough energy to assist Father Man. Until recently, Father Man had done his best to help his wife, but as he got more infirm White Smoke had had to take over their care.

Seeing Father Man so weak and Quill distressed, White Smoke wanted to refresh her thoughts and calm her feelings, so she stepped outside to walk in the cold and dark night air.

The snow had stopped falling and the clouds had parted, partially showing a bright starry sky in the moonless night. She pulled her wrap tightly around her shoulders against a bitter winter chill that blew across the field.

The horses stirred nervously, breathing heavily and shuffling their feet. But before she had a chance to give warning, a raiding party burst through the peace of the camp. Pillaging Comanche warriors galloped in, yelling their hostile cry, grabbing at the women and children. More went directly to the horses, stampeding them away from the camp. Arrows and lances pierced those who fought back.

White Smoke ran back to the tipi. Father Man had gotten to his feet, and was about to come out of the opening with his hatchet in his hand.

"Get back inside," she called to him. "Keep Quill with you." She grabbed a lance and went back out into the fray.

Children screamed as they were carried off. Men and women running after the marauders reaching for their stolen babies were torn apart by hatchets and knives. A confusion of horses ran in every direction, their riders killing anyone they did not want to take. The wounded lay dying in the dirt while others screamed, running for their lives. There were dead and injured everywhere.

At first, the horrific bloodshed overwhelmed her, but then a faint, distant memory worked its way forward, and in that moment her mind cleared. She remembered the terrifying, bloody nightmare of that summer afternoon twenty years before; the slaughter of her husband and her seven-year old son, both falling as arrows rammed through their bodies. She had run toward her husband only to be grabbed by her hair, pulled onto the horse of one of the raiders, and stolen away from her home. Behind, her husband and son lay dead at the front of the house, and she was sure that her three children within it had perished as well.

In front of her, The Red Wing, tall and powerful, with his face colored with dark charcoal and oil, sat high on his huge black horse, whose face had been painted with red striped finger marks that looked like flames. He called out to his men, "Take only the young ones," he shouted as he reached down for a tiny girl who stood next to her dead mother. White Smoke went at him with the lance as hard as she could. The blow to his arm knocked him off his horse, but he quickly got to his feet.

"Run!" White Smoke yelled at the screaming child. *"That necklace, four white claws and a black one, I have seen it before. And that face—I remember that face! It was you! And that is my silver cross you dare to wear on your neck,"* she thought enraged.

The Red Wing's eyes gleamed in the firelight. His huge, muscular body leaned toward her.

"White woman, I will take you for my youngest brother," he said in his language.

"Not again!" she growled in hers, and with all the fierceness of a mother puma protecting her young, she ran at him with her spear. He lunged for her, snapping the lance from her hand easily, throwing it out of reach. He held her by her hair, gripping his other hand tightly around her neck. Her windpipe closed under the squeeze of his thumb, and she choked.

Grappling with both hands against his grip on her neck, she bent back his fingers, but could not loosen them enough to get air, let alone get free. She thrust her fingers at his eyes, but he lifted his head upward and out of her reach. She tore at his buckskin shirt trying to push him away so she could get a breath.

As she wrestled him, she could feel her life force pulling away. His eyes were filled with rage, and she knew he was the terrifying black horse from her vision many years ago. Finally, with all of her might, she kicked him sharply between his legs. He let go long enough for her to grab the knife from his belt, and ram it deep into his stomach. The Red Wing staggered backwards in surprise. He stared into her fiery, blue eyes, then his eyes widened in recognition. She pushed the knife in deeper, and he fell forward onto her, emitting his last breath. When she pushed his body off, it fell to the ground with a heavy thud.

Silence.

Though there was still mayhem everywhere, White Smoke heard nothing. She tore the necklace off his neck, removing the shining silver cross pendant then threw the bear claws into a fire. She pulled the knife from his stomach, and put it into her belt.

Yelps from the other warriors told the rest of the intruders that their leader was gone. The raiding party hurriedly picked up their dead and wounded and left the camp.

White Smoke ran back to the tipi looking for Father Man and Quill. When she tore open the flap, she found Father Man lying face down in the dirt at the entrance. Quill, hunched over him with her freshly cut hair still in her hand, looked up at White Smoke with profound sadness.

White Smoke knelt down beside him and felt his neck for a sign of life. There was none. She turned him over to look for blood. There was none. He had not been a part of the raging battle after all. The heart of this gentle healer could not weather the savagery that was taking place outside.

As was the custom White Smoke took her knife and cut off her own long white hair.

Quiet fell over the camp. White Smoke and Quill took their medicine pouches and went out to see what they could do to help those who had fought so bravely for their families. There were so many dead: mothers, fathers and children. The men who were left gathered together to follow the raiders, riding off to save their loved ones and retrieve their horses.

White Smoke sat with Quill in silence. After a time, they chanted for the spirit of Father Man. His burial would be in a cave, a place that he had loved, near the overhang on the bluff.

Later, in the quiet of the night, White Smoke told Quill what she remembered about her life, her children and when she was taken.

The old woman went over to a basket by the sleeping mat and pulled out the gingham bundle.

"This was yours," she said. "Does it look familiar to you now? The comb was in the dirt near you, the silver chain, in your hand, and that is all that was left of the dress when we found you. The gold ring I removed from your injured hand. There was nothing else."

A shock of recognition radiated through her body. She told Quill that they had been gifts from her family. Her children had given her two identical combs, and her husband had put the chain around her neck at her birthday celebration twenty years ago. "The wedding ring was from my husband, Garritt," she told her.

"Gare...it?" Quill repeated. "You said that when we found you. I did not know what it meant." A cloud came over the old woman's face. "Will you leave now?" Quill asked, staring into the fire. Most of her friends now including her four best friends had gone on to the Place In The Sky, and Quill had come to lean on White Smoke and her family more and more.

She held the old woman by the shoulders. "That family is dead," she told her. There had been a time when Quill was more formidable and would not have allowed White Smoke to be this intimate, but this day when she seemed so vulnerable and frightened, White Smoke thought she needed this affirmation. "They were all killed before you found me. You have been so kind to me for so long that I have learned to love you as my mother," she told her. "When Cougar Two Foot and Swift Fox return I will tell them what I know. But we would like to remain here with you, if that is all right."

Quill lying back on the half empty bed paused then asked, "Perhaps Cougar Two Foot would sharpen my knives?" she said, turning her face away to hide her tears.

White Smoke was not sure what she would do now that she remembered her life. Soon she would go up to the bluff, ask the smoke, and wait for its answers.

36

Quill went into the trapper's fort with one purpose in mind. She needed something to take her mind off the loss of Father Man, and since for a long time, though sporadically, she had practiced reading with White Smoke, she thought she would like to try something other than the *Book of Common Prayer* and the occasional pamphlet from the trapper's fort. She went to buy a book.

"How nice to see you, Quill. What have you brought me today?" the owner of the store asked. She pulled out her finely beaded garments. "Magnifique! Trés jolie! You do the best beading around."

Embarrassed at his profusion of compliments, Quill shuffled from one foot to another. "How is the time of cold and snow treating you, Jacque?"

"Well, though a day or two of sun would make me smile. From the clouds I would say there will be more snow tonight," he said amiably. "But my wife is feeling poorly. Would you look in on her?" He took her arm and assisted her as they walked over to his house around the corner from the store. "Sorry to hear about Father Man."

"He was just an old man, but I was used to him," she said.

Jacque's new wife, a young Shoshoni woman, lay on the bed moaning, holding her stomach. A bucket of filth lay next to the bed, a rag dirtied by it hung on its side.

"Take this outside and clean it, and bring in a fresh cloth as well, and keep that clean," she told him.

"Yes, ma'am. Of course," he said embarrassed that he had not taken care of that earlier, and not the least bit concerned that an Indian woman was speaking to him as if she were his mother. He went out cleaned it and returned with the scrubbed container.

She turned to her patient, "My name is Quill. What is yours?" Their languages were similar enough to understand what the other was saying.

"Share On," she answered.

"A nice Indian name, Share On," Quill smiled.

Sharon explained that her husband could not say her name. "What does it mean–Share On? He said it means pretty flower. Rose of Share On."

"It is a good name for you. You are a pretty flower."

The ailing girl smiled through a grimace of stomach pain that sent her heaving into the bucket once more.

"What did she have to eat for her meal?"

"Some stew from another night," he told her.

Quill looked at the young girl, then at Jacque, "Bad meat." She rummaged through her bag and from within its contents handed him several bunches of herbs.

"She will be fine. Have her drink tea made from these–lots of it. Brew this for me now. And throw away that old stew."

"Yes, ma'am," he stammered as he left.

Quill settled herself. When the shaman began to speak to the girl, the young woman noticed that the sound of the healer's voice seemed to come from within her own body as if Quill were inside her chest.

After a time, Quill came out of the house, and Jacque walked her back to the shop.

"Would you like to taste this sweet?" Jacque asked. "It has come all the way from Mexico," he said opening up the tin. Inside were bits of candied ginger covered in sugar crystals.

"I have come for a book," she said reaching into the tin taking a small bit. She touched it to her tongue. "Hmm," she said, "very sweet, but fiery, too. It is good."

"Come on now. What do you want with writing? You cannot read. Here take another," Jacque said popping a piece into his mouth. "It is supposed to be good for your digestion."

"Give some to your wife then," she said, this time taking a larger piece. "I can read," she stated proudly.

"Naw, truly? You can read? Show me," he said and looked around his shop, "Read that old poster up there." Jacque lifted the hat and satchel that covered it, revealing a yellowed placard.

Quill looked up at the old sign that had been covered up over the years with belts and hats and the like. She had never noticed it before or the sketch of the woman at the bottom. She slit her eyes to get them in focus, and began slowly forming each word as she thought about how it should sound in English, and what it meant.

"Mis-sing," she said glancing at Jacque. "What does 'missing' mean?"

"She's lost," he said.

She began again, "Missing. Vir-gin-i-a, Virginia, Gin-ny Van An-dusson, White wo-man." She stopped and started over, reading it again slowly, "Missing: Virginia, 'Ginny' Van Andusson. Taken in Indian raid near Trapper's Lake, July. If seen contact Richard and Jahn Van Andusson on Silver Leaf Ranch, or through the Trapper's Lake Bank." Quill was pulled up short, and looked hard at the drawing on the bottom of the page and the comb in the woman's hair. "How long has this been up here?"

He looked at the poster and said, "The owner before me said a soldier had brought it. I just left it up. I heard it was the soldier's mother who was missing. You know that lady?"

"How many summers would that be?"

"Well, let's see. I bought the place fifteen years ago, but he said it had been brought in five years before that," Jacque answered, and reached up for the nail, pulling it out and giving her the sign.

Quill was halfway out of the door, when Jacque called, "What about your book?"

"I will come back in a few days to check on your wife," she yelled back.

Quill could not get back to the camp fast enough.

37

Large black ravens sat in the trees calling instructions to their young. The mountains on either side protected the valley where they made camp. It kept the temperature warmer than the summer camps would be at this time of year.

Raccoon sat near his fire in meditation, greeting one of his ancestors who spoke to him about his village. He could not believe what he was hearing.

"The blankets," he said. *"The blankets."* Then in his vision he saw one burst into flame. A Coyote jumped through the fire. He took the burning blanket, and shook it hard, tearing it apart. Raccoon's heart raced as the meaning of the sighting became clear. *"They will die,"* Coyote said. *"The blankets will make them all die."*

He had heard of other Indian communities contracting illness from white men's blankets. The shock of this brought him sharply out of the Quiet. This winter was a particularly cold one, and the men wanted to have enough blankets for everyone. In his vision, warriors were trading horses for them. *This cannot be,* he thought. But again the message resounded in his heart.

"They will all die!" The Coyote kept on, *"Soldier's blankets—sickness in them. Old, babies, mothers, warriors, all will die from the white man's sickness,"* the animal repeated. *"Go. Stop them."*

Raccoon let out a heartbreaking keen that reverberated throughout the forest.

He was hours from the camp. Frothing at the mouth, the horse breathed a labored breath in rhythm with the pounding of his hooves. The young man lifted his body high, to give his horse as much freedom as he could, racing back along the old trading paths toward the village.

White Smoke stood at the edge of the bluff, staring down at the river, barely visible through the mist. Like flooding after a heavy rain, the memory of her life with Garritt and her children had washed over her. That they were all dead saddened her beyond anything she had experienced. She wanted to find the house where they had lived and put her family's spirits to rest. Cougar Two Foot and Swift Fox understood, so they made plans to find her former home in the spring when they were in one of their summer camps.

White Smoke climbed to her Quiet Place, the place with the carved arch in the rocks. Sitting under the overhang above the canyon, she dove into the Vastness and listened to the smoke without interruption. She was intending to say prayers on behalf of her mentor, but today it took a long time to settle into the silence of the All That Is.

She had set her fire just outside the opening. But as she

watched, she could only feel the immense sadness of the loss of her family as well as the loss of her teacher. Eventually though, she settled enough to hear the secrets of the smoke. The essence and urgency of the message could not be ignored. It was disturbing, very disturbing.

Catapulted to her feet, she began to run wildly down the mountain. She slipped and slid on the snowy path down to the river, clinging to branches that broke off in her hands. The images that filled her head were unbearable. Running did not keep them out. Screaming did not keep them out. Exhausted, she tripped and fell at the river's edge and lay panting with her eyes closed.

She felt something near. An animal. Coyote. She dared not move. With its muzzle close to her mouth it took in her exhale. It paced around her sniffing at her whole body, then lay down and waited.

"What do you want, Coyote," she asked inwardly?

She heard. *"We will travel together for a time. Follow me."*

"Where are you taking me," she asked?

"To the gulf between your knowing and not knowing," he answered.

"Who are you?" she queried.

"Your friend," he answered.

"I know you?"

"We have known each other for a long time. In the past you have helped me, and now I am here to help you," he said. *"Be still, my brave friend."* He looked at her with deeply compassionate eyes. Holding her gaze, he instructed, *"Listen to your heart."*

The air was hot, and she was thirsty, so she got up and went into the river to drink the cool water and rinse away the dirt and sweat from her face. Coyote drank his fill as well.

Then the animal led her on a path through the forest. In formation, in the sky above, honking geese flew north. They walked for several hours past the bouncing river waters, and the swirling early summer grasses along its banks. Ahead, in a clearing, in the blossom-filled field was a herd of grazing deer that in unison looked up in fear, then darted away, leaving behind the carcasses of many bucks, does and fawns.

"What has happened?" she asked.

At that, Coyote transformed himself into a human. *"You will know what to do."* She recognized him as the man she had seen when she lay unconscious, battered and bruised after the raid so long ago, and who had been her guide on her vision quest when she became White Smoke. He looked into her eyes and said, *"And your boy still looks for you."* She watched as a white glowing light began to form at the man's heart, flowing outward till it surrounded his body.

From his back, huge black wings opened, lifting the half man, half raven high into the branches of the forest. The light at his heart concentrated into a sharp beacon, which exploded, leaving the sky empty except for a hawk that screeched and dove for its prey.

Quill ran from home to home, from fire to fire calling, "Where is White Smoke?" Shoulders shrugged, heads indicated a direction, but no one had seen her since the morning.

With aching knees and time-weakened muscles she made the ascent to the top of the hill, grabbing at tree limbs that were as gnarled as her hands. She was headed to the bluff where White Smoke went to go within. Her lungs bursting, she came to the overhang. Flames still danced on the wood of the fire, but White Smoke was nowhere to be found.

Looking everywhere for her, Quill called, "Daughter! Where are you?" She waited, but heard no answer. "White Smoke!" she called again. There were only echoes of her voice and the screech of an eagle soaring above. *That is very odd,* she thought to herself, *she would not leave her fire unattended.*

Quill pulled the logs apart, and threw dirt over them, then returned down the long winding path to the village. When she got to her lodge, she slid the folded poster under her sleeping mat.

White Smoke rubbed her head, which ached from hitting a rock. Once again the river splashed its late winter song, leaving ice sculptures along its banks, and frigid wind blew the cover of clouds. She was unsure at first where she was, but soon recognized that she was at the bottom of the ravine just below her quiet place on the bluff.

All at once she understood what seeing all those dead carcasses meant. Horrified, she climbed back up to find her fire had been pulled apart, and dirt kicked over it. But from the charred wood she heard,

"Tell them! Go! Now!"

She raced toward the camp, her heart pounding.

"Oh, Great Father," she prayed as she ran, her moccasins barely touching the icy ground, "they do not know about this disease. They have not seen it on their loved ones. Great Father, spare my people!"

Raccoon galloped into the camp, his face frozen in an expression of horror. Mothers had swaddled their young ones in those death-carrying wraps. Shouting for them to remove the blankets, he tried to tear the infected cloths away with his spear, but the women pushed him back. He threw the ones he could get into the fire. "They will make you sick. Throw them down!" But they did not listen.

White Smoke ran back into the camp soon after, and took up his cry, but no one would believe them.

After fourteen days, however, it began with one, then another, then another. Fever, chills and vomiting swept through the village. Their bodies in excruciating pain, faces disfigured by pustules, men, women and children succumbed to the invasion of the white man's disease. Families gathered around the sick in support, only to contract the disease as well.

Those that remained healthy abandoned the village taking with them their families, horses, dogs and all their belongings.

By now, Raccoon had several wives and many children. "We must go," he told White Smoke. "My family and I will travel north."

She was heartbroken to see her friends leave, and though she longed for Cougar Two Foot and Swift Fox, who were trading at the trapper's fort, she was grateful they had not been home to catch the pestilence.

Quill sat with White Smoke through the long days and seemingly endless nights chanting healing songs, working the energies to move Snake Spirit from the bodies of the afflicted. While White Smoke gathered herbs, which Quill brewed, The Silver Moon and her daughter, Blooming

Flower, helped to gather wood for the fires, rinse out cloths, feed the sick, and help with the care of the families that were left behind. But there were so many—too many for only four women to give care. And soon even The Silver Moon and Blooming Flower could no longer evade the invasive disease and passed away.

White Smoke and Quill, exhausted, began each morning praying for help and guidance. With so many deaths most tipis sat empty. There were but a few tribesmen left. Only an occasional cry from the sick or bark of a dog broke the hushed quiet in the camp.

The next morning, White Smoke awoke to the sound of labored breathing.

"Mother, let me feel your forehead."

She put her hand to the old woman's face. It was burning up. Rivulets of sweat poured down her wrinkled cheeks. The unthinkable had happened. The woman who had been so hearty of constitution and strong of spirit had come down with this dreaded disease. Quill lay on her bedding succumbing quickly to the infection that ravaged her old body.

"Drink this," White Smoke pleaded.

The old woman parted her lips and sipped the tea. The brew soothed her somewhat, but nothing could keep the raging illness from taking its course. It seemed that an avalanche of symptoms was now going to bury the life of her dear, beloved mentor.

With fevered memory, Quill babbled about her younger days of playing on the ridge where she, then called Little Bull, would hide from young Crow Feather, the boy who became Father Man, and how she loved to jump out from behind the trees and hear the boy scream with delight. And when they got older and they had joined together, the playing in the woods was of a different kind. With closed eyes, she smiled admitting that her sons had been made at the bluff under the overhang of stone. But before long, the old woman went in and out of consciousness, and she called out for either Father Man or Pure Heart.

White Smoke, the only person left in the camp without the illness, sat by her side as often as she could. She poured fresh water into a gourd bowl and dipped the cloth in it to wipe the old woman's brow.

"Daughter," Quill croaked waking for a time.

"Try to rest," White Smoke said stroking her forehead with a cool wet cloth.

"I found this," the old woman coughed. "I found this at the trapper's fort."

White Smoke whispered, "Quiet now, Mother."

With difficulty Quill rolled over, reached under the bearskin, and pulled out the poster. "I tried to show this to you as soon as you came back from the cliff, but you were so upset, and then all the sickness began. I think it is about you, is it not?"

White Smoke unfolded the yellowed parchment.

She read about the capture of Ginny Van Andusson. At the bottom were the names of her sons. *They were alive!* She was stunned. "Yes," she said quietly.

"Another thing." She hesitated building up the courage to confess that the Old Man once whispered in his sleep that he had met this Jahn Van Andusson. "I should have told you."

She tried to understand why Quill had kept this from her. Anger rose from deep with in her heart, but erupted silently, giving way to compassion. Quill was alone now, and if her daughter left to find that family, there would be no one here to care for her.

"I understand, Mother. Besides, I did not remember," she said with sadness and disappointment. "Try to rest now."

Through the long night, Quill battled to stay alive, her body becoming agitated, her breathing labored. In the early morning, sitting at the old woman's side, White Smoke finally rested, falling asleep with her head on her knees, but when the light hit the trees, Quill moaned, and she again awoke.

"I am here, Mother," White Smoke said wiping the old woman's fevered brow.

The shaman opened her eyes momentarily. "It is all right, Daughter, I will be with him soon. Father Man is waiting for me. He has been calling to me in my dreams. And my dear grandmother, Pure Heart..."

That evening just as the sun dropped behind the mountains, and the sky was ablaze, Quill surrendered to the white man's illness. With her final breath, the old woman had called out to her husband.

White Smoke took a knife, and once again cut the locks of her white hair. She sat with her mentor as the old woman's body became cold. This woman had saved her life. She had brought her to her home, and healed her mangled body. She had been her rock, her comfort and her teacher. She had been her mother at her wedding feast, and had helped to raise her son. Now White Smoke felt as if the earth had been pulled out from under her. Her life would not be the same without Quill.

She carried the old woman's limp, wasted body up the mountain to where the rocks covered the body of Father Man. She was told to burn it, so she built a pyre. The smoke from the fire curled up and up till she could see it no longer. Chanting and shaking her rattles, she sent Quill's spirit to her cherished spouse.

When she returned to the village she heard, *"There is no one left. Burn everything else! Quickly! Burn everything!"*

She dragged the dead from their tipis and prepared them, laying family members together. Sprinkling the bodies with oil and herbs, she sang the ancient prayers she had learned from her mentors. The pyres were ablaze all over the village. When that was done she lit a torch, touching it to everything that was left: tipis, clothing, bedding, all personal belongings, anything that might have been touched by the sick, including her own home.

Over and over, she had wondered, *"Why have I not gotten sick?"* But she was glad she had not had to leave her family.

She was alone in the village now. Cougar Two Foot and Swift Fox had not yet returned from the north where they had been hunting elk and bighorn sheep. When her family did return they would have to find a new home. In the meantime, she waited.

She built a shelter some distance from the village, and brought in the few items belonging to her husband and son that she felt could be spared from the fire. Her horses and the two dogs were the only company she had.

She tanned the skins of several rabbits, dried the meat, ground tubers, placing the meal in leather sacks, and smoked fish to take on the journey she knew they would have to take. She drove the few horses that were left to the Fort to trade for supplies, and inform the man who sold them the blankets what he had done.

In the midst of the ashes of what had been their village, with the darkness replacing the light as day turned to night again and again, she waited for the return of her family. The time went by agonizingly slowly.

The wind was blowing hard and the air temperature was dropping fast. Jahn tied off his horse, and entered the trapper's store.

"Hello, Jacque," Jahn said.

"Where are you headed there, Lieutenant?" Jacque asked.

"Back to the fort," he said.

"That storm is coming in fast, you might want to stay here tonight," Jacque suggested.

"Thanks, but I want to get a little farther before the night comes. Let me have a sack of beans, salt, jerky, a jar of molasses, and a sack of feed, also, a tin of your pipe tobacco. Hmm. I know there is something else." He looked up trying to remember what it was, when he noticed that the poster he had put up twenty years ago was gone. "You get tired of having that poster up there, Jacque?"

"It was an old Indian woman. Didn't think she could read. But soon as she read it, she made me give her the poster and she tore out of the shop."

"What? When was that?" Jahn asked.

"Two, three—maybe four weeks ago," Jacques answered.

"Where is her camp? Do you know?"

Jacque gave him the directions.

"But you know that storm is almost right upon us. They won't be going anywhere," Jacque said. "Why don't you stay here tonight?"

"A sack of shot," Jahn said, remembering the item. "Thanks. Another time." He paid, and took the supplies out to his horse. His heart was racing.

At long last, White Smoke saw the dark outline of two riders within the shadows of the trees. Her family had been spared. Her husband and her son, healthy and strong, carried many pelts and supplies from their successful hunt and stop at the Traders Store.

White Smoke ran to greet them. "Husband, it is good to see you, and you are looking strong and fit, my son."

Cougar Two Foot looked over the devastation. "What has happened here?"

Swift Fox, now a lanky fifteen-year old, asked, "Where is Grandmother?"

"I am sorry, son," she replied not wanting to speak of the dead. For Swift Fox, it seemed as if the earth shifted, then fell away.

"What about Wind and Tall Stalk?"

White Smoke shook her head.

"Raccoon?" he asked.

"He and his family left as soon as it started."

White Smoke recounted the events of the last days of their beloveds and friends. Then she noticed that over the neck of Cougar Two Foot's horse hung a gray cavalry blanket.

"Where did you get that?" she said, her hand clutching her dress at her heart.

"At the fort," he said looking confused. White Smoke grabbed the shroud and flung it into the fire.

"Mother!" Swift Fox said. "Father traded it for some pelts so you would be warm all winter."

"What have you done? The white man's sickness is in

those blankets!" She gestured sweeping her arm over the charred earth. "They all died from *those*. Did you touch it?"

"No," Swift Fox answered defensively.

"Are you sure?" Her tone was brusque and hard.

"I did not."

"We must leave now," Cougar Two Foot said, looking out at the clouds. "There is a storm coming."

Exhausted, White Smoke took out the hair comb that Quill had returned to her, and ran it through her white hair feeling its prongs run across her scalp. Cougar Two Foot enveloped her in his arms.

"My dear wife, we must get away from here now."

She knew he was right, but she felt a longing for what had been, making the leaving even harder. Wrapping the comb back up in the gingham cloth, she placed the bundle in her sack of herbs.

"What is that?" Swift Fox asked of the cross on a strip of sinew she had tied around her neck.

"Do you like it?" she asked.

"Very much," he said

She took it off and gave it to her son. He hung it around his neck, the silver shining brightly against his dark skin. As they left, she could only pray that Cougar Two Foot and Swift Fox would be safe from the killing blight. Most of their belongings had already been burned with the rest of the camp. Now they gathered what little was left and rode north.

38

Whipped around by gusting winds, the snow blinded Jahn and the cold had crept under his coat, freezing all within it. He had been riding for days, and hoped to take refuge within the encampment that was supposed to be up ahead. The tribe he was looking for was known for being accepting and kind, Father Man's village, the one he had visited so many years before, and where Jacque told him the old woman lived. This time of year the settlement would be around the bend, in the clearing by the river, but when he came around the curve he could not believe what he saw. Every tipi had been burned to the ground.

He rode through the village looking for any sign of life. But there was no human being still living there. At first Jahn thought, *The Red Wing or was it cavalry soldiers?* The harder he looked the more it seemed to be something else.

Bodies burnt together were carefully laid out, one placed next to another. Though all was burned to the ground, he could see that the homes had been filled with everyday items. The devastation in front of him was complete. The sight of it made him physically ill, but he did not dare get off his horse, because he suspected the worst. *Small Pox*.

There in the dirt was the corner of something familiar. He leaned down to get a better look, and in doing so his horse shifted position kicking the object, unearthing it for a clear view. He recognized it immediately. It was one of his posters.

Something deep within him screamed with horror. His mind swam through all the villages he had searched through the years. Now it felt like a heavy door was swinging shut.

Numb, he rode on.

Hours later Jahn sat stiffly on his horse, the ice sticking to his beard, his mouth nearly frozen shut. His journey came to a standstill when his horse refused to cross the icy river.

"Lieutenant!" a voice called from the other side. "That you, Van Andusson? Haven't seen you in a couple of years. Where you headed?"

Jahn coughed, the earth swirled, and he fell from his horse.

Bear and Elk Horn quickly crossed over. They lifted Jahn and leaned him against a tree, brushing the ice from his beard.

"He has a fever," Elk Horn said feeling his forehead.

"We'd best make camp here. Get something warm into him," Bear suggested.

The next day when Jahn woke, he was surprised to see his friends.

"You feeling better there, Soldier?" Bear asked.

"Yes, thanks. Glad you came along when you did."

"We are headed to Yampa River. You?"

"The same."

"Ah, good, join us then. We'll stay here for a day or two till you get your legs back."

Elk Horn asked, "You still lookin' for your mother?"
Jahn shook his head. Later he told his friends about the Indian woman taking the poster from the trapper's fort, and finding it on the ground in the charred remains of the camp. It looked as if no one had escaped the sickness. He told them that he finally understood that his mother was dead.

After a few days when Jahn felt strong enough to continue, they went on together toward Steamboat Springs.

39

With a blizzard buffeting them most of the day, the white powder now up to their horses' bellies, the family rode north away from the deserted camp, their horses fighting against the slipperiness of the uneven road. The numbing cold slowed down their ability to maneuver adroitly, causing them to rock uncontrollably with each step. Trees, boulders, logs were covered, and only the tallest grasses poked above the blanket of snow. All around them was a cemetery of quiet.

Cougar Two Foot spoke very little, which was unlike him. Even Swift Fox was quiet with the cold. All day, White Smoke longed for the comfort of a fire and the advice the smoke could offer.

When they stopped for the night they set their bedrolls under some low-lying pine boughs. Finding dry wood had been nearly impossible, but even so Cougar Two Foot was able to make a warm fire from some branches Swift Fox had found beneath the evergreens. Now they sat in front of it warming their chilled extremities. Supper was light, just some dried fish, because with the falling snow animal tracks could not be seen.

White Smoke unrolled a cloth in front of Swift Fox. "Before she got sick, Quill gave me these. She told me that your grandfather would have wanted you to have them." She handed him a rattle and the beaded bird wing that Father Man used for ceremonies. "He told me often that with instruction, you would make a fine Shaman if you wanted to be one."

He was deeply touched by the unexpected gift, and put them in a safe place within his belongings.

In the morning Swift Fox fastened his snowshoes, slung his bow and quiver over his shoulder, and went looking for game. With all the settlers fencing in land, the animals were also forced to higher ground to forage for food in the harsh winter snows. His cornflower-blue eyes scanned the horizon for any sign of deer, elk, sheep or bear, but he also looked for turkey, grouse or rabbit tracks, though he found none.

After walking for hours, the wind began to blow hard again, and the snow bit at his cheeks. But just as he was about to return to camp, he saw a buck. Not yet aware of the boy's presence, the animal held his head high, his antlers catching the snow, as he sniffed the wind for predators. Approaching the deer from behind, Swift Fox waited till he could feel its heartbeat before he released his shaft.

40

Jahn took off through the snowy woods looking for footprints of game to kill for their supper. Bear and Elk Horn remained in the camp to scrape deer hides, their unexpected bounty from the day before.

Jahn had been walking for an hour or so in the heavily falling snow before he saw the boy. The snow-laden branches almost hid the young man: tall, strong and handsome, with striking blue eyes, who looked to be about half his age. Though the blizzard had obliterated tracks, the young hunter had still found prey, a young buck.

Jahn raised his rifle, but changed his mind. Even though they were many yards apart it felt to Jahn as if there was no space between them at all.

The boy slowly pulled back his arrow, and waited for the right moment. The shaft loosed, the arrow flew directly into the buck's chest. The animal's head jerked back, and it fell to the ground. The young brave knelt by its side, putting his hand on the deer's head. He closed his eyes and raised his face to the sky.

The hunter had not seen Jahn, or so he thought, but when the boy got up, he turned and looked into Jahn's eyes for a long moment before lifting the carcass onto his shoulders, and moving back into the snow-covered branches. He was out of sight before Jahn realized that the silver pendant that was on a strap at the boy's neck seemed familiar. But he could not place it, so shrugged it off, and continued his own hunt.

White Smoke watched diligently for Swift Fox to return. He had been gone only a few hours, but his being out of her sight worried her. When she heard the dogs bark and saw them wag their tails, she felt relieved to see him come through the trees carrying the carcass of a young buck.

"You found a fine animal for us," she told him, hiding her concern, "The skin is thick and strong. The meat will strengthen us."

He put the deer on the ground. "There was a soldier there."

"What did he want?"

"At first, he raised his rifle to the buck I was stalking," Swift Fox said looking up at her face, "but did not shoot. He let me take it."

"What did he look like?" White Smoke asked.

"Tall, dark hair. I didn't see much else," he told her.

"Did he follow you?" Cougar Two Foot asked.

"No. Went on his way."

The snow was already deep and more fell continuously for the next week as they rode away from the infected camp.

Cougar Two Foot grew even more silent than he had been the last few days, speaking only when asked something directly.

Finally White Smoke said to him, "You are very quiet, Husband." His body pitched awkwardly. His face shone with sweat, and his clothes were soaked.

Fearful of the answer, she asked, "Are you all right?"

Before he could reply, Cougar Two Foot jumped off his horse and vomited, and then could not stop emptying his stomach and bowels. She had seen this before and knew what was coming. She was heartbroken. Within days she knew this strong, good man, father to their son, someone she had grown to love and respect, would succumb to the white man's illness. She ran to his side.

Turning to Swift Fox, she said, "Go and get wood. We must make our camp here."

She told him to build the fire some distance away from where his father lay. Together mother and son worked quickly to build a lean-to that would cover their beloved. And even though she knew that separating Swift Fox and Cougar Two Foot was as difficult as keeping the smoke from the air, White Smoke forbade her son to come anywhere near.

"Build another shelter over there!" she barked pointing to a place fifty feet or so from where they stood. "Do not come close."

"But he is my father," he yelled in frustration. "I will help you, Mother," he pleaded.

"And you are my son! Do not come close. Hear me? You must not get sick!"

"What is the matter with her face, Papa?" young Ginny had

asked her father so long ago.

"Stay away from her bed, Ginny. Your mother is very sick, and I don't want you to get it, too," she remembered her father telling her this just before her mother died.

"Stop. Leave it there. Now go back to your camp," she told him. She had to push her son away forcibly more than once. He was angry and hurt by her demand, but he would not cross his mother, so he had built the second camp where she told him. After that he stayed at a distance as she instructed. When he had returned to his shelter, she retrieved the water and food that he had brought.

For several days Cougar Two Foot was feverish, and then his handsome face became obscured by the blisters of the disease.

"Where will you go?" he asked between hacking coughs.

White Smoke dabbed his burning forehead with a cool cloth. She thought for a time, wanting to give him some kind of answer. "As we had planned, north toward the valley where the Yampa grows. You know Long Spear has always told us that we are welcome to join them," she said barely able to think what to do the next minute let alone decide where they would go to live after her husband was gone. "And they have no shaman."

"He likes you," Cougar Two Foot said. "You could be his fifth wife," he said wryly.

"I am your wife only," she said.

"But you will need help."

"I have my son," she said not wanting to talk of it further. "Besides Long Spear is too old and ugly."

"Then you must find a strong cougar like me," he said looking down at his ailing frame and trying to laugh, but it made him cough. Then he said in earnest, "The wolf finds a pack because he knows he cannot survive by himself."

"We can talk of that later. Now you must rest. Take some more of this before you close your eyes." She lifted a gourd cup to his lips. He drank some of the thick peppermint tea she had made to help with the nausea.

"When I am one with the sun–" Cougar Two Foot began.

"Let's not talk of your leaving, please. You are my husband and Swift Fox's father–" She was barely able to speak. She set the gourd on the ground near the palette, and wiped his brow. "Rest now."

"Tell my son," he said between coughs, "that he is a strong boy, fast as the fox of his name, a fine hunter, and someday he will make a fine leader."

With his face puffed with the disease and his eyes merely slits, Cougar Two Foot smiled at her tenderly. He watched how the firelight danced on her cropped white hair, taking in her face fully, tracing it into his memory. Then he turned his head and began coughing again, and though there was nothing left to expel, he tried to empty his stomach once more.

Swift Fox constantly looked toward the lean-to. When he could stand it no longer he went off into the woods to hunt.

For days, White Smoke continued to put cooling cloths on her husband's fevered head, but he had been unaware of the loving care she had been giving him. By the twelfth night, Cougar Two Foot lay under his blanket barely breathing.

At the next first light, when the snow had stopped and stillness still filled the forest, Cougar Two Foot lay motionless. Once again she took out her knife. Taking hold of her hair, she ran the sharp blade across the back of it. She could not believe that her beloved was gone, but she did not cry. *There is no time for that,* she thought. *We must find somewhere to live.*

When White Smoke began to chant for her husband's spirit, Swift Fox was jarred awake by her song, and ran toward them.

"No!" she yelled halting his advance. "You must not come near. Gather dry wood for his mound. Go."

"You are going to burn him, too?" he shouted, taking a step toward his father's body.

"You stay away. Stay far away from this sickness," she called out, waving him back. "Get dry branches!"

Swift Fox gathered wood to form a pyre for the burning of his father's body. Disheartened then angry, the boy took the branches in his two hands, and slammed them hard against rocks. White Smoke waited till her son's fury was spent, then she rolled her husband onto a blanket, and with all her strength dragged him to the top.

She put all of his clothes and belongings on the pyre, including the blankets, his pouch of herbs, his bow and quiver and his knife. Finally she removed her own clothes and placed them next to him.

From the fire, she took a long burning branch and touched it to the funeral mound. Flames licked the blankets, the clothes, his bow and his knife. Finally, it touched his once handsome face then slowly consumed the body. She remained there till all was gone, the black smoke rising into the air.

When all was destroyed, she went to the river, and washed her body in the freezing water then put on the only clothing she had left, her wedding dress, well worn and old. She wrapped herself in a blanket, which scarcely kept out the bitter cold.

For White Smoke time had stopped. She was unable to speak. Swift Fox, too, was beside himself with grief.

"He was my father! He would have wanted me to help!" he yelled at her.

She could not answer him now. In frustration, he got on his horse and rode off.

"Swift Fox, come back!" she called, but he was too far away to hear. "It is all right," she said aloud. "He must not be near this camp of the dying."

The rest of the things she had used to care for her husband she threw into the fire, then got on her horse and rode after her son, barely aware of the frigid air. But when she did not find him, she made camp, and waited for him to return on his own.

Where his Palomino stood, high above the temporary camp, the snow had been blown from the rock. Below it however, the earth was covered with the thick white blanket. Corn Snake had watched as White Smoke prepared her husband's funeral. He had watched as she undressed and burnt her clothes, and as Swift Fox rode away. He waited to see what she would do, and followed her when she left behind the ashes of her husband. But he kept his distance so that she would not know he was there. When she got settled in her new camp, he rode in.

Instinctively, White Smoke reached for her knife when the rider came into the clearing.

"What do you want, Corn Snake?" she said keeping her

hand on her weapon.

"Cougar Two Foot is dead," Corn Snake stated without dismounting.

"Yes," she answered.

"Did all die in the camp?"

"Not all, if they had not touched the blankets or cared for the ill," she told him. "Many left before they could get sick." But she knew what he wanted to know.

"And The Silver Moon?" he asked flatly pulling up the reins to still his horse that danced shifting from one foot to another.

"Your mother and sister–they helped as long as they could, but they both got sick. I am sorry. I did chant for them."

Corn Snake turned his horse to leave then turned back, "Where will you go?"

"Where there is no sickness," she said.

Reaching behind him, Corn Snake freed two large pelts from the stack tied on the back of his horse, one from a bear and the other a bighorn sheep. He threw them at her feet. "You will need these," he said. Then he pulled his horse back onto the trail and rode away. He did not leave, however, but stayed out of sight to watch over her.

The next morning before her fire was lit, a hungry wolverine caught her scent. It hunched down, slowly crawling toward her. Corn Snake pulled an arrow from his sheath and cocked the string. Following the animal with the tip, he let the arrow fly, stopping the predator just as it ran to attack. On the third day, when Swift Fox had returned and would protect her, he rode away. He headed southeast to search for his tribe at Muddy River where it never snows.

Swift Fox sat down in front of the fire saying nothing, and in time said with great difficulty, "I understand." But for the next few days neither spoke, riding the long hours in silence. At night, when they stopped to make a fire, White Smoke would sit with her eyes closed, listening to the voice of the smoke while her son sharpened his arrows or practiced shooting at targets.

One night Swift Fox awoke with a start. His dream message had been quite clear. He was to journey on to the new village by himself. He did not know why, and this concerned him. He had just lost his father, his grandparents, and many of his friends. Now he feared that harm was going to come to his mother.

"I must go to the fort in Steamboat Springs," she told him when he described his dream, "but you need not worry. I will see you again very soon." She was used to this kind of inner instruction, and had followed it as best she could whenever it came. "I will meet you there when I have finished my business," she told him.

What the dream told Swift Fox had been unambiguous. White Smoke knew that her son would be safe and embraced by the new community. Even so, she felt her heart being torn from her body when he turned off to the north. As for Swift Fox, he worked hard to remain strong, and would not let himself look back at his mother.

41

Swift Fox breathed deeply to settle his mind, and looked up the trail. Finding Long Spear would not be easy, for he was only vaguely aware of where they had their winter camp. His mother had reminded him that he was to travel north for two days and west for one.

"Look for 'the fawn in the wood' and you will find the camp," she had said.

For two days, he and the dogs traveled north, the sun's low arc making long shadows ahead of them.

He remembered the many times he had met Chief Long Spear at the annual Tribal Gathering. Since Swift Fox was quite young, he and Long Spear had hunted together during those festivities. Long Spear had been a fine hunter and he enjoyed teaching his young friend the finer points of his talents.

"You must be my eyes now," Long Spear told his young charge at the last gathering. "Mine cannot see the antlers as well as they used to."

"I will guide your aim. Just up ahead is a turkey." Swift Fox

placed his hands over his friends and guided his arrow. "Now," Swift Fox whispered in his ear. The chief released his arrow and downed the bird. "Fine shooting, Long Spear."

"You are a very kind boy," he smiled.

The third day the rain had been heavy, making the trail through the snowy woods slippery and slow. Patches of ice remained throughout the woods, and he knew it could still be cold enough for another blanketing.

That night he made his camp in the opening of a cave by the side of a river. The fire crackled and warmed his chest as he sat remembering the last days of his father. With so much loss he had never felt such sadness, and as much as he tried, he could not arrest the tears that streamed down his cheeks.

He killed a ptarmigan for dinner, and then made his bed for the night. As he fell asleep, coyotes yipped their song in the distance and a white owl screeched to its mate.

Two wolves sauntered out of the shadows through the black circle left by his fire. His dogs had not yet smelled the animals, and were still sleeping. The wolves walked around him, sniffing his breath then leaving their scent. Very slowly, he slid his hand under the blanket, and down his leg where he kept his knife. His hand clenched tightly around its grip, he slowly brought it up from underneath the covers.

In the moonlight he could see the outline of the lupines fighting with each other, and hear the snarling noises they made. The animals pounced again and again, rolling back and forth, mouths open, tongues flailing and sharp teeth bared. Swift Fox kept absolutely still. Then both wolves stopped and turned toward him. Their hindquarters sank readying to pounce. Suddenly they jumped, their mouths aiming for his neck, but when they reached his uplifted forearm, they became soft young pups.

He awakened, and saw that there were no wolves, nor any evidence of fighting. His two dogs stretched and curled up tighter, sighing in their sleep. Even so he reached under his blanket for his knife, and found it next to his leg. He tried to go back to sleep, but his mind raced to the dream again.

The next morning he headed west and began to look in earnest for "the fawn in the wood".

42

Climbing the long winding trail toward the valley where the Yampa root was plentiful, White Smoke began to ramble over her fifteen years with Cougar Two Foot. But she would need to keep those feelings tethered, otherwise she would have to sit on a log and cry till she could no longer breathe, and there was not time for that now. They would not survive well on their own, but would need the companionship of a band.

White Smoke knew that as a shaman and a seer she would be welcomed in any community. She thought Chief Long Spear's would be a fine village to join, and some of her people might have become members with them already. Besides, Long Spear knew Swift Fox well and liked him.

She might have to be delicate, however, about rebuffing the chief's advances, and careful not to injure his pride. But for now, she was heading to the trapper's fort in Steamboat Springs to see why the smoke had led her there. In her bag, she carried some of Quill's beadwork to trade for supplies.

"You need something?" the owner asked in a growly bark from behind the counter of Brother Joseph's Trading Company. His tone was wary and cautious. On his face and hands he had the scars of a man who had fought with wild animals. The opening in his shirt revealed a deep gash, which ran across his chest, and he had some fingers missing.

"Just some beans and salt," she answered. He handed her a bag, and she gave over a necklace. "This will be adequate?" she asked.

"Sure." He looked at her face. "You a white woman, ain't ya?" he queried in English. She did not answer. "They let you out on your own?" Then he saw the bag of herbs she carried in the pouch, slung over her shoulder. "A shaman?" he said in her language. "You white, and they made you a shaman? Don't that beat all," he scoffed, looking at her for a response. Changing his tone he said, "Look, a friend of mine is feeling poorly. Would you take a look at him? I can give you food for it, or whatever you like. He got cut up real bad falling from his horse. I stitched him up, but he's not doing so well. Fever. Chills."

"Show me," she said flatly.

A voice bellowed from outside, "That winter beast has finally gone into its cave. I do believe we have had the end of the snow!" The door swung open, and Bear and Elk Horn strode in. Laden with pelts of all kinds, they threw their hides down on the counter.

Bear greeted the trader with a broad grin, "What will you give me for these, you old cheat?"

"What moth-eaten hides you got there?" he replied fingering the pelts and counting each kind, "Seventeen deer, sixteen sheep, three elk and twenty-five rabbits. Is that all?" He waited. "Oh yes, and one gnarly bear. This one attempt to eat you for supper, Bear?"

"Naw, Joseph, he was waitin' for some more of your fingers."

Joseph, balling what was left of his hands into fists, squared off with Bear pretending to spar with him.

White Smoke interrupted, "Your friend who is sick, where is he?"

Bear and Elk Horn looked to see who had spoken then leaned in and whispered to each other all the while looking at her with curious eyes.

"Right age," Elk Horn remarked. "Has his eyes."

Finally Bear had to ask, "How old are you, miss, if I may ask?"

Looking at Joseph, "Your friend?" she said.

"You are white, are you not?" Bear said. "I only ask because a friend of mine, his name is Jahn Van Andusson, has been looking for his mother most of his life." He looked to see if there was any recognition. "She was taken when he was a young boy." He hesitated a moment before asking, "What is your name? If I may ask."

"What?" White Smoke said in English. "What did you say?"

"My friend, Dutch, has been trying to find his mother for years. Your name, if I may ask? I mean no offense, ma'am, but might you be Ginny, Virginia Van Andusson by any chance?" he asked politely, staring at her face.

White Smoke could not believe what she was hearing. *This could not be true. Certainly, they must be referring to someone else. It could not be her son they spoke of.* It would be much too painful to be disappointed, so she put him off.

"I must attend to this man's friend," she said indicating Joseph. "Where can I find you when I am finished?" she asked.

"At the saloon, most likely," he answered.

"You will wait for me there. I will come to you. We will

talk then."

"Sure," Bear answered confused. "Won't wait long for you, so mind you show up."

She knew that Jahn was alive, but that this man knew her son? Her mind raced, and she felt dizzy. She followed the shopkeeper to the back room. Looking at her hair, cut in honor of mourning, he said, "I am sorry for your loss, ma'am." She did not respond. "My friend is up to no good mostly, but I am kind of used to his bein' around."

Lying on a pallet was a man with deep knife wounds on his arms and chest, and an arrow had gone through his shoulder.

"Nasty fall," she said. "Fire here and here," she said pointing to the injuries that were red and filled with pus. "Let us be for a time. I will meet you in the store when I am finished."

"Yes, ma'am. Miss," Joseph asked, "*are* you Ginny Van Andusson?"

"I am," she said, "or I was."

"Well, ain't that a fresh wind," he said slapping his knee. "Wish I could see your son's face when he sees you again."

When she left, the injured man was sleeping comfortably.

"Let him rest, and be sure he drinks plenty of water," she told Joseph.

"What do you need here?" he said looking around his establishment.

"I will come back tomorrow. You can give me supplies then."

White Smoke went quickly to the saloon to look for the trapper called Bear and his friend. There was a roar of hollers, whistles and unkind remarks when she entered the bar, not friendly places for Indian women. One itinerant gathered up his money from the table where he had been gambling and made his way to where she was standing. He pushed her back against the door with his hips, putting his hand on her breast. "How about giving me a little sugar, squaw."

Elk Horn came up behind him, pulled him off her, and kicked him in the stomach. He crumpled onto the floor gasping for air. "Bear says to meet him outside." Bear sat at the water pump waiting for her.

"Are you Ginny Van Andusson?"

"You are a friend of Jahn Van Andusson?" she asked.

"I am, ma'am."

"What do you know of him?"

"He is a lieutenant in the cavalry out of Fort Garland." Bear looked hard at her. "Your face, even the shape is the same."

White Smoke could not settle her racing heart, and her mind could only jump senselessly from one thought to another.

"Where did you see him?" she snapped.

Elk Horn could see that the woman was getting agitated.

In a calm voice, Bear answered, "We met near Fort Garland."

Elk Horn turned to Bear, and said to his friend, "Those eyes are just like his, intense and that bright shade of blue."

"You are truly Ginny Van Andusson?" Bear asked, looking more closely at her face.

"I am."

"The three of us came here together," Bear said with rising excitement he could no longer contain. "Dang! Wait till the lieutenant hears about this!"

White Smoke wanted to know everything. But she did not know this man and his friend, so she kept quiet.

"When did you see him last?" she asked more calmly now, feigning less interest.

"Known him for years, but saw him a few weeks ago. Like I said, the three of us took the trail through the mountains here to Steamboat Springs. He went back to Fort Garland already, probably there by now. It is something he does every few months—goes back and forth." He stopped to take in her face carefully. "You really are Ginny Van Andusson?"

"Yes," she said definitively. "Your name is Bear?" she asked. He pointed to his scar. "I see."

Elk Horn leaned in to Bear's ear, "Does she want to come with us?"

"Ma'am, Ginny, or," he stopped as if to say, what is your Indian name?

"White Smoke, but Ginny is fine," she said in halting English with her tribe's intonation. "Though forgive me if I do not answer right away. I have not heard that name in many years."

"Elk Horn and me will be goin' to Fort Garland in a couple of weeks, once the weather clears and that sun shines more than the snow falls. Would you like to come along with us?"

She settled her mind for a moment, noting nothing unpleasant from them in regards to her.

"I will join you, but I must go north for a time first, then I will meet you here," she said in English.

Swift Fox would be waiting for her, and though she longed to see if this was truly her son, she knew that Swift Fox would need the reassurance of her company so soon after his father's death, and she needed his comfort as well. This would also give her time to ask the smoke about how to best meet her son who was now a man.

The next morning before leaving, she checked on her patient at the Yampa Trading Company.

"He was pretty restless during the night," Joseph told her. "But he seems better today."

"Good. Give him more tea to help wash out the poison," she told him.

She looked at his wounds, spread on more of the herbal salve and re-bound them with clean bandages. In The Quietness, she held his spirit to help him heal then went into the store and chose a few items, including a buckskin dress for her journey. "I will take these."

"A fair trade," he said good-naturedly. "Good day, ma'am. Ginny." He tipped his hat. "And thanks again," he said nodding toward his friend.

"Keep the wounds dry," she told him again in English as she left.

The huge buck stood at the top of the hill. The striped shaft of an Indian's arrow whizzed past Jahn's face into the animal, the arrow piercing directly into the lung. The buck fell, thudding heavily to the ground. The Indian did not seem to be aware Jahn was there, for as the animal labored to gasp its last breath, the boy rushed past him toward the downed creature. He, on the other hand, could not help but notice the boy's bright blue eyes.

Drawn to him, Jahn walked over to where the boy was crouching over his kill. The hunter had closed his eyes and muttered something, then lifted the carcass over his shoulder. But before he left he turned to look at Jahn, and their eyes locked. It was only then that Jahn saw the oversized silver cross floating at the brave's neck.

Reaching for it, he barked, "Where did you get that?"

"From my mother," the boy answered pulling away sharply.

Jahn awoke before his hand could touch the familiar ornament.

Birches swayed in the morning breeze, and early flowers poked their way out of thawing earth. Traveling at a comfortable pace, Swift Fox took the path that wound up the mountainside snaking back and forth in its ascent. Even though there was still snow on the ground, the trees below were a billowing cloud of new green leaves making a breath-taking vista of the verdant but still white-capped mountains, their snow cover melting into loud waterfalls cascading into raging waterways below.

White Smoke could sense her son. It was not Swift Fox that she felt in her heart at this moment, but Jahn's strong spirit. She closed her eyes, and told him inwardly, *"My dear son, I will find you, but now I must join Swift Fox, your brother."*

She kicked her horse to quicken the pace. White Smoke wanted to catch up with him before he got to the rock formation that looked like a fawn waiting for its mother. By afternoon she would be there, then it would only be a half-day's ride to the new camp.

A harsh wind blew, reminding her that the night would still be quite cold. This had been an early spring and could still turn back into winter with no warning.

Before the sun began to set, she saw Swift Fox ahead and whistled. He turned, and she was greeted with his smile.

Cougar Two Foot, Quill, Father Man and their friends heavily filled their thoughts. Neither wished to dishonor the dead by speaking about them, so conversation was limited.

"The weather is good for us," she said looking at the clear sky above.

"What did you find in Steamboat Springs?"

After a long pause she said. "Coyote Medicine. It was not what I expected." She was silent again, weighing what to say. Later when they stopped to rest, she broached the subject of her other sons. "Do you remember that I had another family before I came to live with Quill and Father Man? And that my two oldest boys live?"

"Yes," he said with some hesitancy.

"I met two trappers in Steamboat Springs who know my second son, Jahn. You can understand that I would want to see him, can you not, beloved boy? So once we are settled I will go to find him. The two men that I met there, Bear and Elk Horn, will show me where he lives."

"Is that safe? I should go with you."

Swift Fox knew that most mountain men had unsavory reputations, and he remembered what his mother had said about being sold to trappers. But what rattled him even more was the reminder that he had two white brothers.

"Let me think about that. We do not have far to go now, and it has been a long day. I feel rather tired."

With heavy hearts, they rode in silence, neither wanting to speak again of her other family or of Cougar Two Foot. White Smoke longed for the warmth of their tipi, the familiar voices of Father Man and Quill, and the sounds of her friends in the village as they prepared the evening meal.

Swift Fox pointed toward the wisp of smoke rising above the trees ahead of them.

"Horse Blanket's people," she said.

Eager to get to the village, they went into a gallop.

The community had experienced many losses causing great hardship: illness, raids and the ever-present cavalry seeking them out. Now it included only fifteen families along with the chief's three wives and their young children. With so few to hunt, wintering in this hollow would be a challenge. And because there were not enough men, the women would be both householders and hunters.

As they came to the edge of the forest and into a clearing, they saw tipis with smoldering campfires, but no people. They found tracks along the winding path that led upward to a clearing where they saw what was left of the group: old men, women and children, and only a handful of boys, a few older but mostly younger than her son. In a crevice in the rocks was a burial mound of their chief, Horse Blanket.

White Smoke and Swift Fox looked around for the familiar faces of those they had met each year at the Tribal Gatherings.

"White Smoke! Hello!" a voice called from within the group. It was Rain. Over the years at the annual celebrations, they had become good friends. She found that Rain was a strong woman with a clear head. She was fun, gregarious, and playful and an unconscionable cheat at games, who enjoyed the game of cheating as much as she liked the game of winning. But today her tone was dark and frightened.

"You have come just in time." She looked at Swift Fox and then to White Smoke, but seeing White Smoke's cropped hair, she did not need to ask about Cougar Two Foot. She asked, "Will you join us in chanting for Horse Blanket?"

"I would be honored," White Smoke said.

James Little Chief and Rain's youngest son, Sagebrush, pounded the big drum with a slow and constant beat. White Smoke took out the quartz-filled rattle that glowed in the dark when she shook it, the one given to her by Father Man, as well as the feather wand she had made. She lit sage and smudged the corpse, waving the pungent smoke over the dead chief's body. All watched as the smoke rose into the sky. The group sang until the entire circle felt satisfied.

After they returned to the village, White Smoke asked Rain about what had happened.

"Raiding party," she answered somberly. "Stole horses, killed Horse Blanket, and took our strongest and best hunters for slaves."

"High Cliff and your oldest?" White Smoke asked concerned. Rain also had three daughters: Big Eyes and Little Fawn, who were quite a bit younger than her son, and Warm Blanket who was nearer his age.

"Senawahv was kind," Rain answered. "My men were not here when it happened."

"When was this?" she asked.

"Two days ago," Rain answered.

"Where is your shaman?"

"Died in early winter," Rain answered. "Did our best without him, but Horse Blanket took an arrow in his chest. Nothing we could do. Bravely stayed with us for several days. Some say they saw him rise into the sky when he passed," she said rolling her eyes. "Now we have no chief, and the men that are left are old or just babies," she exaggerated. "How are we going to get along? Join with another village, I suppose," she said, disturbed at the idea.

White Smoke told Rain they would stay with her family for a day or two till the people could get their next move sorted out.

A new chief would be chosen immediately. The tribal council would gather around the fire and discuss their options. Each person would state his choice and considerations before a vote was taken.

While Swift Fox and the boys went into the woods to hunt for the tribal burial feast, White Smoke spoke with the women, telling them of the sickness that occurred in her village, and that she and Swift Fox were going to join the people of Long Spear.

"Come with us," White Smoke suggested.

"Long Spear?" one of the women said. She looked first at Rain and then back at White Smoke. "You will not find Long Spear or his people any longer. The crow tells us that he passed from a soldier's bullet, and that many in the village were killed at that time. The others are hiding from that infestation that combs the forest with their long guns, looking for 'renegades'," she said in a wry tone.

"You will be safer with us here than trying to find them. Stay here with us," Rain said. "We need a shaman, and you will bring us good luck. I know it."

Between the onslaughts of white settlers overtaking the land, the animals fleeing deeper into the forest, and renegades stealing their horses and men, the band had been feeling like beaten down grass. The introduction of White Smoke and her son into their group seemed like a healing tonic. The other women nodded in agreement, their eyes full of hope.

White Smoke sat quietly then told them, "I will discuss this with my son, and ask the smoke for an answer."

The boys returned, leaving the carcasses for the women

to cut up for the feast.

White Smoke asked her son to walk with her. She told him of Rain's suggestion, and asked his thoughts.

Swift Fox picked up a few stones and threw them into the woods, aiming at nothing in particular. He had been looking forward to seeing his old friend, and now he was dead from a white man's gun. This band needed them, for sure, but also he and his mother needed a community.

"They are good people," was all he could get out.

"And will you be all right when I go to find Jahn?"

"I would prefer to go with you, Mother, but these people need a good hunter, and if nothing else I am that."

"Thank you, son. Let us go sit and see what the smoke has to say."

It was rare that his mother asked him to participate in her ceremony so he felt honored to be asked at this time when there was so much at stake.

That afternoon the feast in honor of the fallen chief began. The smell of venison roasting over the fire filled the air with a tantalizing smell. They joined in the celebration for a while, and then excused themselves to find a place to be quiet. They made their fire high above the camp on an overlook that opened onto a view of the vast valley below.

Almost immediately he heard, *"They have called, and you have come. They have asked, and you are the answer,"* it repeated. Swift Fox felt a deep sense of purpose come over him as he came to know this.

"We will stay here," he said. "It is a good place for us."

The observance should have been over for some time, but it had continued while all awaited the decision. As soon as White Smoke and her son came into the clearing, the chanting and drumming stopped.

As Swift Fox spoke the crowd quieted. "This is a fine place to build our nest." The crowd breathed a sigh of relief. Rain took White Smoke to the family shelter to make room for her things. Excited to have her friend stay, she began to tell White Smoke all about each of the families, their strong points, weak points and who had been taken.

Swift Fox talked quietly with his friend, James Little Chief, "The men that have gone after the raiders–how many were there?" A silence fell. All were listening to his words. Swift Fox stopped when he realized that his was the only voice. "I speak out of turn," he said.

"Go on," said one of the men.

"Three, and they have yet to return," Strong Tree answered. Even though still a young man Strong Tree was built like an old white ash that stands tall in the forest.

"We must go after our people," Swift Fox said. "Who will go with me?"

Eagle In The Sun, Strong Tree, Black Hoof and Deer Spirit gathered weapons, mounted their horses and rode off with him.

Deer Spirit, who was an excellent tracker, took the lead. "I still see their path. Look for this," he said pointing to a half curve made by a horse that had a chip out of its hoof.

They rode hard to catch up to the raiders, and within a day they could see the tracks more clearly. Strong Tree, the eldest of the group, and Swift Fox rode together, each feeling the other as a trusted ally.

"There," Strong Tree said pointing ahead to two mounds in the path. One man lay slumped over a rock, blood coming from his neck; the other had a tomahawk wound in his forehead. "Raven and Green River." It sickened him to see the dead men.

"Green River is Deer Spirit's brother," Eagle In The Sun told Swift Fox.

"Raven has made a sign in the dirt," Black Hoof called. "A cross then a circle."

"The pass," Strong Tree answered, "where the opening is through a rock arch. He is telling us where they were headed."

"That is good for us," Black Hoof broke in. "We can cut across up ahead and catch up with them in a day."

"John Birdwing," he said looking everywhere. "They must have taken him," Eagle In The Sun said solemnly.

Angered by his loss, Deer Spirit sped down the trail. The others followed.

The next day they came to where the river flowed through an arch just as in the drawing left by Raven.

"Let's go up that ridge," Swift Fox told Strong Tree. Both climbed up the rocky hill and looked over.

Seeing the flicking of a horse's tail, Strong Tree pointed, "There. We will curve with this side of the river."

Swift Fox and Strong Tree circled till they could see the men clearly. Seven warriors had made their camp by the river. The five men they took as slaves were leaning against a tree, their hands and feet bound, the stolen horses tied nearby. Swift Fox signaled again, and the other men came up beside them.

"They will see us if we try to swim across," Strong Tree observed.

Black Hoof found a large log along the river's edge. "Help me pull this in."

Hiding behind it, they swam toward the camp. Slowly and

carefully, they eased themselves up onto the shore. Swift Fox closed his eyes, and imagined he felt the heat of a fire near his skin, and his body was warmed by it. The others followed, also taking the chill from their bodies.

Through the trees they could see the camp.

"Strong Tree and Eagle In The Sun, you go for their horses," Swift Fox said. "Black Hoof and Deer Spirit come with me."

Strong Tree hid behind a large boulder then silently slipped behind the man who was on watch. Before the raider had a chance to fight back, Strong Tree drew his knife across the thief's neck. Blood gushed from the wound as he was lowered to the ground.

Above the camp were several pines with branches that would make for easy climbing and offer an unfettered view of the area. The three men quickly scrambled to the top. Swift Fox signaled to the men below to let them know they were in place.

Aiming their arrows downward, Strong Spirit and Black Hoof waited for Swift Fox to fire. His arrow shot from above landed directly into the man's back between his shoulder blades, and the man slumped instantly without making a sound. Black Hoof and Deer Spirit left their targets lifeless as well.

That leaves four, Swift Fox thought.

The horses tethered to the trees began to breathe heavily as Strong Tree and Eagle In The Sun untied their leads. When they slapped them to a run, the commotion woke the others, who dove for their weapons.

Eagle In The Sun continued shooting while Deer Spirit and Swift Fox climbed down from their perch. With a tomahawk in his hand, Deer Spirit charged, but was stopped when an arrow landed in his arm. Swift Fox pulled back his bow and shot one shaft after another, allowing Deer Spirit to get behind a rock and yank out the dart. He then took up the bludgeon with his good hand.

One of the raiders lifted his tomahawk to land it in Deer Spirit's chest. Eagle In The Sun galloped into the camp, charging with his spear readied, and threw it, stopping the marauder in mid-swing. As he fell to the ground, the man looked in shock at the pole protruding from his stomach.

Strong Tree rode up behind one of the two remaining men who, while reaching for the knife in his belt, began to turn. But he was too late, for with a hard downward blow, Strong Tree rammed his knife into the man's back.

Swift Fox caught the arm of another man whose knife blade was inches from his neck. Black Hoof jumped on the man's back, knocking him away. The two men struggled till Black Hoof took him to the ground. Four men stood above the marauder with arrows cocked pointing at his heart. Black Hoof pulled the man's head back by his hair and pushed his knife to the man's throat, ready to end his life.

"No!" Swift Fox called.

"Let me kill him," he said pressing his knife harder, a red line forming at the blade. "He would have done the same to you."

"That is enough killing," Swift Fox said. He dropped deep into The Awareness then told the thief, "You tell your chief that he may hunt for food here, but that is all. We are no longer his prey. Now you had better go before these men tear you to bits." Reluctantly, Black Hoof let the man up, and the bandit ran away as fast as he could.

That evening, with the band surrounding the campfire, they told everyone the story of their fight.

The next day while the council met once again to discuss the choosing of their new chief, Deer Spirit and Rain came to where Swift Fox was sharpening his knife.

"You are very young, but you are a very brave man. We honor your strength and prowess," he told him.

"You would have done the same," he answered offhandedly. "What conclusion did the council come to?"

"Swift Fox," Rain interrupted, "we have talked much, and all of us agree. You are not only a brave and strong warrior, but a compassionate man as well. You make decisions quickly, and are not afraid to speak your mind. With your skills, we think you would be a fine chief."

The small collective had gathered around him and hooted their agreement.

"What about Eagle Hunter?" Swift Fox asked.

"My husband is a fine man and a good hunter, but he is not a leader," Rain offered.

It was not a surprise to either Swift Fox or his mother. The day before, while he was in meditation, Swift Fox had felt the mantle of responsibility fall on his shoulders. He was not sure what that would mean, and though they had not spoken of it to each other, his mother knew this, too.

"I am honored at your request," Swift Fox answered. "But I am too young, and do not know this land or your people. I think Deer Spirit knows all of you and this mountain. He should be chief, and if he will have me I can be second in command."

White Smoke was always proud of her son, but this day, she wished that Cougar Two Foot could have been here to witness their son's wise choice.

45

Deep snow blanketed the trail. Pine boughs hung with giant frozen crystals glimmering in the light of the stars.

Holding tightly to its neck, Jahn rode a huge buck that had a full rack of clear, amber colored antlers. While the animal foraged, it shook the snow off its back, nearly sending Jahn into a snow bank.

An Indian boy with bright blue eyes that shone in the dark and hair that burned with fire, illuminating the snow-covered trees, stepped into sight. He drew an enormous diamond-tipped arrow that gleamed in the moonlight, but then changed his mind and loosened his bow. And even though it seems it had been the boy's intended kill, the buck was not afraid of him.

Attached to a blue leather strap, floating above the boy's chest was a gigantic silver cross. Jahn reached out for it, but the boy grabbed the necklace away from him, and Jahn woke with a start.

46

"I will leave now to join Bear and Elk Horn. Rain says you may stay with them until I return if you like." She promised Swift Fox she would come back by the time the young bucks grew their antlers. The next morning she packed up her things and rode back over the trail. The sun shone like a fire in the sky, and she marveled at the beauty of the vista before her, the place where she had felt her son, Jahn.

"*I am coming for you,*" she told him again.

On the third day she entered Brother Joseph's Trading Company once again.

"Hell's fire, I did not think I would see you again so soon," he replied.

"How is your friend feeling?" she asked.

"Mighty fine, ma'am, mighty fine. Thank you for asking."

"Bear or Elk Horn, have you seen them?"

"You might have missed 'em, ma'am. They had expected you back last week. They came in yesterday for grub 'n' provisions sayin' they was takin' off this mornin'. You might check at the hotel though, see if they're still there."

The hotel clerk looked at his book. "The man with the

scar, you say? Naw, he's still here. He was going to check out, but said he was expectin' some woman to show up and was only waitin' one more day." He looked up at her, "That be you, miss?" White Smoke was already out the door.

Through the glass of the saloon window she saw Bear and Elk Horn, who had been drinking heavily and were now deep into telling stories of their expeditions. She decided to wait till morning to let the men know she was here. She walked back to the Trading Company, and asked Joseph if she might sleep on the mat in the back of his store.

"Make yourself at home. Water's in the jug and I can bring you something to eat if you like."

"I would like that, thank you," she said.

He disappeared for a few minutes, and came back with a bowl of thick soup and some bread.

"I am goin' to lock up now. You can get out through the back if you need to. No one knows it, but the lock on that door is broken. Been meanin' to have it fixed," he laughed. "Be back at dawn to open up. Good night now."

The next morning before the sun had come up, she stood outside the saloon eating jerky, waiting for her companions.

"Ay, there you are. We have been waiting for you for more than a week," Bear murmured sleepily. "Almost gave up on you."

Elk Horn was equally hung over. "Let's get something to eat first. You coming in?"

"No," she said not wanting to cause a commotion inside. "I will wait for you here."

Feeling more like himself, Bear patted his stomach and stretched as he came out of the eatery.

"Here's somethin' for you," he said handing her several slices of squash bread and a piece of elk. "You really are

Ginny Van Andusson?" he asked.

"I was once," she told him taking a bite of her savory meal. "How far are you going?"

"I would say we split ways at Fort Lyon. That about right, Elk Horn?" The Indian agreed. "Not one for talkin'," he said indicating Elk Horn, "but he is as loyal a friend as anyone could have."

The three mounted their horses, pulled their mules and headed toward Fort Garland.

47

After a long day, they stopped to rest, but there were still many miles to cover before she would get to the fort. White Smoke fought hard to keep herself calm, but anticipation of seeing Jahn after all these years pulled her in so many directions she could hardly contain her emotions.

Once again Bear began to tell the story of how Jahn and Elk Horn saved him from drowning in the icy river. *Is this the third or fourth time,* she wondered? With each telling the story got more fantastic. *Soon Jahn will be walking on water,* she thought. Elk Horn gave her a knowing smile.

"He is a good man, that Jahn. Like him quite a bit," Bear commented.

White Smoke enjoyed his command of her tribe's dialect, but what she truly relished was hearing about her son.

"Elk Horn, how did you and Jahn meet?" she asked hoping to learn more about him.

Bear explained how Jahn had come into the saloon and had been wound up by the story of a white woman living with natives that he had been telling. "He thought it might be you, ma'am," Bear concluded.

"Do you have any family, Elk Horn?" she asked, raising her hand to stop Bear from interrupting.

"Gone," Elk Horn said. "Bear is my only kin."

"A deep wound for you," she said to him.

Elk Horn said, "They are with me in the rustle of the leaves, the splash of the river, in the play of wolf cubs on snow." He stopped for moment thinking of them then added, "Bear is good family."

"We are brothers, indeed," Bear said lifting the bottle of whiskey to his lips and before handing it off to Elk Horn asked, "You want a swallow, ma'am?"

"Not right now," she said lying down to rest. She noticed Elk Horn's eyes betrayed him as they glistened with unshed tears.

When Elk Horn went into the woods to relieve himself, Bear came over to her. "A ways back he had a bit of bad luck," he whispered loudly. "Two wives and three children all killed by soldiers. He was not there to take care of them. After that he went wanderin' in the mountains by his lonesome for 'bout ten years. I told him he should come hunt with me. Been doin' so ever since."

Finally, the cabin was only an hour or so away. "The sky is filled with dark thunder," Elk Horn said pointing to the east where they were headed. They picked up the pace and reached the shelter just as the rain started pelting them once again. The little building tucked deep into the woods was a welcome sight for all. But for White Smoke it was almost impossible to comprehend that Jahn had slept there.

"The three of us have stayed here together a couple of times. He is just about too tall for the bunks," Bear laughed, unhitching his horse and lifting the gear from his mules. He pulled one of the boards that had come loose from the makeshift barn roof and hammered it back in place with a stone, while Elk Horn got the fire going in the stove. Too excited to eat, White Smoke took only a mouthful of the dried meat she had brought with her, foregoing the strong smelling soup the men offered. After dinner Bear went out to find more dry wood.

"The lieutenant has missed his mother very much," Elk Horn began. "Looks for her everywhere." White Smoke felt a pull on her heart. "He is a pup with an injured paw. Will bite if you get too close, but longs for relief from the pain." Then he said, "He will do the same with you, even though you are the person he has been searching for all his life. And he looks for a woman with auburn colored hair. He will be surprised to see that it is white."

Bear kicked open the door, his arms full of dry wood. "This ought to keep us warm through the night," he said. "If the weather holds, you should be lookin' into your son's eyes in a couple of days. You must be excited as a cat chasing a mouse to be seein' both your sons."

"Have you seen his brother yet?" Elk Horn asked. "Richard, is it? Jahn says he still lives at the old place."

"At Silver Leaf? No, I have not," she said surprised to know he was still at the property. "And my daughter, Holly?"

"I am sorry, ma'am." Bear shook his head. "I thought I told you."

"No." Her heart sank. "It seems very much like a dream that I will be seeing Jahn and Richard again. Jahn was only ten years old when I was taken, Richard, fifteen. Holly. How old was Holly?" She hesitated. "Three years younger than Jahn. James was just a baby," she sighed. "Richard and Jahn, they are grown men now."

White Smoke tried to imagine what Jahn would look like. As a child he was slight and a bit scrawny. Now as a thirty-year old man he would have filled out. *And Richard. Is he broad-shouldered and tall like his father, or is he short and stocky like my side of the family?*

"What does Jahn look like?"

"Dutch?" he said distracted by his own thoughts. "Oh, he's about my height, tall like me. Lanky though. His hair is the color of a chestnut bay. Nice looking man by a woman's standard. He can be a bit stiff, but he is a man you can count on."

'Dutch' was what people used to call her husband.

"Hey, Dutch," the men would call out to Garritt. "Are you going to play cards with us tonight?"

"Only if I win," he would tease back. "You boys coming to church on Sunday?"

"Only if you win," they laughed.

Garritt would not play, and they would not come, but the good-natured jesting went back and forth often. When they needed Garritt for a birth, a wedding or a funeral, he was right there.

The three all settled down for the night. White Smoke pulled the blanket tightly around her face and closed her eyes, but sleeping was not easy for her. The closer they got to Fort Garland, the more restless she became.

All day the deluge of rain had been coming down so hard that you could hardly see a tree through it. After days of rain, the ground was so soggy that the horses fought for a foothold. What had started as a trickle of water across the road had become a raging torrent, making the way impassable.

"Come on, my friends," Bear said pulling the reigns sharply to the left, "Let us go up a bit higher and see if these rivers are less formidable and the road clearer," he said, laughing his wry laugh.

Even in this mess he can keep his mood bright, White Smoke thought.

The mountainside shot straight up. Mules, being smaller and closer to the ground, had an easier time getting up the hill. But the horses panted hard, struggling for purchase on the muddy, crumbling rocks. After much effort they finally reached the top of the cliff.

"Phew!" Bear guffawed jumping off his horse. "Surely did not think we would make that hill."

He took hold of White Smoke's bridle and held her horse while she dismounted.

Elk Horn stood on a boulder to look down into the ravine they had just traversed.

"Looks worse from here than from down there looking up."

They had been riding since daybreak, and it had been a long day when the three stopped to make camp. The grassy slope next to the trail was perfect for their animals to feed, and a thick grove of Juniper trees kept them from feeling the cold evening wind. Elk Horn and Bear walked deeper into the woods to scout up dinner, while White Smoke went to gather wood. It was not easy, but she did get a roaring fire going and heated up some coffee.

"You all by yourself, squaw?"

White Smoke jolted, swung around. Two white men on horseback, neither one a hunter or trapper, ambled up the trail. Both men were dressed in over-worn, cast-off army clothing. One was beefy with wiry unkempt red hair, while the other was skinny and tall.

"Lordy, what have we got here? Look at that, Red. She's a white. Bet there's a big reward for her return. How much do you think she's worth?"

White Smoke picked up a thick stick to defend herself.

"Now lady, we don't want no one to get hurt. You go ahead 'n' put that stick down."

The skinny one pulled a handgun from his belt and pointed it at her chest. "He said put it down."

White Smoke dropped the wood at her feet. She was afraid to call out for fear these men might kill Bear and Elk Horn, so she said nothing, but scanned the forest for signs of their return.

Red took the rope from around his saddle horn and threw it to his partner.

"We'll take some of that coffee you just made, and then you'll be coming with us, miss. Don't bother with no funny stuff. That Injun and the trapper was way over the hill when last we saw. Make it tight, Clem. She's just Indian enough to get out of a knot."

"I is Clem and this here is Red. Now tell us your name, miss," said Clem.

White Smoke was silent.

"What is your name?" This time the man called Red pulled his gun, and pointed it at her head.

"White Smoke," she said in her tribe's language.

"Your English name foolish woman!" he yelled.

"My name is White Smoke."

"She don't speak English no more or what?" Clem asked.

"Don't matter. Someone will be lookin' for her, and I will be gettin' the money for it."

"No one is looking for me anymore," she said in English. "It has been twenty years since I was taken. My family is dead, and by now my friends will have forgotten me."

"Hey," the skinny one said. "She do speak English."

"That's what you say. I imagine there is a handsome reward for you. Always is when a white woman is returned. Not that they always like gettin' home again, but that is not my problem," Red laughed.

The men drank the coffee then gathered the horses and mules. Dizzy with this unexpected event, she could not think what to do. Against her will, Red put her on a horse, and she headed back to Steamboat Springs.

Off in the distance, the sound of singing from a church service wafted through the woods. Ginny remembered her family attending her husband's church, and her young children getting fidgety in the pews as their father gave his impassioned sermon.

"Why don't we take her there, Red?"

"Out here? Not a big enough church." He turned to Ginny. "The larger the church the more reward they has to give. Don't matter if you even be from that church. They just pays out." His laughter rang out like a jagged saw.

After a couple of hours, they stopped to rest and warm up over a fire.

"Now, miss," Red told her, "we might as well be friendly since we have a couple of days ride to Steamboat Springs. Tell me your English name." Red took a bite of the hardtack he had in his saddlebag. He threw her a biscuit, then handed her a cup of coffee.

"Now, now, don't you be throwin' that at me or Clem neither, unless you want a heavy beatin'."

"Knowing my name will not do you any good now," she

said. "No one is looking for me."

Blood red streaked the evening sky. By nightfall, they had travelled far enough that White Smoke was concerned that her companions would not be able to find her, if they had come looking. She was so close to finding her son, and now this. And what of Swift Fox. She may never see him again. It felt like a knife pushed deep into her heart. She tried to settle her mind, but it would not behave.

Gone several hours, Bear and Elk Horn had walked the trail back to their camp, but when they got there they saw the horses and mules were gone and so was White Smoke.

"What the hell?" Bear began, seeing the coffee was drained and the fire had gone out.

"She wouldn't go anywhere voluntarily without that," Elk Horn said pointing to her medicine bag that still lay on the ground near the fire. "Two horses coming in this way, and five leaving," Elk Horn indicated.

"Bounty hunters, most likely. They can't be far ahead," Bear said.

"You stay here in case she comes back. I will go." Elk Horn took off down the trail running as fast as he could. He did not want White Smoke to get too far away or he might never find her.

He ran until it was so dark he could hardly see the road. His lungs bursting and his muscles crying out, he stopped for the night. He tried to sleep, but only tossed and turned fitfully, memories of the loss of his wives and children playing out in his dreams. At first light, he was back looking for the trail.

They rode on for most of the day. All the while White Smoke was looking for a way to flee. When nothing presented itself, she began to feel like she was falling down into a deep unclimbable ravine.

Ahead was a platoon of soldiers who had stopped at a stream bank, their horses taking water. The soldiers looked fatigued and ill, some had rags wrapped around their feet to keep them warm against the slushy rain soaked snow, and most had scarves tied over their hats and around their chins. All were miserably soaked to the bone.

As they rode to the front, she looked at every soldier's face hoping to find her son.

While Red went to the captain, White Smoke leaned over toward one of the soldiers. "You know Jahn Van Andusson?"

"Yeah," he said warily.

"Is he here?" she asked.

"Back at the fort," he answered. "This lady knows Van Andusson," he said jabbing his buddy in the arm.

"What are you doing there, miss?" Clem yanked on the reins of her horse. "You keep to yourself now."

"What's goin' on here, Captain?" Red turned to the man in charge.

The Captain explained that his squadron was killing off renegades who had been plundering farms and ranches. The truth was that most had merely been hunting food.

"Who might that be?" the soldier asked Red, pointing to White Smoke.

"White woman. Been with Indians for years. Returnin' her home."

Their pace was measured because the horses were tired

out and the men more so. They had been going for many weeks, and it had been nothing but wet and cold. Supply wagons had been bogged down by the weather, and had not gotten to them, so the men were hungry as well.

"You mind if we ride along for a bit?"

"Suit yourself," the weary Captain answered.

Elk Horn finally caught up to where the soldiers had stopped for the night. He kept out of sight.

But he was not alone. One of the army's Indian scouts saw him. Throwing his body off his horse, he knocked Elk Horn to the ground. They fought knife to knife, till each knocked the weapon out of the other's hand. Bare-fisted punches landed strongly on both sides. But the scout was young and strong, and his blows landed well, making Elk Horn's mind swim. At first, he could not get his bearings, and he got a bad slash across his arm. But his years had taught him to be aware of all that was around him so when the younger man charged he ducked to one side of an old pine. The scout turned, and Elk Horn pushed him hard against the tree trunk, impaling him in the back on a broken limb.

While the platoon slept, Elk Horn sneaked down the hill to where the animals were tied. Carefully and quietly he unleashed their horses and mules, and took them back into the woods.

In the morning, Red and Clem awoke to find the animals gone. "Who's the son of a bitch who let our horses loose, and the mules where are they?" Red called out. "Clem, go see if they are up ahead."

Clem ran looking for them amongst the ones tied to the line. When he came back empty handed, Red blamed him for not tying the steeds tight enough, and told him to go looking for them. White Smoke looked furtively for any sign of Bear and Elk Horn.

The platoon saddled up then went on its way, leaving White Smoke and Red alone on the road.

Meanwhile, Clem's horse slipped and slid making its way up the muddy bank. Over a nearby hill, Clem found the missing animals tied to a branch. He pulled his rifle out of its holster and cocked it. Elk Horn had climbed a tree, and waited till Clem rode under him. When he passed, Elk Horn jumped down knocking him off his horse, but Clem was quicker than Elk Horn expected, and he pulled his gun, firing it, hitting Elk Horn, who dropped to the ground clutching his side. The bullet had gone through cleanly. And though the pain was excruciating, he did not lose consciousness.

Clem untied the horses and began down the hill. Elk Horn pulled his knife and with all his might threw it at the man's back, hitting him squarely between the shoulder blades. Clem dropped to the ground and did not move again.

Elk Horn found some moss, made it into a ball and packed it into the bullet hole. He wrapped his belt tightly around his waist over the wound then tied the slash on his arm with his kerchief. He retrieved his knife and went down the hill toward Red and White Smoke.

After a while Red became impatient. "Now where is he? Those horses couldn't have gotten that far in the night." Finally he said, "I am not waiting any longer. Looks like you'll be walking, miss," Red said pulling on the rope at her wrists then winding it around his saddle horn. "Clem will just have to find us. Besides, more money for me if I don't have to split your dowry with him," he laughed and clucked his horse up the road, pulling her along behind him.

Filled with adrenalin, Elk Horn ran down the long hill, jumping over fallen branches and around tree trunks, diving onto Red, pulling him off his mount, taking his rifle and pistol. He threw himself up onto the horse then pulled White Smoke up behind him.

"You better catch up to that patrol or you will be walking a long way by yourself," Elk Horn said. "No need to look for your friend. He will not be returning." Red hesitated. "Go!" Elk Horn said pointing the rifle at Red's face.

Red ran up the road, not knowing if he would be able to catch up with the patrol, but feeling it was the better option than waiting to see if the Indian was going to let him live or not.

"You are hurt," White Smoke said.

"It is nothing. No time to stop now," Elk Horn grunted.

They gathered the horses and mules. After a full day of riding without stopping, they arrived back to where Bear was waiting. The storm had gotten worse and both were wet to the bone.

"Glad to see you, miss. Elk Horn, You all right? You look—"

Elk Horn, whose skin was the color of fire ash, slowly collapsed and fell from his horse.

"He's been shot," she said, "but he would not let me tend to it." White Smoke had known from the smell coming from the injury that the bullet had not only perforated his side, but had nicked his large intestine, which was putrefying inside the wound. She also knew no amount of encouragement was going to make the sickness leave to find a new home. Even so she got her medicine bag, and began to work her healing. White Smoke sang a healing chant for Elk Horn, and then one for Bear, to sooth his anguished soul.

Later that night, Elk Horn began talking with the tongue of the poisonous snake that filled his body. When his fever climbed during the night, she knew that it was only a matter of time.

Bear unable to be still, paced and drank whiskey till he finally dropped off to sleep. When Bear woke in the morning, Elk Horn had already passed.

White Smoke told Bear of Elk Horn's last words, "'He has been a good friend. Tell him he has been a good friend to this Indian.' He wanted you to know."

As the sky finally cleared, they found a small cave where they placed his body, covering it with rocks. She sang a chant. Then they packed up the horses and mules and continued on with their journey.

48

Bear had kept Elk Horn's knife, his bow and his sheath of arrows, and added the carved talisman of an elk antler that his friend had worn around his neck to his own necklace holding the Zuni pendant, the silver bear with a star on his back. Now he was feeling the loss of his friend acutely as if there were a gaping hole that he fell into and was tumbling downward forever, never hitting bottom. Telling and retelling the stories of their exploits seemed to help him weather this grief.

"I know he did not say much, but I do like to talk, and well, he was a good listener. He understood me like no other," he smiled then looked away. "You know we don't owe nothin' to anybody," he said. "Lotta men owe the company where they buys their gear. We always paid outright," he rambled on. "Best money was for beavers, but they's hunted out now, even so we have managed to put away a little money. Been talking of openin' The Bear 'n' Elk Saloon near Fort Garland: Plenty of travelers and army folk coming through there. Could make good money. Don't guess he would mind if I used it for that." He went on without stopping, telling her of Sylvia Waters. "She's a pretty little thing, real curly hair and dark brown eyes. I could not keep from lookin' at her from the moment she walked into the saloon." And how he wanted to get married and have children, how Sylvia could help him with the saloon and not have to pleasure men anymore. He was thinking that he would like to be called his given name, Myron. Then he was unusually quiet in a reverie.

But to White Smoke the air felt fresh. The warming sun broke through the clouds once again, streaming through the leaves, speckling a playful pattern on the ground. The birds were singing, and all felt calm except for her heart, which seemed to swell to bursting at the thought of seeing her son.

"You have been married, ma'am," Bear broke into her memories.

"Yes, twice," she stated matter-of-factly, but not sure why he was asking.

"I have known many women. One at every camp and fort," he said boasting slightly. "Well, ma'am, I was just wonderin'…I have spent a good deal of time sleepin' out under the stars, in tents and tipis, climbin' mountain trails, huntin' for bear, deer, elk and sheep," he said. "I guess what I am gettin' at is that, well, it has been a very long time since I resided indoors all the time, and never have lived with a woman."

"Oh, I see." White Smoke said, amused at his concern. "You will be warm and dry," she laughed. "But that is not what you are asking me is it, Myron? Perhaps it is best to ask the lady what she wants from you. You need to tell her what you would like as well. It is a partnership, Myron, an equal sharing," she said knowing that most marriages were anything but that.

"Do you mind my askin'? Your two husbands, were they

the same kind of man?"

"Yes and no," she replied. "Both men felt deeply about what they believed in. Both were exceedingly kind to me, and were good and loving fathers to their children. Cougar Two Foot was reserved, talked quietly, and made his judgments after much thought. Garritt, Jahn's father, made up his mind quickly. He wanted to be fair, but sometimes he acted without foreseeing the consequences, if you know what I mean. They lived their lives differently. You can understand that?"

She clucked her horse to go over a fallen branch. "You spend some time with your girl and find out what kind of person she is. She will find she is a lucky woman to have you as a husband."

"Thank you, ma'am. Your words mean a lot to me." They rode in silence for a long time. Then Bear decided, "We will make camp here. If we get an early start, we might make the fort by sundown. I know you would like that."

She prayed that Jahn had not gone on patrol before she could get there.

"There she is!" Bear called. The fort stood ahead, its walls glowing orange in the setting sun. White Smoke wanted to gallop straight to the gate, but she knew that the approach to Jahn would have to be more circumspect than a full buffalo stampede.

"Ask the officer on duty, and he will tell you where Jahn is. I will go to the tradin' post to unload my pelts. After that, you can find me at Jessie's Place in town or at the hotel," he said as he pulled his mules down the path toward the gate. "Good luck, Ginny."

"Thank you for all your help," she said.

"My pleasure, ma'am."

White Smoke hitched her horse to the post and looked for the guard on duty, who stood above the entrance looking down at her. She asked to see Jahn Van Andusson.

"He ain't here," the guard said testily.

She told him she would wait, and stood in the courtyard looking up at him, like a vulture waiting for an animal to die. The guard shifted from foot to foot, wishing he could run from her scrutiny.

49

Within the hour, Lieutenant Jahn Van Andusson bounded up the steps, stood next to Jacob, the guard on duty, and looked down at the woman staring up at him from the compound square.

Ginny's heart nearly stopped when she saw him, because she would have known him anywhere. He was a combination of her looks and his father's.

Jahn noticed that her buckskin dress and moccasins were generously decorated with colorful beads and quills, and her white hair, cropped unevenly to the shoulder, shone like a brilliant beacon in the setting sun. Like most of the Indians, the skin on her face was weathered and brown. He thought her to be nearly sixty.

"Who is that?" he asked.

The guard shrugged. "Been askin' for you. Been there maybe an hour. Staring up here the whole time. Damn unsettling."

"What does she want?" Jahn asked. "They always want something," he sniped under his breath. The guard shrugged again. But Jahn could not take his eyes off her.

"Lookin' for you. Didn't say why. Don't think she's dangerous though," he smirked.

"No, but with them you never can be sure," Jahn said. "She must want something," he said again under his breath. Finally he yelled down to her, "You down there. You have pelts to trade or you want blankets? Trading post is down that way," he pointed. "Food? Go to the commissary."

He went back into the barracks, slamming the door behind him. But the urge to see the woman in the yard overtook his reservations, and he burst through the door again, leaning over the railing, yelling, "What is it that you want? Make it quick. I am not in the mood to linger here."

Ginny, choked with excitement, struggled to hold her feelings in check. "Jahn Van Andusson," she snorted gruffly. Her English was sure, but carried a thick accent.

"What do you want with the lieutenant?" the guard barked.

"Come down here," she said to Jahn. She held back a knowing smile, her eyes squinting in the bright evening sun. "Come down so we can talk," she stated again. "You will want to hear what I have to tell you."

"I wouldn't be so sure of that," he shouted.

"You were ten when he took me," she said.

"How do you know how old I am?"

"I know, Jahn, because my name then was Ginny," she hesitated knowing that the truth would be jarring, but then said, "Virginia Van Andusson." She stared at him with her now somewhat grayed cornflower blue eyes watching as he grappled with this truth. The lieutenant nearly fell over the railing. Catching himself, he adjusted his hat.

"Ginny Van... Can't be. She is dead. Stop playing with me. What do you want?" he said snarling at her, this time feeling aggravated and angry. "Everyone around here knows my mother's name was Virginia Van Andusson. You heard it somewhere, and you want something now. What is it? Tell me or go away and leave me be!"

She said slowly and with great assurance, "My name is Ginny Van Andusson, Jahn. I am your mother."

No, he screamed to himself, *she is not my mother!* He looked at her intensely. "My mother is dead!" And his jaw clamped tightly shut. That inner demon that rested in his chest lifted its snarling head once more. Jahn grabbed the railing to keep himself from collapsing.

"Old woman, do you hear me? Do not try to pass yourself off as her. My mother is dead! She died twenty years ago. Twenty years ago! I have looked for her for all that time, and never once have I seen anything that would indicate to me that she is alive."

Jahn was so enraged that he ran down the steps toward her ready to strike or strangle, he had not decided which. He stormed toward her looking intently at the woman standing before him.

"Where did you come from?" he barked.

But when he got closer to her, his stomach twisted. *No, it cannot be*, he said to himself. *She is dead. Is she not?* He was so inexplicably drawn toward her that if he had wanted to back away, he would not have been able to do so. He stared at her finally allowing himself to see what had caused him so much consternation: the shape of his nose, the color of his cornflower blue eyes, even the line of his eyebrows, all were just like those of this woman.

All these years he had asked about her everywhere, searching through the mountains for clues, following stories of white women living with Indians only to be disappointed over and over. There had been no signs. Nothing. None. Only his intense perseverance kept him going. And only very recently had he been able to stop looking. Now welling up inside him were feelings of shame and fear.

She stood in silence letting him take in what he had heard. A quiet intake of breath and a slight lean forward were the only indications of her immense interest in his response. Her face held a small smile, as she knew that this information would be a shock from which he would need to recover.

He calmed himself. *I certainly do not know this woman*, he thought. "Go on now. Leave me be," he growled tiredly. "If you want to trade, you know where to go." And he turned back to the barracks.

He could not know how fast her heart was beating from seeing her son for the first time in twenty years. She had thought all her family had been killed, and now she was facing her own, if reluctant, child. She longed to take him in her arms, but the smoke had told her he would resist, and he would need time to adjust to the verity of this information.

"Listen to me, and I will tell you everything I remember about that day." She looked at him solemnly. "We shall go somewhere alone," she stated.

Her tone was commanding and intense, and her movements harsh and sharp. Her demeanor was not that of someone he would trust and certainly not of the mother he remembered.

"That day?" Jahn asked testily.

"The day I saw James and Pa killed, Jahn," she said.

"Lieutenant Van Andusson to you," he said harshly continuing to ignore her request. Not ready to accept what he had just seen, he yelled at her, "I am not your son! Whoever you are, it is a cruel joke coming to me like this! Everyone knows about that day, at least everyone on the mountain near Silver Leaf Ranch! Go back where you came from."

"Jahn, let me speak with you alone," she said waiting for him to erupt.

He could hardly contain his fierce rage. Then the woman standing in the courtyard began to sing slowly and quietly as if it were a lullaby:

> *Come, Thou Fount of every blessing,*
> *Tune my heart to sing Thy grace,*
> *Streams of mercy, never ceasing,*
> *Call for songs of loudest praise…*

The sound of her voice singing that hymn stung Jahn straight to his heart. *Why that one*, he said to himself feeling the whole of his life having been held by the incidents of that terrible day? He interrupted her and barked, "Why do you sing that song? How do you know that hymn?"

"The same way you do. Remember? We sang it before Sunday dinner. Your Pa liked it. His voice was a bit tuneless, but we covered his sour notes with all the love we had in our family. Now we shall go somewhere private to talk," she said with finality in a tone that made him want to obey.

His feelings jumbled like the swirling of leaves in a mountain windstorm. He wanted to run, bolt from this woman and the memories of his tormenting nightmare: the hooting of the marauders, his father falling with arrows in his chest, the screams of his brother–and his mother. He felt lightheaded, and he could not make his thoughts come out in words. The only thing he had found after the raid was one of the hair combs that he and his siblings had given her on her birthday. He gritted his jaw closed in an attempt to keep all the memories at bay.

"Wait here," he said and he went inside a door. *How could this old woman be my mother*, he thought. And yet there was something about her that felt so familiar.

He opened the door and stepped back out into the sun.

"All right," he said not able to say no to her anymore. "We can go to my quarters. Follow me."

Jahn led her to the building that housed his room. It was quite unusual for him to have anyone come into where he lived. Even his friends knew to wait for him to come out before trying to engage him in any way.

The room was small, but extraordinarily tidy, everything in its place, and nothing extra. *His life, whatever it was, was lived outside of this place*, she said to herself.

She looked around the room, and took a seat on a chair by the dresser. But Jahn did not know what to do. Like a bird looking for a place to rest, he went this way and that, and could not find a spot to land. She waited. When he finally sat on the chair behind the desk, she began to describe what their life had been on the mountain on Silver Leaf Ranch. Even though her tone became more like the mother Jahn remembered, he still fought with himself over whether to believe her. He had spent so much time wondering if she was alive and worrying she might be dead, that to have her actually in front of him was beyond his comprehension.

Searching for the English words, she began, "It was a beautiful spot for a house. Overlooking a meadow, it sat on a knoll with a creek down the hill. The land needed little clearing, with only clump of big pine trees around the side of the house and a stand of aspens fifty feet away in the front," she told Jahn watching his every response for a sign of recognition. "A deer path ran right through the front yard going toward the river. We had a garden fence tall enough to keep critters out, and had ample wildlife to eat even during the winter. A very different life from where we lived down at the edge of the mountains," she said forgetting for a moment that Jahn had lived there, too. "Garritt and Richard built the house for us to live in," she continued. "We had a big room with cubbyholes for your sleeping mats, and an alcove for our bed with curtains for privacy from the main room. Your father fashioned a rocking chair out of saplings from the trees out front. That rocker had a peculiar wobble, but you babies did not mind. You went to sleep without a fuss even with the chair's lurching. You were easy children to raise."

Jahn felt himself fall back into his childhood, into the life before the raid when he was happy and carefree, when he, his brothers and little sister played in the woods, and when on many warm days he lay on the ground watching the silver-backed leaves of the aspen trees shimmer in a summer breeze.

"Your father and Richard had dug a cold cellar." *If they just could have hidden down with the jars of jams, salted meats and potatoes*, she thought, but they had been caught unaware. "It was a beautiful, warm summer day with the grasses already yellowed from the heat. I was hanging laundry," she pressed on hoping Jahn would respond. "You young'uns were playing in the house. Garritt had just fixed the latch on the garden fence for the third time, and went into the house to get James and go down to the lake to fish. But terrible high-pitched yelps broke into our peaceful existence with The Red Wing's raiding party swarming over the property.

As he ran back to get his gun, your Pa yelled for James to get into the house. Running up the stairs, James tripped over his fishing pole, and began screaming at the top of his lungs.

An arrow missed your Pa, hitting James in the throat. Another went into his small head. Then three arrows pulled your father down.

I was devastated. My little boy and my husband lay on the ground murdered. I tried to get to the house, but The Red Wing grabbed me by my hair. I swung my fists, but was not able to loose myself from his grip. He took me away, Jahn. He took me away from you."

The memory of those days filled Ginny's mind: Her hands tied at the wrists, exhausted and hungry, her eyes barely open from the beatings The Red Wing had given her after she had tried to escape. Ginny had walked behind his horse for hours. Then they met three trappers.

"Well, looks like you have had good huntin', said The Red Wing,. And who would that lovely lady be for?" asked the trapper who kept his head shaved clean so no Indian would try for his scalp.

The Red Wing pulled on her rope, making her trip over roots on the trail. "She's for my brother's family."

"She be mighty pretty," one of the other trappers whispered implying what his interest would be.

"Got a lot of spirit, looks like," another man said eyeing her all over.

"What'll you take for her?" the bald trapper asked.

The Red Wing weighed his options. This woman had been nothing but difficult, refusing to eat, running away at every turn. He was not sure he wanted to pass that on to his brother.

"What will you give me for her?" he said.

The three talked then the bald one answered, "How about a blanket?"

The Red Wing pulled on the rope and his horse started forward.

"Now hold on, maybe I can sweeten the deal." He and his two

comrades put their heads together again. "How about two blankets?"

"Show me," The Red Wing said. The men brought forward the barter. "And a rifle and a sack of shot and powder," he added.

"You ask a lot," the bald man hesitated, "but ok," and he handed him the gun and the ammunition.

The bald trapper yanked Ginny to the side of his horse. "Come on up here, you pretty thing. You are ours now." And he pulled her up behind him.

But she did not tell her son all that had happened. She did not say that that night the three men drank whiskey and boasted to each other about how easy it was to procure this pleasure. Each man had his turn, and finally after enough whiskey they fell asleep. Her clothing was torn and her body ravaged. She knew that this was what she had to look forward to until they tired of her and either sold her or killed her.

With her captors heavily asleep, she saw an opportunity to escape. She began to inch her way toward the knife in the bald man's sheath he had at his waist, but he snorted and turned over onto his side covering the weapon. Very careful not to wake the dogs, she moved through the door and slipped into the woods.

"When I was far enough away from the camp not to be heard, I ran as fast as I could, but fell into a ravine injuring my hip and shoulder," she explained. "That is when the People of the Mountain found me. After that I did not remember anything for a very long time."

Jahn noticed the ring on her finger.

"Where did you get that ring?"

"My teacher gave it to me at a special time many years ago."

Jahn felt a sickening recognition come over him.

"Turn around," Jahn said.

"Why?"

"Please."

Ginny turned and as she did she ran her hand through her hair, and he saw once again that cluster of women, the one who had white hair, and the man who had stopped him.

"I have heard about you after all, and in fact, I may have actually seen you. Though I refused to believe them, everyone had told me you were dead," he said dropping into the chair. He felt ashamed that he had ultimately given up on her when she had been alive all the while. She seemed to understand his thoughts.

"Now do not blame yourself, Jahn," she said. "How were you to know? I did not know you were alive, and if I saw you I may not have known who you were. At that time I did not remember much of what happened that day or even my life before the raid."

Jahn said looking off into his past, "I thought if I joined the cavalry I would have a better chance of finding you."

He shook his head, then put his face in his hands and began to weep. He felt ten years old again. His mother stood near, not knowing whether to hold her son or let him be. After he calmed down, they talked into the night.

"Write this down," she had suggested. It would give him a chance to digest what he was hearing, and then Richard could read it as well. Before she got up to go back to make her campsite with the villagers living outside the fort gate, she told him, "You will take me to Silver Leaf. We will go tomorrow. Sleep well, Jahn." Just the sound of his name coming from her mouth felt strange but comforting.

The uncovering of ancient wounds and the reuniting of souls torn apart exhausted both Ginny and her son. The healing would take time, but as a shaman she had learned to be patient. A time of mending was before each of them, and she was grateful.

Ginny came back in the morning and knocked on her son's door. He had not slept well, and had gotten up early to read the pages that he had written the night before. There were so many questions he wanted answered; at the same time, the comforting embrace from his mother would have meant the world to him, but he could not ask for it.

Ginny had recounted to Jahn how she had met Bear and Elk Horn, and that she had grown to admire the two men.

"You met them? How extraordinary!"

"Bear talks a lot," she stated. "His stories get larger and more exciting with each telling." They both laughed at this. Then she told him of Elk Horn's demise. "Elk Horn was a brave and loyal man. He saved my life. By the way, Bear told me he has come to Fort Garland to settle down."

"Settle down? I never thought that he would ever give up trapping," Jahn said.

"The death of his companion has been very hard on him. He may change his mind, but I do not think he will. Also, he mentioned a Sylvia Waters. Someone you know?"

"Yes, Sylvia," Jahn said remembering the last time he saw her, when he first met Bear and Elk Horn, and that Bear had mentioned interest in her. "He wants to see her?"

"Yes, he seems quite enamored." Jahn snorted in disbelief. "Do not judge, my son. Love comes when it comes. He is getting older. Be happy he has found it now when he needs companionship the most."

She told him Bear's plan for opening an eatery and

saloon.

"Well, that would suit him," he said. "He could tell his stories to every unsuspecting traveler who comes in."

Both were amused at this image.

"He said he would be at a local eatery."

"Jessie's Place?"

"Yes, that is what he said."

"I should go find him to give condolences." Jahn said and walked his mother to the Livery before finding Bear.

As he entered the establishment, and even though the noise was deafening, above it he could hear Bear aggrandizing one of his exploits with the saloon crowd cheering him on. *A tavern is a good idea,* Jahn thought.

Bear stopped midsentence when he saw Jahn, and bellowed, "Wonderful news, Dutch!" Bear looked around the saloon and with a wave of his arm announced to all, "The lieutenant has found his mother! Alive!"

"Well done, old man." "Congratulations!" "How about that, Lieutenant!" rang throughout the room.

Jahn knew that in the time to come he would be happy to tell the story to all who asked, but right now the newness of the encounter made him feel raw. Most likely Bear would recount it as well making the elements larger with each telling till it became an epic fable.

Ginny walked into the livery to find the owner.

"You are Jack Beckman?"

"Yes, why do you ask?" he said annoyed at being questioned by an Indian.

"Lieutenant Jahn Van Andusson. You know him?"

"Of course, for years. And who would you be?"

"My name is Ginny Van Andusson, I am his mother."

Jack's jaw dropped a good three inches.

"Jahn's mother?" he said in disbelief. "You are kidding, right?"

"I do not kid," she answered.

Ginny saw that on the farrier's arm was a welt the size of an egg. "How long has that been there?" she asked pointing to the inflamed boil.

"A few days. Came up all of a sudden. Hurts like the devil, too."

She reached in her pouch and pulled out a small, sharp knife.

"Hey, what do you think you are going to do with that?"

"I can help," she said. "I am going to let out the poison." Before he could say 'wait a minute', she took hold of his arm, and made a small cut in the boil. Foul smelling pus oozed out. "Do you have water and a clean cloth, one that is just washed?"

Staring at the deflated bulge, he went outside to rinse his arm under the water pump. "You are his mother?" he called. "Really? He has been on your trail for twenty years."

"Our paths have finally crossed," she said, holding back her own excitement. "Now, wipe that dry with the clean cloth." She took his arm and gently rubbed a bit of salve on it. "Keep it dry for a day or two and it should be fine."

"Thank you, ma'am. That thing has been bothering me for near a week." Beckman scratched his beard. "Son of a gun. Well, how can I help you, Ginny Van Andusson?"

"My son tells me you have the best horses in town. Is that true?"

"I aim to please," he said confidently.

"I would like to buy one," she said. "I will pay you with

beaded clothing, good quality."

"Yes, ma'am, I have a number of good ones in the paddock. Chestnut Sam there, he is a fine steed," he said pointing to a large and sturdy horse. "Tell Jahn he can buy me a couple of meals at Jessie's to pay for it."

50

His mother had talked a long time about her life, and Jahn had been hard put to get it all down. Her recollection of her disappearance, as well as many of the memories of her life with the Yampatika Utes, filled many sheets of parchment.

In the morning, rousing himself from his bed, he struggled to pull on his pants and boots before heading to the latrine. The sun was bright and the sky clear when the bell rang loudly calling all recruits to muster. The clang of that bell meant assembly in the yard, so he hurried back to his room to finish dressing. He was still putting on his jacket when he ran out the door. After assembly, he headed for the mess hall and ate breakfast. When he came out of the building, he heard the voice of a woman calling his name, and turned to look.

"Jahn Wolf Van Andusson! Jahn! There you are!" she said again. "Hello." He looked at her blankly. "Has it been so long that you don't remember me?" she asked. "Oh dear, you don't. Lizbeth George, Jahn. I would recognize you anywhere."

He stared at her face, looking for the thirteen year old he had left behind. He had not seen her since he left to join the cavalry more than ten years ago. An awkward but attractive girl when she was young, she had turned into an astounding beauty, and for a moment Jahn could hardly breathe.

"Lizbeth, of course! How nice to see you again."

"An Indian woman at the store told me that you were here," she said seeing his shock. "She seemed to recognize me, but–"

"Did she have white hair?"

"Yes. I did not think I knew her, but she seemed very familiar," Lizbeth said.

"Long story. What are you doing here?" he said quickly changing the subject.

"Through Mrs. Sumner I found out that the fort needed a teacher. I wrote the captain, and he gave me the job!"

"That is wonderful!" He was flustered, and felt inarticulate. "I mean, how nice to have old friends live so close by. Can you walk with me for a moment?"

They fell easily into each other's step.

"I have not seen you. Have you not been home? But then, of course, I was teaching at the Barden Settlement School for Indian Children. Do you know it?"

"I have heard of it. Was it a good experience for you?" he asked.

"I missed my friends, but essentially, yes."

"I have been home," he broke in, "but because my time is so short when I am there, I have not seen my friends as I would have liked, just Richard, mostly, and of course, the Sumners." *I can see that was a mistake*, he said to himself. "They do tell me the news of everyone so I did know that you were away," he said, barely able to contain his attraction. "Will you go back for your things?"

"No, I have already brought my belongings with me. Will

you be here for a while or do you have to go into the mountains right away?"

"I may go on patrol," he said not wishing to explain. He reached into his pocket and pulled out a leather folder. "Do you remember giving me flowers the day I left to join the cavalry?"

"Yes," she said, somewhat embarrassed, remembering her tears.

He opened the billet and there, crumpled from so many years in his pocket, were a few petals of the wildflowers she had pressed into his hands. He explained to her that he needed to talk with his captain but wanted to see her upon his return. She had much more assuredness than she had had as a young girl. Though he did not want to leave her side, Jahn tipped his hat and headed toward the captain's office.

"Lieutenant Van Andusson, what can I do for you?" Captain Chattwick asked warmly as Jahn walked in. Chattwick had been in the cavalry since its inception. Now he would be giving up his post, or so his wife hoped. "That is astounding, Jahn!" the captain exclaimed after Jahn described the reunion with his mother. "After all this time! Who would have thought you would actually find her?"

"She found me, sir," he said. "I would like to take her to where we used to live so she can see my brother, Richard. That is, if you can spare me."

"How long would that take, Lieutenant?"

"Two weeks?"

"See if Lieutenant Marshall will cover for you." Keeping his eyes on the papers on his desk he added, "Take whatever time you need, son. It must be wonderful for you, Jahn," the Captain said in a fatherly tone.

"It is, sir, but quite a shock as well."

"I can imagine. You have been looking for her for a long time," the captain acknowledged. "And son, living with savages changes a person. I am sure I do not have to tell you, she is not the mother you knew."

"No, sir, that she is not."

The captain shook his hand. "Come to me when you return."

"Yes, sir," he said saluting. Then he went to find his mother.

51

Jahn and Ginny left that afternoon. It would take half a week to get to the river that flowed by their house. Once they came to it and followed it north, if the weather held they would be on Silver Leaf Ranch a few days later.

Jahn noticed his Mother was an excellent rider. She had not been when the children were young, but had been a woman who lived in a cultured settlement most of her life.

While they rode, she told her son more about her life, and when they stopped for the night she had him write it all down.

"You write too slow," she chided.

"You talk too fast," he retorted.

He did not remember her being this impatient with him when he was young. Memories began crowding his mind:

"Supper is ready! Jahn, take Holly and James to the pump and wash their hands. Wash your own while you are at it," his mother said tousling his hair.

"Whose turn is it to say grace?" his father would ask.

After supper they would sit by the fire to listen to their father read a

story from the Bible. Then they would all sit around their mother while
she asked them about their day. Then Ginny would herd the young ones
toward their sleeping mats, tucking each one in, giving each one a hug
and a kiss.

"Mama," Jahn remembered asking. "Are you happy we came
here?"

"I am happy we are all here together," she replied.

"We will always be together won't we? I mean nothing is going to
happen to us, right? I have heard the Indians steal horses and kill
people."

"Now do not worry, son. Your father and I will take good care of
you always," she had said, reassuring him and kissing him goodnight.

Now his mother was like a spring gushing forth
everything that had been stored in her head about her life. As
he watched her talk he thought again in disbelief and wonder,
"This woman standing in front of me with white hair and a wrinkled
face, who is mostly Indian, is my mother. My... mother." He listened
intently and wrote as quickly as he could. He felt surprised,
yet filled with curiosity hearing the stories, and found that
knowing what had happened to her eased the sadness that he
had felt all his life.

The weather was cooperating, making the days sunny and
cool, and the nights dry as well. They traveled easily over the
rocky mountain passes and down into the green valleys.

"Richard was always like your father," she began one
evening. "Garritt was a stubborn man, and when his mind
was made up that was that. I would have been quite content
to stay in the settlement, in our house near your school and
the church. I had friends there who were dear to me, to all of
us. But your Pa got wanderlust, and wanted to build a
homestead in the mountains. After we argued about it for a

time I gave into his dream of starting afresh. Do you remember any of that?" she asked him, the English language flowing more easily for her now.

"I remember the arguments, and the packing up. But I was not worried about moving," he told her. "Where we lived in the mountains was beautiful. I did miss my friends though."

His whole life Jahn had remembered only one version of Ginny Van Andusson, the mother that she was when he was very young. She had been vibrant, affectionate and fun, laughing easily, and always singing a song. Now she was somber and intense. *But then*, he thought, *I am not the carefree boy that she knew either.*

Jahn still found it hard to believe that this could be his mother. His mind churned: *This is a stranger in front of me, more Indian than not. That was too long ago, and we cannot pick up where we left off. She does not seem to be expecting that, but I am not sure what she wants or what I am willing to give.*

"Oh, my dear Holly. I told Bear that when I did not see you, I feared that inside the house you were all dead, but he said she was with you boys. But now she has passed," she cried. "Tell me what happened."

"Holly was not very strong after the attack," he explained. "Nothing could make her laugh anymore. Barely spoke a word," he told her looking into her sad eyes. "The simplest things she could not do for herself. We had to bathe her, feed her, and change her clothes. She got sick often," he said. "The last time Holly got ill we had to grind up her food into a mush just so she could get it down. And she would not take much of it, nor the water we gave her. She lingered for months it seemed, in bed, in a pool of sweat, staring into the dark. Finally, her head churned back and forth, and she could not stop screaming. The cough turned into pneumonia. She quieted, becoming still, looking out into nothing. In the end, her eyes brightened and a smile came to her lips, and with a shushing sound, the air left her lungs." He found it was a difficult truth to tell even after all these years. "She had just turned eight."

Ginny was stunned, the losses compounding on each other like an avalanche. The pain of Holly's death hiding deep within her could not make its way to the surface. For a moment, Jahn thought that his mother had not heard him. But when she stood up he could see the anguish on her face. All she could do was stand by her son looking up at the sky, which had cleared to reveal a starry night.

"Mother, Father Man, your teacher," Jahn started.

"Father Man, yes? He became like my father and his wife, Quill, like my own mother. They were very kind to me," she broke, remembering her mentors with fondness.

Jahn said. "I think I may have met him."

"How is that possible, son?"

"It was about ten years ago."

He told her of going into the village, and how Father Man had taught him to fish with a spear.

"He never said anything to me about meeting a soldier. Oh, Jahn," she gasped when she realized how close she had been to her son. "But as I told you, I did not remember anything then. So if you had found me, I may not have recognized you."

They rode throughout the day telling each other about their lives.

"Tell me more about Richard," Ginny asked as they came close to Silver Leaf.

To Jahn, Richard was a drowning man who would not

reach for the rope that could save him, so Jahn weighed his response before answering.

"He lives alone at our old home, buying and selling horses. He is particularly good with animals that need a bit of care. Seems to know just what is needed to make them strong and able to work again." He hesitated, fearing he might begin complaining about Richard's drinking.

The sky was clear and blue, the day warm and inviting, the sun sending dappled brilliance through the trees. They stopped at a riverside to rest and let the horses drink.

"I think he is very lonely. He does not see many people except–," he hesitated.

"Yes?"

"Sometimes he goes to town at night," he said trying to tell it without saying anything directly.

"Oh, I see. Well," she said understanding his meaning. "I can hardly wait to see him. He is not married then?"

"No, not yet. He wants to be, I think. He often talks about Melina, a teacher in town. I think he likes her. And from what I have seen, she has a twinkle in her eye for him, but he cannot see it, so keeps his distance."

The smoke had been very specific. Let Jahn introduce his mother to Richard. He would not accept seeing her at first, especially if she were alone. He would feel that he was seeing a ghost.

52

They arrived at Silver Leaf Ranch in the early afternoon. The excitement that Ginny felt at being on the homestead again after all these years blotted out her seeing how rundown the property was. Though the barn looked different than she had remembered it, the garden, though filled with vegetables, was overgrown with weeds, and the buildings looked like no repairs had been made for years.

"The barn is much bigger, is it not?"

"Yes, Richard has been adding on to it as he gets more horses."

Jahn started up the steps to the house.

"I will wait outside. You go in and let him know I am here."

She stood looking around the property, reliving what it had been with a meticulously weeded garden bursting with vegetables at the side of the house, and the milk can at the front door overflowing with flowers from the seeds she had brought with her when they first moved. *Oh, dear, I see*, she thought as she began to notice what it had become. *Richard does need a wife.*

Richard's voice rose in volume from inside the house.

"What are you talking about? Who is that woman?"

Ginny heard a murmur that was Jahn's calm and quiet explanation to his brother, and Richard's shouted response.

"Oh really! And you believe her? You just want her to be our mother. Mama is dead, and has been for twenty years! When are you going to accept this? I do not care who she says she is, I am not going anywhere."

Jahn came out of the door shaking his head.

"He will not even come out to meet you."

"You water the horses, son and get them some feed," she said. "I will wait here."

For more than an hour Jahn tended to the horses while his mother waited in front of the house. She sat down on a stump and closed her eyes:

Before she knew it, she was walking in the forest along a path. She could feel a wolf's eyes watch her from within the trees, following her every movement. The breathing and the beat of its heart were in rhythm with hers.

Finally, Richard broke through the door, slamming it hard against the wall of the house. She took a slow breath before opening her eyes. At first, he stood on the porch staring at her, his face contorted with confusion and rage. He ran down the steps past her toward the barn, then turned back to face her. He was not as tall as Jahn, more ruddy, and thicker in the middle. *He takes after my family*, she thought. His hair had been dark like hers, but now it had some white peppering in amongst the auburn strands. His eyes were deeply set like his father's, leading to a smooth cheek.

She reached into her pouch to pull out the hair comb

that they had given her so many years ago.

"Do you remember giving me this on my thirty-seventh birthday?"

He stood silently, taking in the Indian dress and moccasins that she wore, and looked at the hair comb. His eyes filled. But not yet ready to accept the truth, he became enraged.

"Because he has been looking for our mother for so many years, my brother wants to believe that you are her, but you cannot fool me that easily," Richard yelled. "I do not know who you are or where you got that comb," he said grabbing it from her hand and throwing it down, "but you had better leave us alone."

"You have been alone for twenty years, son. Is that not long enough?"

He stepped forward, his fist raised to strike. Ginny closed her eyes in anticipation of the sting from his blow.

Jahn yelled from the barn door. "Richard, stop!" He ran up the hill and stood between them. "Richard," Jahn said more gently. "Stop, please."

Richard turned away from both of them, his fists still held tightly closed.

"You are so easily fooled, Jahn," he said through a clenched jaw.

"It is all right. Richard needs time to take it in, just as you did," Ginny said.

Ginny looked through her memories for something between them that only Richard would know.

"My son, when you were very little, we said our prayers together," she said. "Your father came in first to kiss you goodnight, and then you and I would kneel at your bedside. Do you remember?" Richard fidgeted still breathing heavily.

"We said the same prayer every night. 'Dear Heavenly Father, bless our family—the ones that are here, and the ones that have gone, and those yet to come. Keep us safe in your blessed arms. And thank you for...'" she thought for a moment, bringing the scene to mind. "And then you would add something of your own," she said, amazed that she could remember it at all.

"When Jahn was born, and you were but five years old, you told me that whatever happened you would take care of your baby brother. Do you remember telling me that?"

"Yes," he said then challenging her, "and what did you tell me after that?"

"I told you that angel's wings would cover you, keeping you safe from harm. And that no matter where you were, God would be looking after you."

No one else knew of this conversation, not even Jahn.

"And I believed it for years—until that day." He was silent for a long time before he was able to articulate what he felt. "When those Indians came," he stopped, trying to keep his feelings from overwhelming him. "I— "

"That is all right, son," she said looking at him with tender eyes. "What are you trying to tell me, Richard?"

"It is just that I, I never went out to help. Pa was out there and James, and you—" he wilted onto the stump. "I could not! My legs," he blurted. "I could not get my legs to move. I should have grabbed my gun, and shot those damn Indians dead. But—I, I hid. I hid," he burst into anguished tears. The pain of this immense guilt had overshadowed any of the fine qualities that he might have seen in himself.

"You were only fifteen," she said. "You did what you could. What if you had gone out? You might have been killed, too, then what would have happened to Holly and Jahn? Oh, my dear son, you did the right thing." She held him for a long time while he released his pent up grief.

"I understand how you feel, Richard. We have both been on a journey. Mine took me away for such a long time," she said, "but I am grateful that it has brought me back to you." Richard picked up the comb from the dirt, wiped it off and put it into his mother's hair.

Later that day, Jahn and Richard walked their mother to the top of the hill where there were three painted field stone grave markers, one that read, "Garritt 'Dutch' Wolf Van Andusson and James Wolf Van Andusson, Father and Son, Beloved and will be missed," and the smaller headstone Richard had also painted. It was inscribed "Our Dear Sister, Holly Virginia Van Andusson, held in the arms of angels."

The sadness of seeing this place crept up on Ginny like a hunter on its prey. Before she could harness any strength against it, it overtook her, and she fell to her knees. From deep inside her, a chant welled. At first her song was barely audible then its power rose, and she sang it louder and louder. The boys looked at each other concerned.

"What was that?" Richard asked her.

"A prayer to help them on their way," is what she told him. Later she would come to this mound and sing a proper ceremony for this family: this husband and son and daughter.

53

The rain clouds from the day before had cleared and the sun was warming the air. Mother and son wound their way along the riverbank heading for town, their horses stepping in unison. The hooves and the occasional whinny beat a steady but playful rhythm.

Memories of Ginny's life at Silver Leaf Ranch played in her mind, bringing up many questions about friends: Bethany and David George, Colbertha and Sean.

"And the Sumners?" she asked Jahn, "Sara and Henry? How are they?"

Even though Sara Sumner was more than thirty years older than Ginny, she and Sara had become fast friends in those first years on the mountain. Jahn pulled out the watch Henry had given him to show her the inscription.

"He gave this to me when I joined the cavalry. He has gone on now—about three years ago—from a heart attack. Mrs. Sumner is living with Adam and Jessica Finnian and their three children. Colbertha and Sean live with Conor's family."

Ginny dropped into The Silence for a moment, and then lifted her gaze to her son.

"Take me to Sara," she announced.

"All right, Ma, but she is quite old now and her memory is not what it used to be. Do not be surprised if she does not recognize you."

It was an hour's ride to the Finnian ranch. All the while, she told Jahn stories of Sara and Henry. Some of the stories were familiar, as he remembered reading about them in an early entry in his mother's diary:

When we first arrived on Silver Leaf Ranch (our home), new neighbors, Sara and Henry Sumner, came by with baked goods—several pies and loaves of bread. Sara knows that kind of cooking is not going to be easy till we had an oven.

She and I have gotten on like sisters from the moment we met. I love her no-nonsense attitude, rambunctious laugh, and playful sense of humor.

Their children, all four of them, were lost to diphtheria. Can you imagine? Losing one child must be hard enough to recover from, let alone four. I don't know how she was able to manage the grief.

Sara's way has been to become an aunt to our children, showering them with affection whenever she comes over. They are surprised, I am afraid, but I have explained to them as best I can, and they have accepted her caring with good grace. I think they have even gotten to like it. Now when Sara comes to visit, they greet her with devotion. It is rather sweet.

Sara and I have spent many hours together planning and making quilts, sewing clothing and the like. I have grown to cherish her friendship like no other.

Henry feels a bit too old for Garritt, but they remain cordial, if not gaining a sense of camaraderie. They both enjoy telling and retelling stories about their hunting expeditions. Standing in front of the fire, having a glass of whiskey together, they act out their adventures, and are on the trail once more, courageous hunters of the wild...

"I can't wait to see her," Ginny broke Jahn's reverie.

"Ma, remember what I told you. Sara may not recognize you at all." After all, his mother had changed significantly. Besides, Mrs. Sumner was so forgetful now that she did not always remember Jahn when he came to visit.

When they arrived Sara Sumner was sitting on the Finnian's porch looking out at the turning leaves. The young Finnian children, playing a game, ran in and out of the door. Sara seemed not to notice the commotion.

"Sara?" Ginny said. She moved toward the old woman with deference and caution not wanting to startle her. Quietly she said her name again. Sara Sumner did not change her gaze, but remained looking over the field in front of her. Not till Ginny knelt down and touched her hand did Sara's head turn to the woman who had spoken.

Sara stared, her eyes intently looking over the landscape of Ginny's face trying to locate the name that went with it. She looked up at the woman's hair.

"It has turned now," Ginny said, running the comb through it.

After a long moment, reaching up, Sara touched it. "White," she said, stroking Ginny's head like a child stroking a baby animal, then she cupped the woman's face with her hands, looking deeply into one eye then the other. She held her gaze, taking in all that was in front of her: the tanned face, the white hair, the leather dress and moccasins. Slowly, Sara wrapped her arms around the woman's shoulders and drew her close.

"We thought you were dead. We all thought you were, but here you are. Ginny."

Sara closed her eyes, and held her friend for a long time. Neither one spoke. Then Ginny's eyes filled and tears made their way down her browned cheeks. She began to cry quietly at first, Sara, too. Then the tears gushed: tears from the pain of many years ago, tears from the lost lives of her beloveds, tears for the life she never had, and finally for the one she had lived.

Sara rocked her gently. "Now, now, Ginny-Girl, everything is all right. You are home again, and that is all that matters." Ginny felt the warmth of Sara's embrace, the love of an old friend encompassing her, and for the first time in a long while she felt at home. Now she was overcome with weeping. "There, there, my friend, it was not your fault," she said continuing to rock her tenderly. "Oh, you are alive! Ginny-Girl, you are alive! We have heard nothing about you for all these years. Tell me where you have been." Looking at Jahn for the first time since they arrived she added, "Your children must be so happy. And now, Ginny-Girl," Sara gushed with full-hearted joy, "you are here!"

All the years seemed to melt away, and she was for this moment once again Ginny Van Andusson, a young mother with four children and a handsome preacher for a husband. It was a disquieting feeling. She was nearly sixty now, and certainly never expected to outlive her children, let alone two husbands.

Sara Sumner was frail and weak. Her hearing was almost gone, and it seemed that she did not see well either.

Not wanting to tire her friend, Ginny got up to leave. "I will come again tomorrow, Sara."

"I am not letting you go just yet, Ginny-Girl. Jahn, go in and get us some coffee and some of Jessica's tasty sweet bread."

Twenty years had passed since Ginny had seen her friend. There was so much to say, but where to begin, and how to explain all that she had experienced.

"They were kind to me," she reassured Sara. "I have lived as one of the tribe. The work is hard, but I was not alone in it. Everyone works hard."

Jahn returned with the treats, offering some to Mrs. Sumner and then his mother. "Thank you, Jahn, now sit," Mrs. Sumner said to him. "Have you seen Richard, Ginny?"

"Yes, I saw him for the first time yesterday."

"Good. Oh, there is so much to tell you, and I want to hear all about your life. Promise me that you will come by again tomorrow so we can talk at length."

"I promise."

After a while Sara said, "Ginny-Girl, go in and ask Jessie for my wrap, will you? The breeze has come up, and I have a bit of a chill."

"She's not the same, your ma," Mrs. Sumner quickly told Jahn when Ginny went into the house. "Your mother went into that storm an innocent young woman and came out different, but–strong. There is something, I cannot put my finger on it, something that spooks me a little. It's as if she looks not at me, but–into–me," Mrs. Sumner said shifting in her seat. "Well, who would not have changed with all she has been through? Oh, my dear Ginny," she said almost to herself, "I cannot believe she has returned. What an unimaginable surprise. You must be so happy, Jahn!"

Mrs. Sumner had always spoken of his mother as a wonderful person and her best friend. Her stories, which she had begun to repeat over and over in the last few years, had kept Jahn connected to the mother he remembered. But through those years, it was Mrs. Sumner who had been the one to bandage his knees and put the balm on his sad heart.

For the next few weeks, Ginny sat with her friend in the afternoons. Sometimes they talked, but more often Sara Sumner just looked out over the trees and wild flowers growing in the field. On those days, Ginny sat with her in silence.

54

His mother had left that afternoon for the Sumner's. Since she had come, she had said nothing about his drinking, and Richard was grateful not to be confronted. Going to the bar in town for whiskey was a pleasure that Richard often suffered for the following mornings. He had tried to stop drinking before but had always returned to it. Now Richard was determined. Oddly, on this day, he had no desire to start. As a matter of fact, he almost felt repulsed at the idea.

He carried an apple box into his house, and began gathering the empty liquor bottles, dumping them into the container and carrying it through the door. As a gesture of his intent, he threw the bottles, one by one, against a boulder that lay at the edge of the woods. Glass flew everywhere. But when the last bottle was in his hand, he hesitated. It was a full one. He pulled the cork, smelled its contents, and for a long moment, was not sure he would be able to break this one, too. But with great resolve, he smashed it, liquor anointing the rock and the earth below. He went back up to the house and sat heavily into the rocker.

The next morning he roused himself early, splashed water

on his eyes, and went to the barn to clean out its stalls. He worked hard through the afternoon, fixing fences and taking the horses through their exercises. He made a small supper for himself then cleared the table. With his shirt pressed and pants clean, he combed his hair as a finishing touch. He had even polished his boots. He was to meet with Melina Malachek, and he had an important question to ask her.

All the way to her house he rehearsed what he wanted to say. "Will you be my wife?" He shook his head. "Will you marry me? No, not that either," he said aloud. "What would you think about our getting married?" He wondered how many ways there were to say it.

When Richard arrived at her house, Melina's family was on the porch relaxing after supper.

"Good evening, sir," Richard said to her father.

Gus Malachek was a solid if not handsome man, who had worked the land and made a good living. His wife, Sabina, a tall, slim, attractive woman, had a figure that did not betray that she had had three children. Next to her sat their twins, Frederick and Gustov, who they called Junior, who were a year older than Melina. They were strapping young men who helped work their father's farm.

"Ma'am. Boys," he nodded.

Melina was thirty-two and Richard, thirty-five. *Not too old to be marrying for the first time*, he hoped.

"Good evening, Richard. A fine night," Gus said looking out at the reddening sky, his face stern and unmoving.

"Good evening, sir. Hello, Melina." *She is so beautiful*, he thought.

"Hello, Richard," she said demurely.

Then he asked, "Would you walk with me?"

She stepped off the porch, looked back at her family, and

hid a smile. Her father leaned over to her mother and said, "Looks like a freshly polished apple."

"Now Gus, be kind. He is trying at least," she whispered.

"I am just saying that even a polished apple can have a worm in it. I do not know if I like him coming around."

"I know what you are saying, Gus. But he is a good man, and will be a good provider, and besides Melina loves him."

"I expect that will be true on the days he is sober." Gus leaned back in his chair. "I wasn't sure she would ever find someone. She's been so picky." He took a puff of his cigar. "I was just hoping for better."

"Now, Gus, the drinking does not happen too often," she admonished. "Melina says he drinks only occasionally. And you wouldn't want her to marry someone who she didn't care for."

"Yes, that is true. I just wish that when he drank it would not be to excess," he reminded her.

Richard, pretending he did not hear their conversation, took Melina's hand. They walked along a path, and came to the tree where they had stopped many times to sit and talk. He lifted her up into its crook.

"I want to ask you something. I mean, I have been thinking about my life and I—well—I was wondering if," he halted. His mouth went dry, his stomach tightened into a knot, and he could hardly breathe. "Melina—I know I am not the best catch for a girl as fine as you. I do make a good living with my horses though," he started.

"Yes, Richard, you do," she confirmed.

"I—I know I have not been the steadiest of men, but I think that could change if, I mean, well, would you consider being my wife." *There*, he thought, *I got it out!*

She looked at him with the sweetest face he had ever

seen.

"Are you sure, Richard?" she teased.

"Yes–I am very sure. More than sure," he exclaimed. And he started once again, bending down on one knee, "Melina Louisa Malachek, would you do me the honor of being my wife?"

"Richard Wolf Van Andusson, it would be my pleasure."

They kissed, and held the embrace, his arms around her waist, hers around his neck. He promised to honor her all his life. "But we shall say that properly in a church just as soon as possible. How about next week?" he said without thinking.

"Richard, I will need a dress. I cannot make one in a week."

"My mother will help you, she sews very well. I feel like I have been waiting all my life for happiness to begin, and I do not want to wait another minute. Can we get married a week from Saturday then? That is ten days."

She thought for a moment then sighed, "All right, Richard."

Richard wanted to be sure his mother was there for the wedding, and he had a feeling she might not stay with them as long as he would like.

Jahn had been walking in the woods for hours, revisiting all the places where he and his siblings had explored, played and roughhoused. But because he no longer held that childish innocence, it was both endearing as well as upsetting. The last twenty years had not only aged him, but had left him feeling empty and incomplete. He had been searching for his mother for so many years, and now they were finally together again. But it was not he who had found her. She found him. He hardly knew how to look at his life with his purpose completed. Who was he now? He felt there was no one who could understand what he faced. That feeling was unbearable.

He went to speak with Sara Sumner. She sat on the porch staring out at the trees. Though he was not even sure that she was able to hear him this day, he spoke of it anyway.

Divulging his dilemma, even to Sara, made him feel weak and lost, and he could not withstand the disappointment he might see flow across her face, so he did not look at her while he spoke.

When he finished his thoughts there was silence. Sara did not move, nor utter a word, but just when Jahn got up to leave, as his back was turned to her, she said, "My dear boy, how could you feel any other way? For so long, you have longed for her return, thinking of nothing else. Your whole life has been spent looking into the empty hole her disappearance left. You must be patient, dear. Those feelings will dissipate. The darkness of that time will fill with the light of those you love, and who love you. Dare I say, Jahn, that you will be happy for the first time since the raid?"

She sat quietly for a moment. "Come here," she said finally, opening her arms. Jahn knelt down next to her, and let her embrace him. "You'll see, son. Your life will—well, it will feel renewed." She stroked his hair as they held each other then asked, "Did you tell me you saw Lizbeth George?"

55

"Where is my clean shirt?" Unfolding piles of clothing, Richard sprinted around the somewhat tidier house looking for the white shirt he had washed to wear for his wedding. "And my pants. Where are they?" he said throwing clothes on the floor as he tried to unearth the new pants he had had made for the occasion.

He was a whirlwind of confusion, too excited to be rational, and too happy to care.

"Your pants are hanging on the door, and Ma has your shirt. She's darning the hole in the cuff."

His mother brought in the shirt and showed Richard what she had done. "It was too big to close, but I think you will like it."

With her finest stitching and beading, she had made a patch to cover the hole.

"Look at that. Thank you, Mother," he said slipping the shirtsleeve over his arm. It was not what he had expected, but he quickly saw how beautifully drawn the design was, and how looking at it gave him a feeling of strength.

"Jahn, did you polish my boots?"

"On the floor at the end of your bed."

Jahn and his mother stepped aside so as not to get run over by Richard rummaging through the house.

"Do you have the ring?" Richard asked.

Jahn felt in his vest pocket. "Yes."

"What am I forgetting?"

"Your brain and this," Jahn said handing him the freshly brushed hat.

Jahn wore his military uniform, which he had whisked clean as best he could. Jessica had lent Ginny one of her dresses for the ceremony. It was covered in soft peach colored flowers, something she would have loved when she was young. Her bright white hair, loose, was pulled back from the front of her face with the two silver combs that she had been given so long ago.

Jahn looked down at his mother's beaded moccasins.

"Mother, your shoes!"

"I know, son," she told Jahn, "I tried on the shoes that Jessica lent me, but they hurt. These are much more comfortable."

With a hint of exasperation, Jahn sighed, "Are we all ready now?"

"What time is it? Do I have time to shave again?"

"Again, Richard? That will be the third time," Jahn teased.

"I want to be sure it is smooth, and that I did not miss any spots."

"Richard, get in the buggy. Let us not keep your bride waiting," his mother chided.

He jumped into the buggy lent by Conor George and his wife, who had decorated it with ribbons and flowers. "Do we have everything?" he asked.

The little church had filled up with friends and families of the bride and groom. Many had not seen Ginny yet, and were looking forward to that as much as to the wedding. When Jahn walked his mother down the aisle to her seat in the front, a spontaneous ripple of applause went through the congregation. Ginny looked up and smiled at the faces of those she passed. Some she recognized, but others she did not. *I guess I do not look the same either*, she thought.

Adam, Jessica and Sara arrived in their buggy. Before they got out, Jessica spread the shawl and wrapped it around the old woman's shoulders.

"Thank you, my dear," Sara said.

"Sara, you sit on this chair, and we will take you in," Adam told her.

"Ah, my chariot!" Sara said with flourish and an upward sweep of her hand. "Thank you, my handsome steeds." Adam and Conor carried her through the door.

"Careful now, this is special cargo you are ferrying," Sara burbled with delight. "Now put me down right in front. There, with Ginny," she insisted. "What a special day! Your boy is finally getting married!" she said with a mischievous grin.

"Hello, Sara, I see you are feeling well. I, for one, am glad he waited so I could be here," Ginny answered.

"Of course, Ginny, what was I thinking? Forgive an old woman's joke," Sara responded.

"The joke was on me."

"Ginny-Girl, he did not know you were alive. Well, I dare say from what you have told me you did not know that he was either," Sara said, distracted by the thought.

Ginny turned to Sara and took her hand.

"You have been a real friend. Both Jahn and Richard have told me how much care you have given them over the years."

"They are good boys, Ginny. How could I do otherwise?"

Mrs. Sylvester began to grind out music on the pump organ for the processional and everyone turned to look at the bride.

Melina stood with her father in the doorway. Her dotted muslin dress was pristine white except for a slim pink trim at the edges of her sleeves and at her neck. A fine lace shawl, which had been her grandmother's, covered her head and shoulders. When she walked down the aisle on her father's arm, she carried a bouquet of tiny pink and purple wild flowers in her steady hands.

When the minister called out, "Now I pronounce you man and wife." Richard breathed a full breath, and kissed his bride.

"You look so beautiful, Mrs. Van Andusson," he told her. She took his arm and they walked back through the church.

"Congratulations, brother!" Jahn said enthusiastically, slapping him on the back.

"Congratulations on finally getting married, or that I did not faint before it was over?"

"Perhaps a little of both?" Jahn smiled.

The party was held on the church lawn under the trees and a clear, bright, warm, late spring sky. The Malacheks provided the food and the fiddler. Everyone enjoyed a good dinner and lively dancing. Much to Jahn's surprise and relief, Richard did not drink.

"Where is mother?" Richard asked looking around for her.

"She is probably here somewhere," Jahn answered

looking over the guests.

But Ginny had quietly disappeared from the gaiety, ridden back to Silver Leaf Ranch, walked up to the burial ground, and sat down in front of the gravestones.

"I want to talk with you, Garritt," she said. "Our oldest boy got married today. I think he has married well. Melina is a patient and understanding woman. Richard loves her a great deal, and I think he will turn out to be a good husband."

She sat for a moment thinking about her life. "I do not blame you any more, Garritt. How could you know what was to come into our lives, or that yours would end so early? Senawahv–um, God," she said using the word she thought he would understand "has plans for us that we do not know."

She sat quietly. "I think of you all the time now, and James and Holly," she said. "The boys? We have Sara and Henry to thank for taking care of them. You tell Henry for me, will you?"

Then she took a breath and looked up to the sky. "I got married again, Garritt. Cougar Two Foot was a very good man. He was kind and considerate, and he did love me deeply. You would have liked him, I think."

As she sat by Garritt's headstone, she could feel his presence. Then she was filled with the sense of Cougar Two Foot, as well. "Seems you two have met," she said aloud. As if in a painting, she saw Garritt standing with Quill and Father Man on his right, and Cougar Two Foot on his left. As he lifted his arms a light moved from his hands in an embrace around the three shaman's shoulders.

In that moment, she knew that it had been Garritt who had sent them to her, that he had been looking after her even in death. She walked back down the hill to the house feeling completely and profoundly loved.

The wedding couple would be returning to the house soon, and she wanted to do something for them before they came home. The great room of the house was a jumble of strewn clothes, dirty plates, glasses, dust and dirt brought in by muddy boots. It took some time, but she managed to refold the clothes, wash the dishes, sweep out the room, and put flowers in a vase on the table before Richard and Melina came home. She was just throwing a blanket over the clean bed covers when she heard the buggy drive up and Richard outside talking with his bride.

"Well, Mrs. Van Andusson, we are home," he said.

"So we are, Mr. Van Andusson. So we are."

Hearing this, Ginny smiled, and slipped out the back door, then walked her horse up the road, and rode toward Adam and Jessica Finnian's, where she and Jahn would be spending the night.

Within a few minutes Jahn rode up next to her, "I thought I might find you here," he said. "Mind if I ride along with you?"

"I can think of nothing better," she smiled.

56

Swift Fox climbed up to the quiet place he had found on the mountain. From where he was, he had a view of the whole valley below and could see if anyone was coming toward him long before they knew that he was there. He had made it a practice of coming to this spot to clear his mind.

He had thought of his mother often, and was concerned because she had been gone for such a long time. When he saw her again, he would not tell her that he was worried about having brothers who were white and that she might choose to live with them. To push away those feelings he went hunting. The small footprints of a rabbit were clearly showing in the soft earth amongst the webbing of pine needles. He put his kill over the fire, and waited for it to cook for his evening meal.

As his fire blazed, he watched the smoke drift up into the leaves of the trees. But he was not his mother. His way was to listen to the wind. Feeling it brush across his face, hearing the leaves swirl in its path, he took in the whisperings of its wisdom.

57

"Seems like Mrs. Sumner has been getting more and more forgetful," Jahn said to his mother.

"Have you noticed it, too?" Richard added, "Jessica says some days Sara will not wake easily, and it scares her."

"Yes, she has her clear days, and ones when she is not lucid," Ginny confirmed, looking out at the leaves. "Our lives are like the leaves of the trees coming in bright green, growing through the summer, then turning colors, drying up and falling off," she said, "or like the sun that rises, travels across the sky then sets." She waited a beat and then said plainly, "Sara's sun is setting."

Jahn had sensed this as well. Thinking that he would be losing Mrs. Sumner made his heart feel heavy.

A few days later Ginny told her sons, "Come with me. Sara needs us today."

Richard went to get the wagon from the barn, and called for Melina to join them. The four rode out to the Finnians'.

Jessica was standing out on the porch wringing her handkerchief when they arrived. "Oh, you came! I am so glad. Sara said you would. Saw it in her dream, she said. You had better hurry though! She has been asking for you."

They went into the house expecting the worst, but to the boys' surprise, even though Sara looked weak, she was sitting up in her bed looking alert and cheerful.

"Hello, Sara," Ginny said gently sitting at the edge of her bed. "You are ready?" She took her friend's hand. Now becoming glassy eyed, staring at nothing, Sara nodded her head and smiled.

"I have brought the boys, Sara." She turned to wave the boys closer. "Step forward you two. You know she does not see well."

Mrs. Sumner opened her arms. Richard leaned in, followed by Jahn, to give her their customary embrace. Her strength waning fast, she fell back heavily onto the pillow. Adam and Jessica and their three children stood next to the bed, each leaning down to give her a kiss or a hug.

For a few minutes, Ginny closed her eyes, and quietly sang a chant then she bent down to whisper something into Sara's ear. Sara smiled an understanding smile. The family stayed by her side into the night. When Sara Sumner breathed for the last time, Ginny leaned over her friend's body and tenderly kissed the cold cheek.

Jahn asked later, "What did you say to her, Mother?"

Ginny was still for a long time thinking about what to tell him. "I told her that she is not alone. We had talked many times about what comes after this life," she explained to her boys. "I told her that even her ancestors' ancestors were joyfully waiting for her to arrive."

"How do you know that?" Richard asked.

"Some things I just know, son."

Both Richard and Jahn felt heavy with this loss. Mr. Sumner's passing had been difficult enough, but now Mrs.

Sumner's death had added to that weight.

"I will make the arrangements for her funeral," Richard told Adam.

58

"Boys, come with me," Ginny said. "I want to talk with you." They walked to the riverside and along its bank for a few minutes before she broached the subject.

"I was gone a long time, and as you know I did not remember much of my life except that your father was dead, and that I thought all you children were as well. Jahn already knows this, but Richard, I want to tell you this so both of you understand.

"After five years of living alone with Father Man and Quill, I learned to love another," she told them. "He was a good man, kind and loving." She let that sink in a moment before she said, "And we had a son. Swift Fox. He is your half brother. He is a good hunter, and a bit headstrong like the both of you. I think you would like him."

Jahn thought about the years he had spent looking for his mother. Learning about his mother's new life and new family had jumbled his mind, tearing him apart. Hearing this once more made the beast in his chest churn. It stung Richard, too, and even more so when he found that he had a sibling. Both were silent, feeling confused, angry, and betrayed.

"You married an Indian?" Richard yelled. "They were the ones who took you away!"

She looked intently at her two sons. "I know this is not what you expected or wanted to hear. They were very kind to me. They saved my life."

Richard paced and threw rocks into the water. Jahn stared at his mother.

"He had been my spouse for fifteen years before he died of the Pox. His name was Cougar Two Foot. He was a good man," she said, "a shaman, like me."

"How old is he," Richard stammered, "this Running whatever his name is?"

"Swift Fox," she said calming herself. "He is fifteen."

"Where is he now?" Richard queried.

"Near Steamboat Springs on the Yampa River."

She told them about how she and Swift Fox had come upon the group in their time of need.

"Does he have red in his hair like you had?" Jahn asked looking off into the distance.

"Yes. It also streaks when the sun bathes it in the summer. And he has our blue eyes as well. He has been teased for it."

"I was on my way to Steamboat Springs last winter, and saw a young boy hunting a deer," Jahn began. "His eyes were blue like mine—and yours. He was a fine hunter, downing his buck with one arrow into the lung. I did not think much about it, but I kept having dreams about him," Jahn admitted.

That they had almost met astounded Ginny, but then she remembered Garritt's help, and she understood.

Jahn's gift for *knowing* was beginning to grow. She would have to think how to nurture it. He would not sit on a mountaintop for many days as she had done. But there was time now that she knew where to find him.

Richard. How to help Richard? she wondered. His self-doubt fueled his battle with alcohol, and that would keep him from settling into the Big Nothing with ease. She would have to approach his learning differently. But there was time to figure that out, too.

One thing she knew was that she wanted her sons to meet Swift Fox soon. When they were ready she would bring them to her village.

59

Early in the morning the day after Sara Sumner's funeral, Ginny packed up the few things she had brought with her to the house. Spring flowers were beginning to open and bears had come out of hibernation weeks before, so the Tribal Gathering would be very soon.

"Mother, where are you going?" Richard asked.

"I must go to my people," she told him, "and your brother is calling for me."

"Your people? We are your people. We are your family. Surely you can't mean you will continue to live with those savages," Richard said.

"Yes, my dear son. They are not savages. They are the stitching that holds the cloth of my dress together, and they have been so for a very long time." Then she tried to explain. "For so many years, I wanted to return to a life I could not remember. It was all I thought of, and all I dreamt about, but I had no choice but to make the most of living with The People."

"So stay here with us, Mother," Richard cried.

"Try to understand when I say that I am no longer that

woman who lived here on the ranch with your father and you children. I am quite someone else. It was not till I got here again, and realized that what I have to give, I can only give in my tribe. It would not be welcome here."

"You do not know that. People here have always loved you."

"They did not know me." She was resolute, and Richard could feel it.

"When will we see you again?" he asked.

Richard seemed nervous and was getting agitated. Melina took his arm.

"Ginny, please stay. There is room for you here," she said for Richard's sake.

"Ma, please stay," Jahn echoed.

"I must go now," she answered.

"How will we know where you are?" Jahn asked.

"I will hear you when you need me, and I will come." Then looking at Richard and Melina, "I will return after the winter, at the bloom of the first flowers, after your boy is born," she said mounting her horse.

Both sons looked at Melina who smiled in surprise and recognition that what she had suspected was true. Without another word the boys' mother disappeared into the mist of the morning air. Richard and Melina watched till she was out of sight, but Jahn got his things together as quickly as he could, and followed. Mother and son rode together till the sun was high, and Jahn had to turn south toward Fort Garland.

One day in the following spring, Jahn walked to his friend's house. He knocked and waited for an answer. Sylvia, pregnant, was wrapped in a green shawl, her hair neatly pulled up into a bun. She wore a white and green muslin dress that was closed up to the neck. She looked rested and beautiful when she opened the door.

"Hello, Jahn," she said

"Sorry to bother you. Is Bear–I mean, Myron–is he here?"

"My!" she called back into the house. "Honey, Jahn is here!"

"Hey there, soldier! How are you?" Bear asked, taking Jahn in a big rambunctious embrace. From the look on Jahn's face, Bear could see that Jahn was upset. "What's going on, Jahn?"

"May I speak to you in private?" Jahn asked.

"Bring us a glass of something, Honey," Bear said. "Please."

Sylvia went back into the house and Bear stepped out onto the porch.

"Everything all right?" Bear asked again.

Jahn felt self-conscious asking for help, shifting from one foot to another several times, then walking back and forth.

"You got girl troubles there, lieutenant?" Bear asked trying to get the conversation started.

"No," he said. " No," he said more emphatically. Then he explained he was to meet his Indian brother for the first time. He was apprehensive and had been wrestling with his feelings for days, sleeping little and eating less. He wanted to please his mother, to have the meeting go well, but after spending so many years enraged with Indians, letting that go was not easy, and he was not even sure he wanted to.

"Well, you are in a pickle," Bear laughed. "I understand why you might rather jump him with a knife than bring him into your family. But Jahn, he is your brother. He's kin."

Jahn took a deep breath, but still felt the beast writhing in his gut.

"How does Richard feel about it?" Bear asked.

"Last time I saw him, he said he would not go. But when Ma came for a visit, I think she encouraged him otherwise. Me too, but now that it is time, I feel less sure." Jahn stepped to the edge of the porch and looked over the street. "I gotta go, don't I, Bear?"

"'Fraid so," Bear answered. He pulled out two cigars from his pocket, and handed one to Jahn. Striking a match on the sole of his foot, he touched the fire to Jahn's and then his own. "Will do you good," he said.

Sylvia came out with the whiskey, and they both took a draw from the bottle.

"Now you boys wait. I brought glasses." She set them down and poured a round, then returned to the house, leaving the container.

"It will do you good," Bear repeated. "He's part of the story of your mother, of you and of Richard, an important part. And surely you would not have wanted her to be alone all those years? Isn't it better that she had someone to love, and someone who loved her? Seems natural they would have a child." He took a big gulp of whiskey, then puffed on the cigar. "Want me to ride with you?"

"Would you?" Jahn said with a feeling of relief.

"You'll want to bring gifts for your mother and brother as well as the chief and his wives. I will help you with that. All right. Let me tell Sylvia, " Bear said taking the bottle and the two empty glasses. "I'll meet you at the store at daybreak. We'll buy what you need then. Goodnight, Jahn. Get a good night's sleep," he called as he went into the house.

The next morning, without thinking, Jahn put on his uniform as usual, then changed his mind. Slowly, deep in thought, he undid the buttons of his coat and slid it off. He removed his boots and took off his pants. On the bed were the civilian clothes that would replace his uniform, leaving all trappings of being a soldier behind. He met Bear at the trapper's store, and they bought the gifts and foodstuffs they needed for the journey. He was to meet Richard at the bend in the river near the trapper's fort, and they would travel together to their mother's camp.

"I am not sure this is a good idea," Richard said when they met him. "I have my guns handy, and a couple of knives hidden in case those Indians get a wrong idea."

"He always this jumpy?" Bear asked.

"He's all right," Jahn said. "Mostly, he's hardheaded."

It was only after some time that Richard remembered that Bear had been the trapper that sold him his first horses.

"You were a scrawny young buck back then. Jahn tells me you are good with the ailin' ones. That true?"

"I do all right." Richard had the same beast residing in him that had followed Jahn all his life, and it was none too happy about this adventure.

On the third day the three men came within a few hours of the camp. The horses were jumpy, mirroring the feelings of at least two of the men on their backs.

Through the woods came a lone rider. His face was

painted, and he was wearing fine clothing, a shirt of the best skins and highly beaded leggings.

Bear slid his hand down to the butt of his rifle. Jahn and Richard did the same. The Indian stopped before they felt they had to defend themselves.

"I am Raccoon. Your mother has been waiting for you. You are Jahn, and you are Richard." he said with assuredness indicating first Jahn and then his brother. "Who is this?"

"He is my friend. Known as Bear. My mother knows him," Jahn said.

"We have heard many stories of this man. You have strong Medicine. It is not many who would still be alive after facing a bear. You are a welcome visitor," he said. He turned his horse. "It is not far."

The next hour no one spoke till Bear broke the silence, regaling the riders with tales of his trapping days.

Finally, Jahn interrupted. "What is our brother like?"

"Save it," Richard sniped.

"Easy there, Richard," Jahn said.

Bear jumped in, "I heard he is very much like his father. Cougar Two Foot was a fine man, a healer like your mother. Well thought of throughout the tribe," Bear said. "Your mother said members of many bands came to him for healing."

"I suppose mother *had* to marry him," Richard quipped.

"Like the honeysuckle vine, each twisted around the other for strength," was all Raccoon would say. One does not speak of the dead.

Richard scowled, keeping his gaze forward. Jahn felt years of tears well into his chest. All the time he had been searching, she was making a new family. It was more than he could take. To push those feelings down, he pulled out his pipe, stacked the tobacco then lit it.

"You are making ceremony?" Raccoon asked.

Jahn looked confused. "Oh, the pipe. Hmm, yes, in a way," he said.

"I will join you." Raccoon pulled out his stone pipe, filled it with some aromatic grass, and lit it. The smoke from both pipes wafted upward into the trees.

Within a few hours the village was visible, twenty or so tipis. When they rode in, everyone stopped to look. The men dismounted and walked the rest of the way into the camp. The children gathered around the horses and stared at the men. Richard pulled out a small pouch. He opened it, and poured its contents into his hand. "Would you like some sweets?" Jahn translated it. Richard placed a crystal of sugar in each young palm then ate one himself. *That went well*, he thought.

"I am Rain," a tall woman with a generous smile said as she strode forward. "I am your mother's friend. She has been waiting for you. Your brother waits, too, but it is as if he stands on a sharp rock without his moccasins," she laughed.

I know the feeling, Jahn thought.

"I also like sweets," she said. "Do you have any for an old woman?" Richard reached into the sack, and handed her a piece of sugar. She smiled and popped it into her mouth. "Come with me," she said escorting them to their mother's tipi. "White Smoke!" she called. "The boys are here!"

Ginny ducked out of the home, and when she saw her boys she opened her arms, embracing each one warmly. This was not going to be an easy meeting, and she knew it. "I am so glad to see you both. And Bear! How nice to see you as well. Boys, your brother will be back any–ah, there he is."

As they again embraced their mother, a young man rode

up. The sun behind his back blinded Jahn and Richard when they looked up at him. He did not dismount.

"This is my son Swift Fox. This is Jahn and Richard."

"Nice horse," Richard said. "Strong legs."

Swift Fox said nothing.

It was as if they were standing on different mountaintops, and she was not sure how they would traverse the distance between them.

Swift Fox looked hard at Jahn, searching his memory. He knew that face. He had seen him somewhere before. Then it hit him. He put his hand to his throat, grasping the silver cross he wore at his neck. "He is the same, mother, the one who did not shoot."

"He remembers meeting Jahn in the winter," Raccoon said to Richard in English.

Something in Jahn let go, and for the first time in weeks he felt relief.

"You are a fine hunter, brother," Jahn said in Ute.

"Your reputation is not that good with my friends in the tribe, soldier," he countered.

"I hope to change that," he said, knowing that it would not be easy.

At his mother's insistence, Swift Fox and Raccoon took the visitors hunting along the ridge near the ravine. Mountain sheep had been spotted there, so they hoped to bring home some good meat for supper. Bear was happy. He had not been hunting like this in a long while.

Swift Fox felt self-conscious in front of his white brothers. He was considerably younger and felt that gap strongly. The instinct to honor a man's years he held at bay.

He thought, *these are white men, brothers or not. How can I trust any white man after all the broken promises they have made to my people?*

The white men had rifles, while the Indians brought their bows and arrows. They spread out, walking through the forest.

"This would be a perfect time for them to make a mistake, and shoot one of us instead of the sheep," Richard whispered to Jahn.

"For mother's sake, let's hope that that is not their intention," Jahn said. "And don't you go having any wild shots either, brother."

Several rabbits crossed the path ahead. Both Indians shot their arrows before the white men could lift their rifles.

"Dang," Bear whispered. "They are quick!"

They walked on for several miles, when a wild turkey fluttered its wings. Once again, the Indian's arrows left before the white men could get a bead. Jahn had shot arrows before, but only enough to know it took great skill to do it.

They continued on, but no tracks could be seen, so they headed for the ridge.

"Halfway down the cliff," Richard said.

Leaning hard into the rocks, placing each foot carefully, three sheep traversed the side of the mountain.

"Too far," Raccoon said. "We could not get there before they will get to the top."

Jahn pulled up his rifle, aiming it at one of the sheep. He cocked his gun, let his breath out, and shot. The sound reverberated through out the canyon. Instantly, the animal fell where it stood.

"Not too far for a gun," Richard said. "And my brother is a crack shot."

With one end of a rope wrapped around a tree, holding

tight to it, Jahn scrambled down the rocks to where the sheep lay and tied the rope around it. They hauled the body up the embankment then sent the rope down for Jahn. He wrapped it around his waist and arm, and they all helped to bring Jahn up the cliff, but suddenly, the branch holding the rope snapped off, and Jahn dropped. In an instant, Swift Fox dove for the rope, grabbing it with his bare hands. It tore at his skin, but he did not let go. Raccoon joined him, as did Bear and Richard. The men carefully raised him up the rocky cliff, onto the flat top.

"You all right there, Dutch?" Bear asked.

"Yes, I am fine," he said dusting himself off. "But your hand," he said to his brother. He pulled out his kerchief and wrapped the ripped flesh. Jahn knew it must have been painful, but Swift Fox did not indicate so.

After they tied the sheep to a pole, Raccoon and Swift Fox hoisted it on their shoulders and carried it back toward the camp.

High above, a mountain lion lurked, watching the men with the kill. Furtively, it followed them till it found an overhang just above where they would be walking. He hunkered down, waiting for the right moment.

By this time the men were tired and ready to be home.

"Let's rest here for a moment," Bear suggested. "Catch a breath." The men lifted the sheep off their shoulders, and stretched their bunched muscles. "We'll be eat'n' well tonight!" Bear laughed, rubbing his belly. "Wait till you see how fast their women will make a fine skin out of those locks," he said.

Bear pulled out some jerky, and passed it around, then Raccoon went into the trees to relieve himself. Richard was about to set his rifle down when he heard a twig snap. Just as he turned, the cat dropped his hindquarters and leapt. He brought his rifle up aiming at what looked like Swift Fox's head. Swift Fox reached for his knife.

"No! Look!" shouted Jahn.

Swift Fox and Raccoon turned in time to see the mountain lion sail through the air. Richard's gun blasted, and the cat dropped heavily at the boy's feet.

"I am a pretty good shot, too," Richard quipped.

That evening, sitting around the fire, the family gathered over the night meal. Many members of the band also came to watch, and to decide if these white men were like so many they had known. Were they here to take the land, put up fences and shoot at them?

The meat was shared with the whole band so everyone was eating well this night, which lead to a general sense of well–being throughout the camp.

After the food was served and a pipe smoked, Swift Fox ceremoniously gave his brothers gifts. For each he had a sharp hunting knife and a stone to sharpen it. He spoke softly to his mother, who handed Richard a pouch. "This is for your wife," she said to Richard. Inside was a beaded medallion very similar to the one Ginny had worn at her wedding to Cougar Two Foot.

Then it was Jahn and Richard's turn to give out the gifts they had brought. For the women, there were bolts of cotton material for making dresses. Plaid patterns or stripes in dark blues and maroons were favorites. For the chief, they had brought a bridle for his horse and a good strong rope. Jahn pulled out a spyglass and showed Swift Fox how to use it. "Good for hunting," Jahn said. For their mother they had brought a comb, a brush and a hand mirror encased in mother of pearl. Bear had brought bags of beans and coffee.

"You are very generous," she said. "Now it is late, and I am tired. Swift Fox will show you where to put out your bedrolls. We can talk more in the morning."

The next day White Smoke caught Bear before he entered the tipi.

"Good morning, my friend. How do you think we are doing?" she asked.

Bear thought for a moment. "Might be easier if your child had been a girl. You know how boys are—always tryin' to be the man on top." Bear looked her in the eye. "I have a feelin' with time the boys will be thick as thieves, but right now they are puppies tryin' to get to their mother's teat first."

The next morning, Richard went with Raccoon to look over the horses. After they left, Swift Fox told Jahn, "Come. Bring that," he said pointing to Jahn's rifle.

The tall boy had long strides, so that Jahn, even though he was tall as well, had to push to keep up.

"Where are we going?" he asked.

"To practice," Swift Fox answered.

In a few minutes they came to a clearing. Hanging from a tree branch was a leather pouch with a red dot the size of a fist painted in the center. It was worn, having been used for target practice for many years, and now had many patches to shore up its holes.

"There. Shoot it with this," and he handed Jahn his bow and an arrow.

Jahn took it, pulled back the bow, and let the arrow fly. It landed in the dirt.

"Again," Swift Fox said.

He took another arrow and cocked it on the bowstring.

Slowly, he pulled back, let out his breath and released it. Again it missed the target, but at least landed in the tree trunk. This went on for a while, Swift Fox handing him arrows, Jahn hitting anywhere but the target. Finally, Jahn asked Swift Fox to show him what to do. Swift Fox laughed to himself, remembering his first target practice with Father Man so many years ago. The same instructions that Father Man had given him, he now gave to his brother.

"Remember, you are the arrow," he said again.

Jahn went inside himself, and as best he could, became the arrow landing in the target then he released the shaft. It grazed the hanging bag.

"Good. Again." Swift Fox handed him arrow after arrow. Eventually, he was able to hit the target, at least one out of five times. "Practice," the young man said. "I was a young boy when I started. I have had lots of practice. You should be able to kill a beast while riding your horse at a gallop, or you don't eat. It's good incentive," he said with a wry smile.

Only then did Jahn remember the wound on his brother's hand. "Shouldn't you keep that wrapped?" he said turning over the hand to see the cut from the rope. There was only a thin red line, not even a scab.

"Mother?" Jahn asked. Swift Fox made a few quick fists, and shook off the question.

"Show me how to shoot that," he said pointing to Jahn's rifle. Jahn remembered what his father and Henry Sumner had said when they taught him, and passed it on to his brother. He set up rocks on a tree branch. They took turns shooting at their targets, both improving with each shot.

All morning Richard had been taking an assessment of the

horses. They were, for the most part, healthy, strong and fast. And he was pleased to have spent the time with Raccoon, whom he found to be intelligent and kind, and a loyal friend to his mother.

Raccoon spoke with White Smoke that evening. "The fissure between your two older sons and their brother is not one that is going to close up quickly. As with most wounds, healing takes time. You need not worry though. The knitting will happen when they are not looking, when other things take their attention. Then one day, they will notice that instead of feeling anger, they will be looking forward to their paths crossing. Before they know it, the bond will be made, and they will be family."

Not wanting to leave his own family for an extended amount of time, Bear had already returned home. Now the time had come for Jahn and Richard to leave as well.

"Be well, Ma," Richard said holding tightly to Ginny.

"I will, son. Give my best to Melina."

"Nice to meet you, brother," Richard said with some hesitation.

Swift Fox looked intently at both men, still trying to read who they were.

Jahn knew that hunting had been poor because the animals had retreated into the mountains, away from all the settlers, so as he got on his horse, he pulled out his rifle and a sack of shot. "Here," he said handing it to Swift Fox. "For those sheep."

Swift Fox's eyes widened as he took the gift.

Jahn hugged his mother and the boys rode off. Raccoon joined them to ride part of the way.

Six months later, Jahn and Richard went again to visit their mother's camp for the ceremony when Swift Fox chose

Rain's daughter, Warm Blanket, to be his wife.

Because so many white men had moved into the area and there had been so much more killing on both sides, the community was wary, making that meeting more difficult for the band. Swift Fox made sure that they saw his acceptance of his brothers, honoring them with a place next to him at meals, and publicly giving them gifts of ceremonial knives and beaded shirts, and smoking the ceremonial pipe.

The first spring after Ginny's return, Richard and Melina had a son, and a daughter came a year later. Jahn married Lizbeth, and they had two sons.

For many years, Ginny would surprise Richard at his home, arriving without warning. She would stay for a time then return to Swift Fox and his family.

Richard battled the demon liquor his whole life. There were many months that he was able to conquer that foe, only to lose again. Ginny gave Melina herbs to help him with the fight. Later Melina told Jahn that she always felt Ginny encouraging her.

Jahn saw his mother often, as she had promised. She would appear sometimes in person, but more often in dreams that left him feeling strengthened and whole. He never again awoke in a sweat from that recurring nightmare, because the beast in his chest had moved on to take up residence elsewhere.

Jahn retired from the cavalry soon after the first meeting with Swift Fox. He could not, in all conscience, continue to kill Indians for the sake of it. He and his family lived in a house that the brothers built on their property, and together they raised horses.

And never again did Jahn see that cantankerous woman, full of demands and expectations that had looked up at him so intensely from the yard at the fort. His mother now carried both the loving softness of Ginny Van Andusson, the mother he knew, and the strength and assuredness of White Smoke, shaman for the Yampatika Utes, the People Who Live In the Mountains.

He was proud to be her son.

60
SILVER LEAF RANCH

1897

Melina and Richard were just finishing supper with their grown children, Jeffrey and Isabel and their families, when they heard coming from the road the neighing of many horses. Melina's eyes opened wide with terror. Richard grabbed his gun, went to a side window, aimed his rifle, and sent a bullet clattering into a large metal pan tied to a tree that stood between his home and his brother's.

Hearing that sound, Jahn grabbed his gun, told his wife, "Stay here," and ran out the door.

Only when Richard looked out the window, did he see that it was not raiders, as he feared, but his tall blue-eyed brother and his family.

With so many ambushes and raids upon their camp, hearing the twang of the bullet caused one of Swift Foxes sons to lift his rifle sighting it at the shadow in the window at the front of the house.

"It is all right. It is Richard alerting Jahn," Swift Fox said.

Richard and Jeffery went out to greet them, setting his gun against the porch railing.

"Swift Fox, it is good to see you and your family. Wolf and Henry, you have come as well? Your parents will be glad to see you," Richard said to Jahn's sons.

"Hello, brother," Jahn said to Swift Fox, slightly winded from the sprint from his house.

"Jeffrey," Richard said to his son, "go tell Lizbeth her boys are here."

"Where is mother?" Jahn asked. But when they did not see Ginny, they realized why Swift Fox and the others had come.

Jahn and Richard and their families gathered at the fire circle outside the tipi they kept on their property for their mother, and listened to Henry, Wolf and Swift Fox's account of their mother's last days. Henry began:

"Van Andusson?" the sergeant major called out as he walked through the noisy mess hall.

"Here," the young blue-eyed lieutenant answered. The sergeant major wove through the crowded dining room to where Henry was sitting.

"Excuse me, sir. The captain wants you in his office right away."

"Thank you, Sergeant Major. Gentlemen, excuse me. I am called to duty."

Good natured and well liked by his men, Henry Garritt Van Andusson, twenty, was an officer in the United States cavalry just as his father had been before him. Joining the cavalry was the only way he could be sure that his Indian family was safe.

As Henry came across the yard, his younger brother, Wolf, who had also enlisted in the army for the same reason, joined him.

"Race you there," Wolf called out as he took off in a sprint. Both men were strong runners, and each was thinking he was going to win.

But the soldier on duty called out, "A tie!"

"Tie, no!" Wolf laughed. "I was a good inch ahead of him."

The men straightened their clothing and entered the Captain's office.

"Good Morning, sir," Henry said, both men saluting. "You asked to see me?"

"And me as well, sir?"

"At ease, men. I have had a request from a Myron Josephson. He has asked for you specifically. Do you know this man? What would he want? He is the saloon keeper, is he not?"

"Yes. He's an old friend of our father's. Perhaps, he has news from him."

"Ah, yes, well, that explains it. Go find out what he wants, and then report back to me. I have an assignment for you."

"Yes, sir," the men said in unison.

Bear was waiting for them outside the gate. He no longer traveled the mountain passes looking for game, but with his wife he ran a saloon, and they had raised five children. The boys greeted their father's friend with enthusiasm.

"What is this about, Bear?" Wolf asked.

Just then Raccoon stepped into their view, away from the prying eyes of the guards. "You must come with me now," he said. "White Smoke asks for you."

The men told their commanding officer that they needed to attend to an urgent family matter.

"Thank you, sir," they both said.

"Go on now, before my mood changes."

"We must hurry," Raccoon told them.

Henry and Wolf said goodbye to their wives and children, gathered foodstuff for their Indian family, and left immediately for the area where their grandmother lived in the warmer months. They did not have far to go. The weather was glorious, with bright sunshine during the day, and clear stars and a full moon at night lighting the Fawn In The Woods.

Within a half-day the Van Andusson men would be at the camp where Swift Fox and their grandmother, Ginny, lived. Over the years both men had secretly made it part of their patrol to visit there, and had become close to both of them, as well as with their cousins, Swift Fox's children, and their offspring.

When they rode into the camp, they noticed that except for some singing at the far end, the village was unusually quiet. The music was coming from the tipi of Swift Fox, where a group of men and women sat just outside, chanting and drumming.

Swift Fox stepped out of the opening. Though his once auburn hair was now streaked with white, his stature was that of a man half his almost forty years. His face showed fatigue and concern.

"Thank you, Raccoon," he said. Then affectionately shaking the hands of both men he said in English, "Hello, nephews. Thank you for coming. Mother has been calling for you."

"Grandmother? Is she ill?" Wolf asked.

"Come, she will tell you herself."

The group began their chant again as the men went into the dwelling.

They found their grandmother lying on her sleeping pallet surrounded by their cousins, the grown children of Swift Fox and Warm Blanket: One Eagle Feather, Water Moon and Snow Goose. The men knew to stand at the back of the tipi until they were called forward.

Warm Blanket had neatly combed their grandmother's hair and dressed her in a fine beaded dress. She wore almost all of the jewelry—necklaces, rings and bracelets—that she had been given by her patients over the years.

Her breathing was shallow and labored, her face wrinkled and her eyes clouded and she looked every bit of her eighty-two years, but White Smoke still carried the energy of a shaman.

Warm Blanket handed White Smoke the pouch she had requested which held gifts for each of these grandchildren.

For One Eagle Feather, she had set aside an ornately beaded ceremonial knife, and for each of the two girls a large beaded necklace. She had painstakingly made these gifts for them, each bearing a symbol of the grandchild's name.

Water Moon helped Snow Goose put on her necklace. She fastened her own, then turned her face away to wipe a tear from her cheek. Silently, the three went to stand with their father.

White Smoke's oldest and dearest friend, Rain, came in to see her.

"Look for me when I come, White Smoke," Rain said, her knees crackling as she eased herself down next to the pallet. "I am so used to having you near, I cannot imagine the sun rising without it shining on your face," she said.

"I will look for you, Rain. I will find your husband, and we will wait together for you to come."

Swift Fox and his son helped Rain to her feet.

"Easy journey, my dear friend," she said leaning on Water Moon's arm as she left the enclosure.

With difficulty, White Smoke asked, "Where are the little ones?"

Snow Goose called outside for the children to enter. At once, on a ripple of giggles, five little children ran in shouting, "Great-grandmother!"

My great-grandbabies, she laughed to herself. "Hello, my little pups. Are we all here?" She counted heads pointing to each as she said their names, "Sun On The Trees, Long Wing, The Flying Bird, Rippling Water, High Mountain. And where is Coyote Laugh?"

The smallest boy burst in through the doorway.

"Here, Great-grandmother!" he chortled.

She gave each of them a small, soft, beaded deerskin pouch filled with river garnets, quartz crystals and bits of turquoise.

Finally, she gave her attention to her grandsons, the Van Andusson men. "Henry and Wolf, how good to see you."

"Grandmother, does Father know you are unwell?" Henry asked.

Swift Fox leaned down and whispered in his ear, "There is not time for him to come."

"We can speak of that later," she said shooing away her son, and taking their hands. "Now tell me about what you have been doing."

The young men sat at her side telling her about their lives. She listened intently, but then the years began to drift together, all that she had experienced floating up into her memory.

She looked up at Swift Fox, who stood above watching her with an unwavering gaze. "It is good," she said to soothe him, "and I am ready for this day." She turned back to Jahn's two boys.

"When my day ends, dear ones, and Swift Fox has put my body to rest, you will take some things back to your father and to your Uncle Richard." Under her gaze, Henry and Wolf felt like children again, and even though they had seen killing and death, they were not prepared for the talk of the end of their grandmother's life. "I want you to tell Jahn this," she said. "It is something he must understand."

Warm Blanket, who was also a shaman, ducked in the door bringing in some strong smelling tea.

"Drink this, it will soothe your body." White Smoke sipped a small amount of the liquid, but struggled to swallow it.

After Warm Blanket gently wiped her mouth, she began again. "If your father had not persisted, we never would have found each other. Tell him that Senawahv, hearing the steady and earnest cry of his heart, informed all creation. Our hearts beat as one, so I was pulled into the path of those who could bring us together again. Do you understand? Tell that back to me," she said.

After they repeated it, she whispered something to Warm Blanket who went to the other side of the tipi. She brought back a bundle, which she handed to Henry.

"Open it, grandson," White Smoke told him. Inside he found two silver combs. "I would like your mother and Melina to each have one of these," she said to her grandsons. From her gnarled fingers, the old woman took off two rings, giving one to each of the men.

She handed Henry a pouch. "These are for Richard's children. And this," she pulled off the large beaded bracelet edged with wolf's fur, that she had worn for many years, "this is for your uncle, Richard." Then White Smoke handed Wolf her rattle, smudging wand and the pouch that Cougar Two Foot had given her, saying, "Give these to your father."

Warm Blanket handed her two beaded deerskin pouches. "Please give these to your wives and children," she told Henry and Wolf. "I have not been able to see them lately, but they are always in my thoughts."

"Grandmother, they would have wanted to be here had they known," Henry replied.

She looked around the room at her family. "Now, all my adored grandchildren, will you leave me with my son for a moment?"

Henry and Wolf both bent down to give her a hug and a kiss. One Eagle Feather, Snow Goose and Water Moon came forward and squeezed her hands. Snow Goose ran back again throwing her arms around her neck.

White Smoke gently brushed her hand over the young woman's hair. "It is all right, my dear."

Reluctantly, Snow Goose released her cherished one. Then all but Swift Fox headed toward the opening.

"Warm Blanket, wait," White Smoke choked. Warm Blanket stopped at the opening of the dwelling, and turned back to the old woman. "These are for you," she said handing her the two gold bracelets that Quill had given her on the day of her wedding. "You will take this also," she said taking a labored breath, putting her hand on the strand of large silver and turquoise beads that she wore around her neck.

Warm Blanket stroked the old woman's cheek tenderly. "Thank you for all that you have given me and my family."

White Smoke took Warm Blanket's hand in both of hers and smiled.

"Now, I will speak to my son alone—just for a moment."

Once all had left the enclosure, she quieted herself. Swift Fox did as well.

Soon after the family left the tipi a rider galloped into the camp. The chanting ceased. Panting heavily, he ran into the circle to speak to Raccoon. Swift Fox went out to see what the man wanted. He said soldiers were on their way to take their tribe to a reservation. All were concerned and frightened. Raccoon suggested that it would be far better for the band to go to the reservation on their own, and avoid bloodshed, than for the army to come, force them to go, and most likely get many killed. Swift Fox turned to the gathering, and told them to pack their belongings and leave. Immediately, they broke down the camp.

His family would stay behind to care for his mother.

"What is it?" White Smoke looked confused when she saw his face.

He did not want to tell her that they would no longer hunt in these mountains nor fish in these streams, but must go to live in worthless flatlands. But she understood. White Smoke looked up at her son with profound sadness. They had been avoiding this day for years. Tears filled her eyes, and ran down her wrinkled cheeks.

She coughed deeply. "My dear son, you are a brave man and a masterful leader," she said looking into the future. "You know that all that you need is within the heart of Senawahv. Make each day dance for you," she told him. "Behind you to give you strength are the spirits of your father, Father Man and Quill, and most deeply, you must know that I will be there. Your ancestors will guide your spear and inspire your tongue. In your heart, you will know that we are with you. My son," she said looking deeply into his eyes, "you are the sun and the stars in my heart. Though I have never wanted to be parted from you, this is the time of my leaving. You are strong, and you understand these things."

As the fire crackled, and the white smoke rose up to the opening in the ceiling, her breathing became even more labored.

He knelt down to look closely into her face. "Mother," he said tenderly, "I am grateful that the time of your leaving has been long in coming."

They sat quietly taking in each other's gaze, connecting on the deepest levels.

"You are a dear and wonderful son." With effort she took off the large silver ring the one with a turquoise stone with gold flecks running throughout, the one that Father Man had given her so many years ago, and slid it onto her son's finger. "When you wear this you will think of your family," she whispered hoarsely.

"Mother, I do not need a ring to remember those I love, but I will wear it with pride as your son."

Now extremely fatigued, White Smoke's head rested heavily on the soft pillow that Warm Blanket had fashioned for her from the pelt of a snow rabbit. The family came back into the tipi, and gathered around her.

"You must all go," she said. "Leave me."

Warm Blanket shook her head. "No, we will not leave you."

"Then sing with me?" she asked.

"Of course," Swift Fox answered. They began a familiar chant, their voices blending soulfully, the sound lifting into the air like smoke infusing the forest.

Outside, and nearly surrounding the lodge, women and children had assembled in silence each holding what belongings they would carry. The men had brought horses harnessed for carrying tipi poles, tents and other belongings, and others had taken the rest of the herd along the path toward the reservation. When they were ready, they left the camp leaving only one tipi intact.

The clear night sky, with its abundance of stars, held a generous moon. Crows that had gathered in the trees chattering loudly during the day had become still, a night owl called, and coyotes barked in the distance.

Her breathing stopped.

Swift Fox went to each member of his family: each child, each grandchild and lastly his wife. "You must all leave now. There is nothing more you need to do here. First we will go to Silver Leaf Ranch then meet up with the rest at Mancos River. Raccoon, Wolf and Henry, help me carry her up the mountain." Then he turned back to his wife. "I will catch up with you."

While the men took his mother's body to the mouth of a small cave, the women put the rest of their belongings on the travois, and left the camp.

Carefully, Swift Fox lay his mother into the indentation, placing her medicine bag in the curl of her body. Each man gathered rocks to cover the opening, then lay branches in front of it, so no one would suspect what was hidden there.

Raccoon told Henry and Wolf, "Talk to the soldiers. Keep them away for as long as you can." They quickly mounted their horses, praying that they were not too late.

"You must go, too, my friend," Swift Fox said. Raccoon rode after his family.

As the wind brushed through the tips of the pines, he looked up, transfixed. Before long, a low resounding voice began to permeate the forest like a winter fog. The escaping families turned to look back one last time. The smoke swirled, the fire crackled, and sparks flew upward. Silhouetted against the blazing tipi, Hears The Wind, also known as Swift Fox, their Chief and shaman sang a death chant.

In his heart, he could feel White Smoke melding with the night sky, mingling with the starlight.

EPILOGUE

For many years, in the lands to the south and west, white settlers and white armies massacred men, women, children, old and young, sometimes in their sleep. The Mountain People hoped those soldiers would stay far away from their precious land, leaving them in peace, but the stormy tide that had first washed over the plains spread all the way into the mountains and valleys of Colorado. The People were forced to defend their way of life. This onslaught meant bloodshed with heinous and brutal massacres on both sides.

Those who lived in the flatlands had already been wrenched from their favorite fields, lakes and streams where their bands hunted and fished. Like White Smoke's village, some of the People of the Mountains, were able to keep from being captured by moving constantly. Out of desperation, her band joined with a Ute Mountain Weeminuche village in the Sleeping Ute Mountain range. But that was to change as well.

The chiefs of the Ute Nation gathered with the military and the government of the United States to sign treaties. With regularity those treaties were broken, and Ute land was taken away.

For those who were caught and taken to reservations, the life of moving with the seasons, following the buffalo, bear, elk, and deer, digging fresh roots, gathering nuts and berries as they had done for centuries, came to an end. They were told to become farmers on the arid, worthless land they had been given.

For most, this new life, a time of melding cultures where the Indians had to learn to live as whites was impossible to comprehend, let alone accomplish. Most were not able to accept the inevitability of the change happening all around them, and suffered terribly for it. It was a clash of cultures. Indians were a nomadic people, and the settlers believed in owning property.

"Many more of my people will be killed with the white man's guns," Swift Fox told the man from the Indian Office who came to negotiate a peaceful settlement to the ongoing war that waged between The People and the whites they considered interlopers. "Not even my white brothers and their sons will be able to stop it."

He had said many times, "The white man is a starving people. The beauty of the mountains with its flowing streams, abundant wild life and beautiful vistas ignites a sun in their chests and fills their being. They believe if they own this land, and hold it tight, they will always feel the fullness of the bear after eating its kill. But this is not the way. They have a hunger of spirit. They must learn to know in their hearts they are one with all that lives, a part of it and not separate from it. Only then will they feel the fullness that all men seek."

ABOUT THE AUTHOR

A. B. Kreglow is an artist of amazing and impressive range. Her creations encompass work as a producer, director, dancer, choreographer, photographer, painter, potter, singing performance coach, composer and author. Creative expression is clearly her passion.

She has worked in film and video production, and her photographs have appeared in *Modern Dance, Dance Magazine* and *The New York Times,* among others. She choreographed for *Washington Square Repertory Dance Company* and *Theatre In A Trunk Productions* at NYU.

A. B. Kreglow danced in New York City for *Fred Mathews and Gary Masters,* and produced, choreographed and danced there for *Amanda Kreglow Presents an Evening of Dance* under a grant from the Deerfield Foundation.

She created and produced *Amanda Kreglow Presents~Dance By...*concerts, which featured the work of a variety of local contemporary choreographers, as well as choreographing works for these performances, and for *SoCo Dance Theater* and *UPside Dance Company* in Sonoma County, California. Her dance "In The Mist of Dying" was performed as part of a TED Talks Live presentation in New York City. Some of her dances can be seen on YouTube.

A. B. Kreglow is a founding member of the Steering Committee for *danceSonoma* with the Arts Council of Sonoma County, California, her home. *Becoming White Smoke* is her first novel.

Made in the USA
Charleston, SC
10 April 2016